forest

of

whispers

Spencer Hill Press, LLC

Contact: Spencer Hill Press, PO Box 247, Contoocook, NH
03229, USA

Please visit our website at www.spencerhillpress.com

First Edition: September 2014.
Jennifer Murgia
Forest of Whispers : a novel / by Jennifer Murgia – 1st ed.
p. cm.
Summary:
A teenage girl is caught up in the witch hysteria in 17th
century Bavaria.

Cover design by Lisa Amowitz
Interior layout by Kate Kaynak
Published in association with MacGregor Literary, Inc.

ISBN 978-1-937053-56-7 (paperback)
ISBN 978-1-937053-58-1 (e-book)

Printed in the United States of America

JENNIFER MURGIA

SPENCER
HILL
PRESS

Bavaria
1627

Also by Jennifer Murgia:
Angel Star
Lemniscate
The Bliss
Between These Lines

For my mother

Related to European villages of old, the term "Hedge Witch" comes from the fact that the average village was surrounded by a hedge or woods. Beyond that hedge was unknown land, beyond their known perception...i.e., the Other World. The village witches of this era usually lived just beyond or just before this hedge. The hedge was a metaphor for someone who practiced shamanistic arts—a walker between the worlds.

Pronunciation Guide to the German Words:

Butterbrot – (BOO-ter-BROTE) – Bread and butter

Chanterelle – (shan-tur-EL-a) – A golden mushroom found in the Black Forest of Germany

Gnädig – (guh-NAY-dig) – Gracious, mercy

Metzgerei – (METS-ger-eye) – Butcher's shop

Mutti – (MOO-tee) – Mother

Öffnen Sie die Tür! – (OOF-nen ZEE dee TOUR!) – Open the door!

Schätzchen – (SHET-zee-en) – Dear one, honey

Schupfnudeln – (shoomf-NOO-deln) – A thick, rolled noodle dumpling

Strappado – (shtra-pa-DOE) – A torture device in which the subject is hoisted by rope and allowed to fall its full length

Thaler – (DAH-ler) – A large, official silver coin used in Austria, Germany, and Switzerland

Tollkirsche – (TALL-kair-shuh) – Deadly nightshade, also known as belladonna

Chapter 1
Rune

My feet fly across the soft ground, away from the footsteps that chase me. With a pounding heart and my skirt gathered in my hands, I dodge my pursuers and run into the haunted forest.

There is just enough time to squeeze myself under a low branch, and while the pines are thick enough to swallow my small frame, my heart beats a painful rhythm against my ribs as a boy no older than me inches closer to the edge of the path—closer to where I hide. Sap-coated needles glue themselves to my cheeks as I hug the closest branch and peer out. One of the boys, the fearless one, raises an arm to signal the direction he believes I've gone. But while his expression is hard, he doesn't dare venture too far from the path; the trees are dark and foreboding, even for a determined ruffian with a fistful of pebbles.

"She's gone," he sighs.

"You mean vanished?" The second boy has joined him. His eyes are wide as he scans the sky, as if I have taken flight and disappeared altogether.

Blood trickles a thin line of red down my ankle where one of the small rocks nicked me, but this childish witch hunt does not frighten me. I am hidden—having outrun them, outsmarted them, like I always do. They call the forest *black* for a reason, and today it has proven true, hiding me well within its cage of branches, safe behind the fear it breathes and the animals who scream their devil calls.

Soon enough, the boys give up their chase and head back toward the village. When I am certain they cannot hear me, I pull myself free from the camouflage and stretch my limbs, noting the small welts that dot my arms. This is not the first time the boys have been cruel. After all, I am the strange girl who lives in the forest, apprentice to the one they say is a witch.

The boys' backs become shadows as they cross the hedge, leaving me alone in the wild, dark space that borders the village—until something warm and unbidden kisses my ear. I turn quickly, spying nothing but the endless stretch of forest. Then it comes again—a whisper, a faint touch against my skin, the gentle glide of fingers through my hair. The trees are still. No breeze sweeps past, yet I am certain I am not alone.

Rune… My name carries on the air, its breathy tone so clear that I know this is not some trick of the mind or emotional game. This is real.

That is all I need for my body to react. My fear explodes inside me, and soon the village is far behind as I dash deeper into the forest, toward my home.

Come to me, Rune…

Against my will, I pause, knowing that what I do is a terrible risk. The snap of a twig startles me, and the birds in the trees fall silent. My arms are chilled in gooseflesh and I know that something, *someone* is dreadfully close. There is movement, and beyond the needles and boughs I see what appears to be a tendril of hair as dark as pitch…as dark as mine. My breath stills inside me, though there is nothing I can do to calm the hammering of my pulse as it races through my veins, as if it too flees from the shadow forming within the trees.

The whisper comes again, closer and from all angles, pelting me harder than any stones those miserable boys could have thrown. It seeps beneath my skin and severs all that is rational from my mind, filling me with a sour horror. A howling wind wrenches itself free from the heart of the forest and sweeps closer, twisting loose branches, lifting tender roots. Leaves fall like rain around my head, swirling, taunting, wrapping me in arms that I feel but cannot see. And then, it is as if the leaves come to life, taking shape, fixing to an invisible, gentle curve of a cheek, the soft definition of lashes against translucent skin. My eyes snap shut and I will the ghostly image away, for I am not certain of anything anymore.

My breath catches in my throat and, somehow, I am able to open my eyes. I know well the tales of the dark forest and the shadows it keeps, for I live with them every day. For sixteen years, Matilde warned this day would come, and I was a fool to believe I could escape it—that I could escape *her*. Just as the forest appears calm and still and dark before my eyes, there is a land that sleeps within it. A land that separates the dead from the living with only a thin veil—a land my mother has woken from, seeking me at long last.

Perhaps it is the shuffling of the birds in their nests that gives me the courage to reach my hand out and test the cool air. I wiggle my fingers, and then, growing braver by the second, I test myself even further and whisper to what I cannot see.

"Mother?"

Only stillness answers me, so I say it again, louder.

"Mother?"

I turn my open hand a few times, clench and unclench my fist, and then…a touch grazes the back of my hand. I am startled at how it feels—so tender, so human—until it tightens to a grip so excruciating I fear my hand will be crushed before my very eyes. Four thick lines materialize upon my skin, resembling fingers. The sight leaves me breathless as fear seizes me. I yank my hand away, nearly stumbling into the thick ferns behind me.

In my ears, my breath is a frantic, terrible force as I run toward the tiny cottage. I hurl myself inside, but she has followed me and rattles against the door, begging to be let in. My fingers find the flimsy lock and work at it until it clicks in place, assuring that I am safe from what I fear the most, and soon, I find I am convincing myself that all is well. My morning gathering, the taunting boys—they have simply unnerved me, for there is nothing but gentle comfort in this room. Burning wood crackles in the hearth. Lavender, Coriander, and Blessed Thistle dry in bundles overhead. The pungent peel of the Bergamot orange boils in the kettle over the flames. Its citrusy aroma fills the room.

"Schätzchen," Matilde looks up from the heavy table at the center of the room. Her eyes are cloudy with age and they linger on my face, surely seeing the fear I try so hard to conceal. "You've been out early."

The fear I felt moments ago dissipates and, with a quick smile, I step away from the door and cross the room, lifting the edge of my dress against the table to reveal what I had collected in the woods just moments before the village boys found me.

"Five in all, not a bad clutch for this time of year, eh?" Matilde's mouth grows wide, nearly all gums. With hands as dotted as the grouse's eggs, she turns each one over, diligently inspecting for cracks. I am sure she hears my sigh of relief that my run through the trees hasn't wasted our meal.

"Did you give thanks to the Mother, like I taught you?" she says, noticing the light-green stalks inside my pocket. I look down and smile at the herbs that have somehow survived the fury outside.

"Of course. You taught me that long ago."

"And why, Schätzchen? Why must we always remain in good favor with the earth?"

I let out a quiet sigh. "We only take what is needed, never more. We should never be selfish with what the Sacred Mother provides for us."

A smile creeps to her lips, and I know I've answered well. This lesson has been ingrained in me since I was a child, yet she still asks me to repeat it. I'd like to learn other lessons, though. I'd like to read the leaves at the bottom of our chipped cups instead of only seeing soggy tea. I'd like to tell the silly girls who sneak off into the woods that they will find love someday, like Matilde does.

Her gentle hand presses against my forehead, taking me by surprise, and I wait for the questions to come. Why was I in the forest so early? Why am I still trembling so?

My fear followed me home, Matilde, I want to say, but I keep silent. I don't give evidence to the one person who has the ability to sense the unseen.

"Rune," Matilde says softly. "Sit with me."

I cross the floor and hold onto her elbow, easing her into the old, worn rocker. Matilde lets her eyes close with a sigh, and I try to remember when she didn't appear so frail.

"I'm an old woman, Rune."

"You're not old, Mutti," I say back, smiling at the old joke. Matilde has been an old woman forever, it seems. I begin to pour the tea that is now ready, then hand her a cup of it, making sure her hands are still before I let go. I bite my lip as her eyes meet mine.

"I've taught you well, haven't I? Well enough that you feel capable and strong?" she asks.

"Yes, you've taught me well, only…"

"Only?" A deep, guttural noise wells up from her throat, preventing her from finishing. I press my fingers to the bottom of the cup, gently lifting it, prompting her to take a sip. When her chest no longer heaves, and the rise and fall of it appears relaxed once again, the question is forgotten, but not by me.

Only I wish I could see the future like you can, Mutti, I want to say, wishing with all my heart that the tiny tea leaves would tell me she'll be all right. But I know they are dark and tea-logged and won't offer any sort of fortune that will ease my worries. Her coughs have worsened these last few months, and I cannot bear to think of the day she is called home to our Mother. Matilde is the only mother I have ever known. How long will

5

she and I have together? Will she see the next snowfall? Or will I spend the coldest, darkest days of the year alone in this little cottage?

I settle myself at her feet and feel her bony touch upon my shoulder. I am not ready to look up just yet, so I stare into the fire and will its heat to dry the threatening tears I hold back. But it is too late, and Matilde knows.

"Now, my Schätzchen, tell me your troubles."

I know she does not need my words to figure out why I am so afraid. Her hand gives my shoulder a gentle squeeze. The air is thick with what I know will come next, with words I can already hear inside my head. She will reassure me that the Sacred Mother bides time well, and then she will ask the question I dread the most—if I have seen my birth mother, if the woman who haunts my dreams now haunts the hours I'm awake.

"Tell me, child. Has she come?"

Her voice is a profound whisper, which makes me look up. There is a light behind her eyes I have never seen before.

I nod.

The sigh that sweeps through her fills the entire room. "I prayed this day would never happen," she says softly. She is as white as a specter, and I am on my feet leaning over her, removing the shaking cup from her hands and wrapping my own around them. "May our Mother help me, I can still see the fear in her eyes as she handed me the bundle."

I watch, wide-eyed, as Matilde stretches her trembling arms out past me. My eyes follow, but I see nothing. It is her memory, not mine.

"You, Rune, you were the bundle I took from her. I promised I would take you and keep you for her, that you would be safe from the others. She knew it was the end. Goddess help her, she knew."

"Others?"

"In the village. There is a reason we don't meet the eyes of those who stare." She pauses, then leans close. "They might remember."

Matilde's eyes seek mine with an immeasurable determination. "Sometimes when a person faces the most trying circumstance, they become stricken like a wild animal. Corner them, and they will do anything to escape. Give them a voice, and they will make the most desperate of promises."

I swallow the lump in my throat. "What promises, Mutti?" But it's clear that she is somewhere else, far away, lost in her story.

Before I have the chance to wonder where, her eyes focus sharply on my face. "Has she spoken to you, Rune? You must tell me."

"I...I don't know." I don't remember exact words, only indecipherable whispers.

But there is fear in every line of Matilde's face, and I cannot lie to her.

"Yes. I think so."

"The boundary has been crossed, then..."

I wait for her to finish, but nothing comes after. "What boundary? What are you talking about?"

"The hedge." Her voice trembles. "She has crossed the hedge."

I shake my head, willing it to clear of confusion. "The hedge between the forest and the village? Is that the hedge you're speaking of?" Surely she is tired, or ill. I'd rather her not be either, just a little muddled. "Please, lie down for a while, won't you? You're not making sense."

The strength Matilde exuded is now gone, and I watch her shoulders slump into their normal bend, leaving her weary and old...and afraid.

"What is it, Mutti? I've never seen you like this before."

"You will need to be very strong, Rune. Stronger than I've ever asked you to be."

"I don't understand."

"The world is changing, my sweet, as it always does. Do you know where your name comes from, Schätzchen?"

"Yes." I pause, thankful that she has calmed a bit. "The stones told you I was coming."

"That's right," Matilde says, remembering. "I rolled the stones that morning, and by afternoon, I had a tiny babe in my arms. The woman who was your mother had not named you. She had the foresight to see that a child cannot be found if it bears no name, so she left that task to me." Her smile grows wide with pride, and I can't help but wrap my arms around her. But something bites at the tip of my tongue, as if I've tasted something sour, or burned it. Something Matilde just said…

A child cannot be found if it bears no name…

Who would be looking?

I resume my position on the floor. Despite my proximity to the hearth, I am freezing inside as I wait for what Matilde will tell me next, though I don't suppose this is will be like any of the stories she's ever told before. This is not a fairy tale meant to hide the ugly truth. I see it in her eyes. I can feel it waiting within the very air of the room, hiding behind the appealing scent of the little orange that tries to sweeten our reality.

There is a knock at the door that makes me jump, and although unsteady, Matilde rises from her chair.

"The Blessed Thistle, Rune." Matilde points to the batch of green on the table. "Quickly."

I sigh, knowing it is the butcher, come for us to cure his stomach pains, putting pause to our conversation.

"Now Schätzchen, be nice to the man. He's promised a good-sized pig for two months' ration of herbs, and you know how I love my black pudding."

I do as I'm told, but find I am biting the inside of my cheek, wishing she and I could spend just a few more moments alone to finish.

The Blessed Mother is not the only one who bides time well, for I feel the dreaded truth deep in my stomach. What Matilde will tell me later will not be just another story.

Whether I realize it or not, it is the one I have waited my whole life to hear.

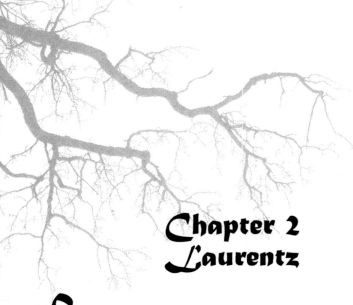

Chapter 2
Laurentz

Eltz Castle, 1627

She is dying. Anyone can see that.

My boot scrapes across the stone floor outside my stepmother's chamber, where I wait. When the door finally swings open, a weary, gray-haired man emerges. "Has there been any improvement, Father?"

Clearly, I know what his answer will be. Still, he humors me and replies, "No, Laurentz. Not yet."

He places his hand upon my shoulder as he shuffles past toward his own chamber at the far end of the hall, and I tense at the unusual display of affection. Surely he has not slept, at least not well. There are few servants in the Countess's quarters these days. We've asked for all who dwell and serve at Eltz to be considerate of my stepmother's needs, to let her die in peace.

That's what will undoubtedly happen.

She will die.

Her chamber will become empty, the house will fall as silent as a shroud, and my father will become a bitter old man. Perhaps that is why I ask after her condition each and every time I see him leave her chamber, such as now. Though I have no real interest in her life, or her imminent death, my fate does rest in hers, and I fear once she has passed, my father will either require eternal servitude of me or ignore me altogether. At this point, I cannot decide which outcome would be worse.

I stare back and forth between the two doors that have just closed, and then find myself turning the corner of the hall, walking toward the other end where another door faces me—the door my mother used to live behind until the day she fled into the forest. My hand skims the handle, but I let it rest there instead of turning it. I will not find her behind it, for she resides beneath the earth upon the knoll outside the castle. My brother lies beside her, reminding me I am all that is left to bear the family name, that I am all my father has left for a son, and every bit a disappointment as he braces himself to endure another loss. He will not speak of the dead we have buried, but leaves them to another time he refuses to revisit. When I ask him of them, it only gives him another reason to turn away.

Shrill, girlish whispers swell from the stairwell behind me. My memories melt away as I let go of the latch and turn to find two red-faced handmaidens. They quickly curtsy and avert their eyes as my presence reprimands their intrusion. The servants at Eltz live in a different world than I, one that is keen on invading privacy. They whisper and assume and speculate from dawn until dusk, sometimes alluding to the rumor that my family is cursed. After seeing so much misery, I don't blame them for coming to that conclusion, for I am certain there may be some truth in it.

It's clear the two girls are up to no good, probably sent on a mission from the kitchen, and I squelch their adventure immediately. One has the audacity to peer up through her dark lashes in hopes of appearing demure, but she will not garner a smile from me just yet. Perhaps later I will visit her chamber, but until then, I stare them down until they scurry away like the rats that burrow beneath the castle.

I take one last look at my mother's door and hold on to the little memory I have left of her. She is forever the faint scent of lemon, the whisper at bedtime, the cool kiss on my cheek, nothing more, and I make my way down to the lower level of Eltz.

"I beg your pardon, My Lord." A voice summons from the bottom of the stairs as I descend, and I am soon face to face with the house messenger who stands in the middle of the Great Hall. Try as I might to recall his given name, it will not come to me, and I stare back at him with eyebrows raised as invitation to speak, hoping his delivery will be swift.

"There is a visitor in the chapel," he announces with a small degree of urgency.

I peer beyond his shoulder, past the heavy brocade draperies that suffocate the windows at the east side of the castle, and see a large ornate carriage waiting outside. Of all days to come, the bishop has chosen this one. I swallow my annoyance, even though I'd like nothing more than to roll my eyes and be on my way, doing as I please. Instead, I nod my dismissal to the man and listen to the light step of his boots as he leaves me alone in the grand room. Even after I can no longer hear him, I make no attempt to hurry off to the chapel. Part of me doesn't care if the bishop waits; he really isn't here to see me. I glance up the elaborate staircase to the landing above and wonder if I should tell my father. I can still feel the pressure of his hand on my shoulder, but ultimately decide against it. He was weary when I left him. Besides, earning my father's respect is crucial, as is proving to him I am more than capable of standing on my own and making him proud. Eltz, and all its affairs, will be mine one day, and proving I am worthy might change things between us. The gesture upstairs was small, yet significant to me. I want to believe my father feels something for me other than blame and disappointment.

The path to the chapel is overgrown in a wild sort of way my brother would have loved. I stop and listen, hard enough that I'm sure I hear his laughter surfacing from behind the vines, and suddenly, I am little again, hiding among the shrubs, waiting until one of us comes close enough to send a thin branch snapping at the other's backside. It is a memory of my childhood that grips me with such force that I quicken my pace and push past the rotund Provence roses my mother once tended. They still bloom as large as cabbages. I pass the Elderberry and the bright orange Calendula. She taught me all their names; my brother had no patience for such things, and I smile a little at the fact that I can still identify them. For years I believed beauty no longer existed at Eltz, that my home was as cold as the bitter winters blowing through all of Germany. Today is different, because the roses are blooming. Because of the little gesture my father has given me, I have reason to notice it again.

I stop still upon the chapel steps and force the thoughts of happier times to the pit of my stomach. The bishop stands at the arm of the front pew with a measured look draped across his face, and I struggle with the reason he is here.

"My boy," he greets me. "But forgive me, My Lord, you are no longer a boy, are you?"

I bristle at this personal observation, for the bishop is not my friend. He is cold and guarded, and always has been, making it difficult to warm toward him easily. I'm sure he is well aware that he makes me uncomfortable, especially since his visit is not a planned one, but still we keep up the charade. I am only here to prove I am worthy of being Electorate one day, and to earn my father's trust.

"Your Holiness." I bend my head. "It's always a pleasure to see you." My welcome is forced, and my words feel as though they are made of a thick, unpleasant substance I am sure he can see. As long as I am respectful and pretend to agree, as my father would, then this meeting should be a brief one.

"Your father?" The bishop looks past my shoulder in expectation.

"Detained."

I watch as he nods, believing the Electorate of Burg Eltz is preoccupied with important business. He doesn't need to know my father has confined himself to his chamber, dreaming of a way to save the wife who wastes away a few doors down the hall. The bishop wipes the perpetual beads of perspiration from his brow with a small square of cloth, and I watch as his meaty hand tucks it somewhere within the thick folds of his robe, where I'm sure it will become lost.

"I'm afraid I come bearing grave news," he says steadily. "Your neighbor, Pyrmont, has fallen."

I stare at him silently with narrow eyes as the cogs of my mind shift. I'm well aware that Eltz's Guard has not been alerted, nor has the morning's breeze carried the telltale horns of a breach, even one that is miles from here.

The bishop can see that I am not following him.

"From Plague, My Lord." He says this appearing as if he too is stricken.

Suddenly, I regret not taking the time to rush upstairs and find my father.

"Are you certain?" I don't mean to question that he could be wrong.

"Nearly half the family," he nods, finding the embroidered cloth again and twisting it to and fro. "I'm afraid the rest will be dead by nightfall."

I grip the worn, wooden pew behind me as I mentally map out the distance between the two castles, noting it is only a half-day's ride from here. I've never seen Plague before, only heard of it, along with stories of the horrible, swift deaths it causes.

"Have you been there yourself?" My face must show I am in the midst of making a terrifying assumption, one that is perhaps accusatory—has he brought the infection with him, possibly condemning us all to a similar fate?

"Goodness no, Laurentz," he insists. "Word was sent last evening to the nearby friary. By moonrise, the surrounding village was wiped clean. It's spreading quickly, and I don't advise either you or your father making the trek to look for survivors. By morning, I suspect the halls of Pyrmont will echo with the silence of death." His words fall, and there is a strange hum between us. More souls will be lost by tomorrow.

It's nearly unfathomable, and I struggle to digest the news. At least a hundred people live within the walls of Pyrmont— the Electorate's family, servants, guests, the armed Guard. Yesterday they were alive, and by sunrise, they will be dead.

"But I believe you might be safe," he says, sounding hopeful. "Eltz is mostly surrounded by the river, with one side exposed to the forest."

"What will *that* do to protect us?" My voice bears no reverence, and the bishop stares at me, dumbfounded. I assume he wants to say something that would make me ashamed and fear God, or both, but I see he bites his tongue, for I am in a position he is not. I stand to become Electorate of Eltz one day, and if Plague is on the horizon, with my father slowly deteriorating, that day could come sooner than either of us realizes.

He turns his back to me and faces the altar. His hand touches his forehead, chest, then shoulders, then meets the other and tents in prayer in front of him. I've offended him. Just as I am about to say something I hope will make amends, he changes the subject.

"I trust you are aware of necessary tactical maneuvers, Laurentz? This is your second year in your father's Guard, is it not?"

"It's my third." I wait for him to turn around, curious that he would discuss military strategies at a time like this. "You speak of the feuds?"

My father taught me several things—never let your guard down, be civil with your neighbor, and stock the Keep. Feuding between territories is as rampant as the wind that rushes through the Black Forest, and like the forest, you should never turn your back upon it. I feel the presence of the door behind me and wonder if I should excuse myself and make my way back. My father worked hard to establish amicable ties with Pyrmont; surely this news will weigh heavily upon him.

"In a way, it is a type of feud, one I firmly believe is responsible for the fall of many places, Pyrmont included," he says.

My mind whirls as the soldier inside me begins to organize all there is to do. If there is a band of vagrants unleashing infection upon the strongest of sovereigns, being prepared is of utmost priority. I mentally ready myself for the tasks ahead—alert my father, the Guard, the servants, and pray the knowledge the bishop has given me will keep Eltz from succumbing.

The air in the chapel is heavy and the bishop's information warrants telling my father immediately, yet he makes no attempt to leave so I can do so. Instead, the bishop moves slowly, and I wonder if he really believes Eltz stands a chance against the affliction. Perhaps he is reluctant to face whatever lies outside.

"Disease and famine have made their mark on Bavaria in the past, and so they shall again. But mind you, Laurentz, nobility has always prevailed."

He is telling me this so I won't worry, but I can't help hearing how his tone has changed from that of a nervous, fearful man to one who speaks as if he has a plan. He paces back and forth before the pulpit, his knuckles bone-white as his hands clutch the cloth.

"The villages surrounding the region are tainted." His voice is low and secretive. "They harbor all manner of contagion and are responsible for many of the afflictions upon this world. Forgive me for being so bold, Laurentz, but you are well aware of the difference between nobility and the *rest of them.*"

"*Them?*"

"Certainly you understand your place in this world, my young Lord, and that the Church has always protected those with souls worth saving."

My eyebrows arch at the words that hang in the air between us.

"It is my understanding that the Church protects *all* souls, does it not?" I make no measure to hide my surprise at his implications of how degraded the villages are. I have grown up knowing my place, knowing *theirs*. Peasantry is not admirable, not by any means, but it should be respected, as should all forms of life. But to hear it spoken out loud, by this man especially, fills this space with the strangest of emotions. I may have grown to be bitter about things—my father, the death of my family, what the future holds for me—but I certainly do not hate the world and wish harm to befall anyone in it.

"What exactly are you saying?" My question implies challenge, and by the grave expression his face holds, I see he is up for it. He plumps around his thighs the fabric that nearly drowns him, seats himself in the first pew, and gestures for me to join him. He studies my expression, and then tells me, "You look like your brother."

I find this hard to believe, because my brother never reached eighteen. He never had the chance to bear scars of disappointment, or of death. He never carried what felt like the weight of the world upon his young shoulders or faced bitterness from the one he pledged to serve.

"You've been through your share of dark times, haven't you, my boy?" he says, making up for the strange silence when I don't answer him. "I am afraid to say there will be dark times ahead as well, but it's best to be prepared."

I give a nod, for preparation is what I've already begun to do, and I cannot quite understand why we are sitting here, speaking of things I'd like to forget, when there is so much at stake. The look on my face sparks a light behind his dark eyes, as if I've just opened a gate that he is now eager to lead me through.

"There is a source for all the wrong in the world, an evil that gives birth to all other evil. Darkness is a sneaky thing hiding among us, undetected. The sooner we stop it, the sooner we will all be saved."

"You mean to say there is something more than the Plague?" I ask.

Murgia

He leans forward and looks into my eyes. "I ask that you keep this between us, Laurentz. As successor to your father one day, you will have an advantage if you are aware of the real dangers among us." The bishop twists the gold band on his finger. "Heresy is at play here. Be mindful of the cunning woman who hides from the others, if you value your soul."

Chapter 3
Rune

My breath is suctioned to the back of my throat, because when Matilde opens the door, it is not the butcher, but a cloaked figure, and my venture into the forest hits me all over again, hard.

"Are you the crone?" a cautious feminine voice pushes through the open door into the small room where we stand.

Matilde and I are silent, and I feel the fine hairs on the back of my neck rise. I do not like the word "crone." It is degrading and harsh, and it bothers me to no end that Matilde assures me she has been called much, much worse. I ignore that she tells me I am much too protective of her and stare at the stranger with enough suspicion for the two of us.

Matilde hobbles forward. "It depends who's asking."

With slender fingers, the woman pulls the grey hood back, revealing a shock of dark blonde hair that frames a clean, pretty face. She is fairly young, but not as young as I, and dressed nicely from what I can see beneath the heavy wrap that covers her.

"Forgive me, I mean not to offend. I was told to follow the path that divides the village from the forest; there, I would find the crone who could help me."

Still feeling the sting from her lack of tact, I let the bundle of Blessed Thistle slip from my hand and rest upon the table.

Strangers have called at odd hours before. It's not unheard of. I suppose it's not as unusual as anyone assuming Matilde is anything *but* a crone. She has lived in the woods for much of her life, preferring solitude to the bustling, gossip-ridden village. What seems strange here is how obviously Matilde doesn't try to hide her discomfort.

I study the woman's face, pay attention to her movements. Her eyes flit around, agitated, while Matilde assesses her in a calculated sort of way. And still, Matilde asks her to step in further. I cannot place what her trouble could be, since she appears neither sick nor in pain. She doesn't clutch her stomach or ask for tea. Matilde takes on a peculiar determination, ushering the woman to one of the few chairs we own, and then setting about to fill the kettle unasked.

"You seek something," Matilde states as she adds more kindling to the fire. It is an odd thing, because Matilde usually doesn't trust guests enough to turn her back to them, although we have very little for her to be interested in stealing. Perhaps Matilde feels confident that I am her second set of eyes and will notice anything out of sorts. When Matilde straightens, kettle in hand, she is very stiff, despite her usual bent stance. "I doubt you will find it here."

The woman is taken aback. "But I've come so far to see you. I am positive you are the only one who can help me with my…my ailment."

I am a little shocked myself. What bothers this woman is apparently invisible to me, and I fear I will never be as trained as Matilde to be able to read another person well enough that they need not explain.

"Mutti, surely we can at least see what troubles her."

I have not intervened before, and the woman eyes me curiously. Surely she wonders why I've called the old woman my mother, and suddenly my face warms at my error. I am Matilde's apprentice to anyone who visits, nothing more. The look Matilde gives me makes me wish I had kept my thoughts to myself, and I feel a strong prickling sensation behind my neck. She slowly walks closer to our guest, who now has a sweaty sheen coating her forehead and temples, causing the ends of her yellow hair to twist and curl ever so slightly. Her face is ashen.

Matilde holds out her hand, palm up, implying that the seated woman should rest her own on top of it. A shiver courses through me, but one of excitement and anticipation, and I cannot help wonder what the delicate lines in her hand will say. Despite the odd air to the room and the look she had just given me, I am thrilled Matilde has not ushered me out of the cottage yet, like she has from time to time. My heart hammers away. I realize I might finally be able to see the old magick Matilde often shields me from. "Folk Magick," she calls it. I've learned a little, but I've often felt there are some lessons Matilde believes I am not ready for. Hopefully, today will be different, and I amuse myself with wondering if this is what I am to be strong for.

"What do you see, old woman?" The woman's ill appearance does not match the tone of her voice. She seems too intrigued by the vision Matilde may or may not be able to see.

Ever the wise businesswoman, Matilde barters, "What are you willing to give me?"

The woman pulls a small purse from beneath her luxurious wrap, and unravels the cord looped around her wrist.

"I will give you two thaler. Will that do?"

Matilde wrinkles her already-lined face and purses her lips at the offer.

"Your palm speaks, but does not reveal that which you wish to know."

The audible sigh from the woman makes me uncomfortable. Matilde is not one for causing annoyance. She's accepted far less for her fortunes, and I wonder what she could possibly sense by insisting on higher payment.

At last an exchange is made. The thin sound of coin against coin chimes as they fall into the open palm, and Matilde's voice rings clear. "Bring the stones to me."

Within seconds, I am at the cupboard on the other side of the room, twisting open the wooden knob and brushing aside the rabbit that hangs there curing. I grab the old drawstring bag sitting at the back. It is filled with smooth, marked stones that shift when I carry it back to her. She instructs the pale woman to come stand beside the edge of the table. The string is untied and the bag emptied; its contents, wrapped in a lumpy cloth, fall to the wood with a dull *plunk*.

Nothing but the sound of three breaths can be heard as we hover over the table. The cloth is unwrapped and within it are nearly a dozen pale river stones, each etched with a black symbol different from the next. Matilde carefully moves the stones aside and spreads the cloth flat. She then turns each stone face down so that the etchings are hidden for now.

"You will take a stone, one at a time, and place it upon the cloth," she instructs the woman. "The stone must be faced down. Do this until all the stones are laid."

The woman's hand reaches out, but Matilde's gnarled fingers stop her.

"Do not be so quick to know what lies ahead for you. You must let your hand sweep over the runes, like this." Matilde's hand hovers just an inch above one of the little rocks. "Feel the stone meant to be chosen first. It will call to you."

It takes a few moments, but soon enough, the woman chooses a stone and places it upon the table.

"This is the rune of Past Influences." Matilde nods her head for another stone to be chosen.

When the second stone is laid next in line, Matilde tells her, "This is the rune of the Present."

As a third stone is settled in the row, Matilde says, "This is the Outcome."

She guides the woman's hand to the pile of remaining stones, and, after two more are chosen, they are each laid above and below the middle stone. "Now, you must turn them over."

I lean over the table with wide, wondrous eyes, waiting to see which stones the woman has chosen. Like our guest, I am eager to hear Matilde interpret them for us.

One by one, Matilde turns the stones upright upon the old, warped table. The woman leans over hungrily. "Tell me, old crone. Tell me what they say." She is too fascinated by the ancient markings to notice how Matilde leans close to me.

"You must leave, Rune," Matilde whispers. "Take the basket into the woods, gather whatever you can, and don't return until the sun is setting behind the trees."

"But…what's wrong? Tell me what to do, Mutti."

I want to stay, because I know something is not right. Twice today Matilde hasn't been well. What if her coughing spell comes back? What if she feels faint? Will this woman know what to do? She shoots me a look telling me I must be on my way. I think I see sadness lingering behind it, only I am too stubborn to try and understand what it could be. All I can see is, once again, I am being forced to leave, just when I had thought everything had changed.

Confused and hurt I hear myself talking back, refusing to do as I am told. "Why don't you trust me to stay?"

Her hand catches mine, but instead of the reprimand I am so sure I will receive, she is soft and pleading.

"Do as I say, Schätzchen. It will be all right."

Defiantly, I take my basket, casting a sharp glance at the woman whose fortune awaits her, and then at the woman who insists I am still too much of a child to witness it. *Fine*, I mutter to myself. I lift my cloak from the nail on the wall and fling it around my shoulders. Then, basket in hand, and doing all I can to ignore the earnest expression Matilde holds on her face, I open the door and step out into the forest.

Chapter 4
Rune

I should be quiet and do what Matilde asked of me, but there is a heavy stone inside me telling me to do otherwise, a wild, willful part of me that is desperately tired of being treated like a child. I am half-tempted to press my ear to the door and listen in on the fortune being read, but I decide I am too annoyed to want to know what's in store for that strange woman. Let Matilde be the one to tell her. Let the woman in the fancy cloak walk off into the arms of a handsome man, or a pouch full of money. I don't really care.

The rushing sound of the stream breaks my thoughts. It calms me, even at this distance, but I cannot bring myself to find it among the trees. Suddenly I am angry at myself. I'm angry at being too young and incapable of what Matilde can pass down to me. I'm angry for being scared this morning at nothing but the wind playing tricks on me.

I am angry for being gullible.

My basket is empty and I don't feel like filling it, but a small cluster of wild mushrooms grows just beneath the Larch tree, and I quickly pull the tender flutes from the soft earth and place them into my basket, just so I can say I gathered something. The forest is dark for such an early hour, as if rain will fall at any moment. I pull my cloak closer and welcome the damp grayness I've stepped into. Perhaps it will wash away the horrible feeling brewing inside me, the one that begs me to realize much of my life has been in the dark. My past, my present, my future—all of it, shadowed as heavily as this forest I have always lived in.

My feet find the trail that leads to the hedge. I usually don't care for market day, but I am drawn to the voices and clamoring I hear from where I stand. There is life there, even if the faces are cold and stone-like. Even if they eye me strangely.

When I am standing at the waist-high wall of green, I am reminded of Matilde's vision, that my birth mother has somehow crossed the hedge, coming from the Other World into mine. My birth mother is dead. The whispers and dreams are nothing but a bunch of fairy tales, and I have been frightened for no reason for far too long.

I hoist my skirt to my knees and squeeze myself through, feeling the sharp sting of thorns hidden between the soft leaves, but I don't care. I don't complain. I am used to scratches on my legs and tears in my dress, and soon, I am all the way through, breathing in all that is the village of Württemberg.

My shoulders are straight and my chin higher than usual as I pick my way around the cobbled square. The air doesn't feel as damp here, and the doors of the houses and stores are wide open. There are fruits, and meats, and cloth for garments, and iron, all laid out for buyers, and I am so caught up in the wonder of it all that I don't take notice of the stares aimed my way. For once, I feel I am part of the town with every right to walk among the vendors and admire.

But whispers do float to me and stop me for a moment, as they always do. I lean over a table of beautiful linen, admiring the handiwork. I will not look up; I am determined not to let it bother me today. Today is decidedly different.

Only I *am* gullible, and I lift my chin just a little to try and peer around me. There are shoppers, just like me, but that is all I can see. No one is whispering nearby, at least from what I can tell.

I hold up one of the handkerchiefs and focus on the delicate stitching.

"It would look lovely on you, my lady."

I am stunned by how she has addressed me, and my face must show it because the woman staring at me gives a little laugh.

"It's too fine for me to wear," I say timidly, and place it back among the others for sale.

"Nonsense," she replies, leaning over the small sampling of cloth she peddles. She fetches the one I've just returned and holds it up against my cheek. "The silver stitches match the sparkle in your eyes quite nicely, just like fairy dust woven between the threads."

This is the first time anyone has seen my eyes up close. I've been too fearful to raise my head any other time, always too afraid to draw attention to myself. I am beaming beneath my skin, and am drinking her praise like it is some strange nectar I cannot get enough of.

"Only a thaler today, it's my special price for such a beautiful lady." She is sweet as she tries to convince me to make my purchase, but I have no money, and Matilde is an experienced trader whom I've followed around this market many times, so I wonder for a moment.

I extend my basket across the table. "I have these delicious mushrooms. Perhaps you'd consider taking them in exchange?"

The woman eyes me curiously, then, bending her head, she peers inside the basket at my offering. "I did spend an entire week on this one. My fingers don't bend the way they used to. Perhaps you have something else to give me?"

I am getting nervous. I am ashamed that all I have to offer in trade are a measly bunch of mushrooms that grew outside my doorstep, that I picked out of spite. Suddenly, I wish I had taken Matilde's instruction to heart and spent more time gathering so I would have a suitable exchange. Quickly, I think of Matilde, and wonder if she has finished telling the cloaked woman all the wonderful things her future holds. They are probably marveling at the message the runes have given, and with a sudden jolt, I am jealous.

Before I realize what I am doing, the words fly from my lips, "These aren't just ordinary mushrooms." Then I bite my tongue in regret, and pull my basket closer, but it's too late, I've already caught the old woman's attention.

"They look like regular mushrooms to me."

"Oh, not by any means," I say quickly, drumming up a way to appear worldly and helpful. "They…"

My brain is whirling madly and yet I cannot think of anything suitable for what these ridiculous mushrooms can offer this woman. Why did I let myself become so enamored with a piece of fabric! I cannot carry it anywhere but in the forest while I scavenge for food. It was a silly idea for me to think otherwise, but my head continues to think, and think, and then, it comes to me.

I stare at the woman's twisted fingers as she holds the fine square I desire, noting how she used a bit of fantasy to entice me.

"They are healing mushrooms." I whisper beneath my breath, half-hoping she cannot hear me, while on the other hand, hoping she does. I'm almost fascinated by the lie that slips from my lips.

"Healing mushrooms, eh? And why should I believe you?"

Why? Why would anyone believe me? Suddenly I can't believe I've woven this incredible story all for the sake of owning something beautiful. "Because they came from deep within the forest, further than anyone has ever been."

Consideration lights her weathered face. She turns toward the hedge I slipped through just a short while ago, and stares for a moment.

"The Black Forest, you say?"

"Yes." I try to sound convincing, but I cannot help my voice from quivering, so I thrust the basket in front of her, hoping it will persuade her as she had persuaded me.

Her eyes stare at the line of trees just past the blacksmith's fire, and I am struck with the strong feeling that she is superstitious, which may just work in my favor. She looks into my eyes, then motions toward the open door behind her, leaning across the basket between us. Bringing her face closer, she whispers, "My daughter is with child, but the fool of a man does not love her," she tells in a tone that is desperate and hushed. "Do you suppose your mushrooms will heal her heart?"

I had expected to persuade the woman because of her hands, yet I'm captured by what she's revealed to me. How horrible to be unwed and expecting a baby, and to be cast aside as well. My heart lurches, and I search within the darkened doorway for a glimpse.

Before I can tell her that I suppose they will, she is speaking again.

"Tell me about where they come from. Is it very deep in the woods? Do they possess magick?"

A strange chill spreads to my entire body. Magick is a word that carries the weight of a thousand stones. I know well that a word is just word, without the meaning small-minded people like to give it, and I am inclined to continue my bartering.

"They grow just past the cottage that is there." This seems to spark renewed interest in the woman's eyes, and I know I've said the right thing. Matilde is well-known for her healing magick, and although it is always in secret that people find her, I've seen how the visitors hold her skills in high regard.

The woman extends the beautiful cloth out to me. "It is yours, then."

Gingerly, I take it, allowing her to spill the contents of my basket into a bowl beneath the table. She gives me a measured look, probably because I am trying to smile back, and not doing a very good job at it. I can imagine my mouth is more twisted in pain than appreciation.

The space behind me suddenly feels as though packed with people, when in fact, it is not. My guilt is suffocating, and pressing, and my breath bursts from me in short jets of panic. I turn around and attempt to walk to the next vendor, even though I have nothing left in my basket to barter with. Somehow I doubt I will find anything else to catch my interest and I quickly make my way past food that now looks terribly spoiled, and horse shoes and tackle that are dented and old. It is as if everything here has suddenly lost its luster. Nothing is as shiny and appealing as it was when I first arrived.

It is a horrible thing I've done. Matilde will be so upset with me. My cheeks are burning as I walk toward the last house in the square, the one that is nearest the hedge. If I cross now, I can leave my worries here. But I am certain all eyes are on me, and if I do cross, they will surely know who I am, and where I've come from. Perhaps my birth mother _was_ a terrible person, and soon the village will piece two and two together, realizing my ebony hair is not an anomaly, that I remind them of someone dangerous, that I remind them of _her._

Do you care if they know?

I have never spun around so fast in all my life, yet there is no one near who could have spoken so loud, or so close.

You've done well...

I am falling ill. Perhaps the woman I left Matilde with _was_ suffering from something after all, and the short amount of time I spent at the cottage was enough to become exposed to it. My hand has been twisting what it holds, and I look down, ashamed. The exquisitely sewn handkerchief is ruined, after what I've done to get it.

This is my punishment for stealing away to the market and becoming a thief. I push myself forward and have one foot inside the bristly growth of the hedge, about to hurl myself into the forest and run for home, when I hear laughter behind me. My eyes catch a hint of black creeping behind the corner of a building. It is a cloak, and my breath stills in my lungs. A few moments later a black horse rounds the corner, its tail flicking away the flies as it trudges along behind the man that pulls it.

The laughter comes again, this time from a different direction. It is hollow and thin, and I spin around, determined to find it. There is nothing. I panic and leap into the thorny border at the edge of the forest.

Chapter 5
Laurentz

*T*he bishop finally prepares to leave, wrapping his thick robe around him as he steps carefully onto the foot iron of the red lacquered carriage. He extends his hand for me to kiss the gold and garnet ring that adorns his chubby finger, and I do so quickly. My thoughts are torn. Do I tell my father of the visit, or sort through what the bishop has just shared with me in effort to understand it better?

The bishop's heated accusations have irritated me. There is something in his words I cannot quite put to rest. If the infection that has infiltrated Pyrmont spreads to the South, where Eltz lies, then I doubt the bishop will return anytime soon. Since today the South is still safe, I must see for myself if the small hamlet nearby is not as vile as he made it out to be, despite the thorny past rumored to be associated with it. That it is still home to the good people my father has worked to earn respect from, not caught in the grip of one woman harboring ill secrets and heresy.

I take the reins of my steed and head toward the thick line of dark green trees at the base of the hill. It is an impenetrable wall that appears murky and sinister as I approach, and my horse whinnies and slows with reluctance. I stroke her muscular neck, whispering words that I hope will calm her, and apologize for not fixing the shadow roll to her bridle before leaving. She settles beneath my touch, and I gently dig my boots into her girth, guiding her through a patch that is not as dense, until we are swallowed whole within the mouth of the forest.

It is like night has fallen before my eyes. I blink, adjusting to the dimness that steals my breath for a moment, and then we are off again, trailing along what appears to be a trampled path. "Shhh," I whisper. If I do this at regular intervals, I find I am not only calming my horse, but myself as well. It's not easy to ignore the tricks my mind conjures as we continue along. This is the Black Forest, the very forest my mother ran into. And when she returned to Eltz, to us, she was dead.

The hooves of my horse clop along, leading me deeper and deeper into the suffocating darkness, and I find myself peering upwards, searching for a sky that is completely obliterated by arching branches. Shadows are cast, creeping along, hiding behind trunks. There are whispers I am sure are not the wind; from both my left and my right, I hear sounds so strange I am convinced they are otherworldly, more than simply the magnified crunching of needles and underbrush.

At last I see a structure forming within the shadows before me. It is small and constructed of crooked stones. The smell of charred firewood greets me as plumes of dancing smoke roll from a stubby sort of chimney in its thatched roof. A cloaked figure flees quickly from the door, and I am certain it is a woman by the slight build and the agility with which she moves. Could this be the witch the bishop spoke of earlier? I am immediately on guard and let my eye follow her to where she disappears between a thick wall of green.

I give my horse a kick, and once again, we are off. The cloaked woman I am following seems to disappear into thin air, and I find myself trapped behind a fence of greenery that divides the eternally dark forest and a seemingly lively village on the other side. Yanking the reins, I lead my horse in a half-circle away from the hedge in order to round back and jump over it, but to my surprise, instead of leaping over the waist-high shrub, my horse rears, responding to the small shriek welling up from the mass of twisted green beneath her hooves. The hedge is alive, and from it a girlish screech rises. Before my eyes the thorny patch sprouts two arms and a leg, scrambling for all their worth to be free.

"Are you all right?" I ask, quickly slipping from my saddle. "I didn't see you!" I extend my hand to help the girl from where she is lodged, her delicate hand hesitantly accepting me. Then, with a couple of tugs and maneuvering, she steps out of the feral shrub line, pulling at the leaves and thorns that cling to her. Her skirt is dotted with dozens of tiny tears, yet she straightens it, bringing her hands to her face for a moment while staring at me with intense brown eyes.

"I didn't mean to scare you. Are you all right?" I ask again.

"Yes, I think so," she says, nodding slowly.

"I'm sorry, I suppose I've pulled you out on the wrong side of the hedge. You're obviously going *into* the village, not out of it. My horse can take you over, if you'd like."

She looks at me with surprise, and I cannot help notice she is stunning despite her current disheveled state. But I am staring too long, and this makes her uncomfortable.

"No. I'm headed the right way." Her voice quivers slightly, but is light and beautiful, like little birds have escaped the dreadful forest and gathered in her throat. I have just come from the forest, spending nearly an hour trying to find my way out of it. Why would anyone wish by choice to go into it? And then I spy her empty basket lying on the ground.

"I suppose you're spending the day gathering?" I reach down and retrieve the basket. "I'm not sure what you'll find growing in there. I would think plants need sunlight in order to grow, but what do I know?"

She ignores the basket I offer her and suddenly drops her eyes to the line of red growing beneath my sleeve.

"You're bleeding."

"Look at that, I suppose I am. Thorns are sharper than they look, aren't they?" I pluck a few thorns from my torn sleeve, flicking them to the ground.

"Let me help you with that." Before I can object, she is pushing my coat sleeve up and rolling my cuff away from my wrist, exposing my forearm, which is indeed sliced and trickling with blood.

"It looks to be clean," she assesses softly, then leaves my arm to scoop something green from the ground, then presses it lightly to my skin.

"Is that…sanitary?"

"It's quite safe," she replies. "It's called Sphagnum Moss. It will stop the bleeding and prevent infection."

Her hand is warm and gentle as it holds my arm still, and I can't help watching her closely, noting how softly her dark hair coils at the nape of her neck, how smooth her cheek appears.

"So something good comes from this forest after all?"

I don't receive a spoken answer, just a hesitant nod accompanied by a slight blush. For all the forest is associated with, I wonder if I've assumed incorrectly, and then, I take a quick glance behind me and see how the darkness creeps along the edge of the tree line, deepening as far as I can see. I am not quite ready to say it doesn't make me uneasy.

"Forgive me," I whisper, hoping she isn't regretting helping me. "My name is Laurentz, or rather, should I say today I am a bumbling idiot. I know nothing of…Stagnant Moss."

She laughs at my terrible pronunciation. "Sphagnum Moss," she corrects me. In an instant, the mood is light again, and I am mesmerized by her agile touch as she treats the cuts on my arm.

My name doesn't seem to register with her, which is fine by me. I'd much rather learn more about her than blurt out the fact that I'm the son of the Electorate of Eltz.

"Rune," she answers back after a few seconds, and continues to press the strange spongy moss into my cut.

"Rune…" I repeat her name, letting it roll on my tongue, feeling how unusual it sounds. My arm feels oddly warm all of a sudden, and just as I am about to ask if I could be reacting to the moss, Rune lifts the green bandage. My skin sticks to it for a moment, then releases. She pulls the moss away.

"There you are," Rune says in a quiet, nervous voice.

I hold my arm out in front of me, and turn it over then back again. There is no blood. There is no sign that my arm has been cut in the first place, save for the garnet stain on my sleeve.

"How…?"

A peculiar look blooms across her face that tells me I'm on the brink of asking too much. She takes the empty basket and steps away from me. But I cannot let it go, and am about to ask again when her face pales. She looks frantically toward the village instead of answering me. My horse stamps her hoof, suddenly agitated. A breeze stirs on the village side of the hedge, then cuts through the middle of it, disappearing into the trees. I am left staring after it as if I've just witnessed something that has a mind of its own; then, I look down at my arm again and touch it with my finger. It is hot, but not feverish or alarming, and my skin is smooth, as if the thorns never cut me.

A whisper of white snagged on a thin branch within the green border distracts me, and I pluck it away between my fingers. It is crumpled, but still delicate, and although the handkerchief briefly reminds me of the one the bishop carried earlier in the chapel, I suspect it might belong to Rune.

"Is this yours?" I ask as I turn to her, but she is gone, and I am left with the shadows between the trees.

Chapter 6
Rune

My side hurts from running, and I press my hand to my ribs once I am safely hidden behind the tree. I peer around the thick branches to see if he's watched me run away, but he is far from sight. I've never spoken to a man before, alone, and I am terrified and thrilled all the same.

Was I too obvious, watching him closely while I tended to his arm? I hope he didn't notice and think me strange. I couldn't help myself. I planned to keep my head low, thank him politely for saving me from the brambles, and make my way home. But he was hurt. I couldn't ignore that. And from the moment I'd pulled at his sleeve to survey the damage the hedge had inflicted, I could barely concentrate.

He was handsome, with a shock of unruly chestnut hair, and very tall, with wide, broad shoulders. The look upon his face was impish, yet he was more man than boy. He was dressed impeccably for a rider—his boots not too soiled, and the knees and elbows of his trousers and waistcoat not too thin, except for where the thorns had ripped through the fabric.

But I should have watched where I was going. How was I to know a person would be on the other side of the hedge, the *forest side* of the hedge, the very moment I leaped across?

Thank goodness he noticed my basket and not the vaporous laughter I'd been running from. It made going along with his assumption, that I was out for a day of gathering, easier than explaining what I was really doing, which was running off to hide from the voices I'd heard. My insides tighten at the very thought that he might have heard. I am certain his horse did, the way she whinnied and stamped.

I let myself steal a few moments, sitting upon the soft pine needles, and suddenly I am unsure of containing the emotions flooding through me—fear, delight, confusion. I only wanted to help him. I can't explain why the cut on his arm disappeared beneath my touch. I've never seen anything like it in all my life, yet I believe I made it appear as if such a thing was normal.

My head is still spinning at the way he smiled at me. He was certainly beautiful for a man, and I wonder if that was my luck today, to find beautiful things I would feel oddly about. Frowning, I reach inside my basket to find the handkerchief gone. I scan the ground, but it is nowhere to be found, and I realize it has been left behind. Maybe it's just as well. I don't deserve it anyway, although it would have been nice to have studied it and quietly learned the stitches on my own. I would like to make one for myself one day, or one I could give to Matilde at the end of the summer harvest, just before the first snow, or perhaps for Yule. It would be something special to have during the cold months, something pretty to look at when the sun is not growing flowers for us to admire.

I stare at the hedge that divides the forest from the village. As much as I wanted to pretend I belonged on the other side today, it is clear to me where my loyalties should lie. I will always belong here, among the protection of the shaded trees, instead of in the open, pretending I am someone I'm not.

I stand up and brush the needles from my dress and apron, then set about scouring for herbs. I plan on honoring at least one of Matilde's wishes, and begin filling my basket while I wait for the sun to sink behind the tree line, just like she told me to.

There are butterflies and dragonflies diving in and out of the dappled light around me. How could I possibly wish to be anywhere else on a day like today? Little white and yellow Chamomile blossoms poke their heads up from the ground between beds of Sphagnum Moss, and I can barely contain my excitement. Matilde will be more than happy to have it once again. Only last week, Matilde used her last mound of the spongy pale-green moss to dress a patient's leg wound; since then, it's been difficult to find enough to replenish her supply. My basket is nearly overflowing, yet I continue to fill it. Finally, when it can hold no more, I add a few strips of Silver Birch bark on top and make my way home.

The sky is a blood-red glow between the treetops when I hear the butcher's wagon behind me. I groan beneath my breath. In the midst of my trek to the village I had forgotten he was still coming today, and of all places to run into him, he is steering his mule up the very path I walk.

"Pleasant evening," I grumble lightly as he pulls up alongside me. I don't plan on standing on this path for the next hour or so discussing the weather, so I hope he is happy with that and continues on.

Unfortunately the wagon creaks beneath his weight and slowly rolls to a stop. Rolf glares at me, and although I've never liked the man, I can't bring to mind why he would appear so rude right now.

"Have you come from the cottage?" I ask, trying to be nice. "I laid out the Blessed Thistle for you. It should help with your...troubles." I can't stop my eye from following the thick brown belt he tries to fit around his middle, knowing his appetite is the cause of all his pain. It is one thing to be wealthy and robust, but to look like him, well, that's another.

He harrumphs loudly, and spits over the side plank of the cart, nearly missing my shoe.

"Do you see what's strapped there to the back of the wagon, young miss?" he hisses.

I don't want to, but I look anyway, expecting to see something bloodied and meaty hanging from the hook, but what I find is neither, and I'm not sure what I am looking at.

I wrinkle my nose. Obviously, this is a guessing game.

"Don't know, do you?" He spits again, and I step back. "It's the swine your…your… What is she to you, anyway?"

"Matilde?"

"Yes, the old woman. She's too old to be your mother, but then again…"

"She's adopted me, raised me. I have no mother, just her."

After all these years of helping him, he still doesn't have a clue. It's really none of his business, but I hope it satisfies him enough to leave, although if he hasn't delivered the swine yet, then it means I'll have a good chance at having him for company on my walk home.

"That there swine's not for sale, at least not to the likes of you and the old crone." He spits again.

"And why is that?" I stare at the hideous, emaciated slab that hangs in front of me. "It doesn't look like a pig. What's wrong with it?"

"What's wrong with it?" he mocks me, repeating my question. "Why not ask what's wrong with all my animals? Why not ask the old crone if she knows anything about that?"

It's not that the pig is no longer for sale. It's how he says the word *crone*, for a second time. It makes my skin raise and feel pinched.

"Is there a problem, sir?"

Rolf looks me up and down a few minutes until I feel my clothing has all but disintegrated.

"My horse fell ill." I watch him twist the leather strap between his meaty hands.

"Well, then I'm sure you'll share your stock of thistle, won't you?"

"My horse is *dead*, Miss. Lying down, hooves up, dead, and it's that crone's fault."

I can feel my eyes widen. He's mistaken. He has to be. Before I can jump to Matilde's defense, he's leaning over the side of the wagon, his eyes bulging as he tells the story. Whether I like it or not, he's got me now, and I'm going to listen until he's through.

"All I know is my horse made a meal out of those little mushrooms just outside your door the last time I was here, and now I'm driving this mule. You tell that old crone she owes me a horse."

My throat thickens. "Did you say mushrooms?"

He looks at me as if I'm a stupid girl, and begins twisting his hands in an effort to somehow describe what he means. "Yes, mushrooms, those little brown things the ground spits out when it's soggy."

Like the ones that grow in the patch just off the step of our front door. The same I picked just this morning and traded to...

I swipe my hand across my forehead. I couldn't have mistaken the variety, could I? I've always paid close attention to what is edible and what is not, and yet I was in too much of a hurry to place something in my basket, regardless of what it was.

The wagon passes, its wheels squeaking as they roll away, the butcher still complaining. My hand is over my mouth and I'm afraid to take it away. I no longer feel sick, but there's something building deep inside of me that I know I won't be able to contain for very long.

Forcing myself to stand, I stare after the wagon as it grows smaller and smaller, rattling along toward the break in the hedge. He's going to the village, of course, to see if he can sell the swine that was meant to be ours, that sickly withered beast Matilde was counting on. Now we'll have to scour and scavenge for small game at night, hoping we find food before larger and more dangerous animals come along.

Only that pales in comparison to what will happen once the butcher reaches his shop. What's much, much worse, is that the first person who wanders into his Metzgerei to buy the swine will hear the story about his poor horse. He'll be happy to tell it from the very beginning, going on and on, because Rolf is quite the storyteller, and eyes will roll because, frankly, it's just a horse.

But when they bring the body of that woman's daughter out of the little house and into the square for all to see, they'll piece things together. They'll look at the butcher and nod with wide, shocked eyes, and all fingers will point to Matilde for something I've done.

Chapter 7
Laurentz

When I enter the village I find that it is small, rank, and full of faces that make me want to turn the other way and leave. It is far worse than the Black Forest, much to my surprise. There is an unmistakable stench that assaults my nose. Flies and the odors of rotting meat and human waste permeate the air around every corner I turn, every open doorway I pass. It's a miserable place, and I'm convinced that the girl I nearly crushed to death at the border is undoubtedly the most pleasant thing about Württemberg.

Each person I pass wants something. Filthy children beg me to fill their open hands. Peddlers eye my clothing, as if they can see right through to the coins that lie at the bottom of my pocket, but what they have to give me in return is meager and unappealing, and I don't invite any offers. Even the horses tied at the nearby fence stare at me with wide, glassy eyes, their sides gaunt with ribs that jut out too far, and I am glad I decided against hitching my own mare at the post to walk around like I had first intended.

The bishop may have been right about what surrounds my home. Württemberg isn't a condemned village yet, but I truly fear it soon will be. This is a breeding ground, a potential hazard for what has already claimed Pyrmont, and Eltz and my family are devastatingly close.

I realize I've made a grave mistake in coming here. This village is as good as doomed, and here I am in the middle of it all.

I pass an open door as I round a corner; from it, a pleading whimper makes its way out to the street. I pull the reins taut, knowing I should ignore what I hear and move on, but the sound is so desperate that I am drawn to it. I dismount and wrap the reins around the sturdiest part of the doorjamb, praying my horse will be here when I return. It wouldn't surprise me if I come out to find her stolen, or even slaughtered. I'm betting she's a more satisfying meal for a good number of people instead of what they are selling on the nearby tables. My boot pauses at the threshold, and then I step inside.

It is dark and damp, almost cave-like, and I am careful where I step because I cannot see what is in front of me. The smell here is worse than outside. It's contained and moldering, and even though I'm repulsed, I force myself to continue, knowing when I find the source, I'll find the voice I heard from the street.

Another plea cuts the thick air deep within, and I press further, careful not to make a sound. I am an intruder in this person's home. I'm uninvited, and if anyone were to arrest me right now, they would have every right to. But I can't help myself.

"Please, just one more bite." The voice carries across the stale air to my ears.

I've made it to the back of the house where the light filters through broken boards in the roof, speckling the bare room. A scraggly woman sits in the corner encouraging someone I still cannot see. She seems intent on holding a distorted brown lump to the other person's mouth. Still concealed, I shift my weight and lean against an object that seems sound enough to support me so I can crane my neck. A second woman lies upon a pile of blankets and rags. She will not part her lips to taste what the other woman offers, but instead moans and turns away, holding her stomach in agony.

"You must try and eat it, you must. It will make you and the infant stronger."

What I've heard shocks me and my eyes scour every inch of the sickly woman's figure. She is as thin as bone, and in the dim light she appears gray and sunken. If this woman is indeed carrying a child inside her, then there is no chance either of them will survive. I think of my stepmother lying in her chamber, knowing she is being doted on and being given more nourishment than this poor woman has probably ingested in an entire year. My fingers rake through my hair as I wonder why on earth I've allowed myself to walk into this person's home, uninvited, and witness what could very well be another human being's last moments.

"Anna, please," the older woman begins again. "It's from the forest. *The forest, Anna.* Surely it is charmed and will help you."

The younger woman seems to brighten at this, and her right eye opens slightly, focusing on the little morsel that I can now see is the shape of a fluted mushroom. Her eye is drawn past the little meal, where the sun moves and reveals me. Our eyes widen at the same exact moment.

"Stop!" I step forward, startling them both. The older one lets out a shrill scream, but not loud enough for anyone from outside to come running, for which I'm glad.

I reach for her hand and take the little mushroom from her fingers. I may not be one to venture out beyond the castle very much, but I do know a poisonous mushroom when I see one.

"She hasn't eaten any yet, has she?" I ask the older woman as I try and look over her shoulder to the younger one for any sign of poisoning. Not that it will do any good—the younger one she calls Anna is already so pale and weak, I'm sure I wouldn't be able to tell just by looking at her.

The old woman stares at me, her mouth wide in what I cannot tell is fear or relief, but the shock passes quickly and she lunges at me for the precious dinner I've taken from her.

"Thief! There's a thief!" she cries louder, and this time, I'm sure someone has heard her. I've only moments to try to redeem myself before the bailiff comes barging in and carts me off to the stocks.

"Stop! You don't understand! This won't help her; it will *kill* her!"

The woman continues to pry my fingers apart, paying no mind to what I've said. She's desperate, and I can only imagine what she's gone through to get this tiny piece of food. There doesn't seem to be any way to make her stop and listen. But Anna's heard me, and she uses every bit of strength she has to pull herself up to her elbows, where she grabs the grubby ends of the older woman's dress.

"Mama, listen to him." Her voice is barely there, just enough to stop the commotion, and I am flexing my fingers around the spongy mushroom that is no longer being wrestled from my grasp.

"It's true. I know you're hungry, but you can't eat this." I hold the mushroom up to make my point. "This isn't a Chanterelle. It looks a great deal like one, but trust me, this will do great harm if either of you eat it."

The woman slumps next to Anna, weary over the ordeal. How long has it been since either of them have eaten?

She buries her face in her apron.

"It's an easy mistake to make," I offer, pocketing the mushroom to prevent further harm, "especially when you're hungry."

She rests a frail hand upon Anna's arm. "These eyes of mine fail me all too often. I am desperate for us. If you had a husband to provide for you, I wouldn't worry," she says to Anna, which brings a weary sadness to the younger woman's eyes. "I only wanted to believe in the magick for a little while."

"Magick? Mama, you don't make sense."

"The girl told me the mushroom came from the forest," then the woman lowers her voice, "near the cottage."

"Did you say 'cottage?'" I interrupt, and the look on their faces is more than fear.

"Who are you?" the woman asks me. She rises to her feet, but I can't tell if she's about to attack me again or not.

"Forgive me, my name is Laurentz. I'm traveling through your village, and I heard cries coming from your home. I never meant to intrude."

The old woman nods a subtle gesture of forgiveness. This surprises and relieves me, and I stop looking over my shoulder in expectation that I'll be removed from her house.

"But what of this cottage?" I continue. "Is it the small cottage just outside the village?"

The look in Anna's eyes is soon guarded, revealing to me that I shouldn't know of what goes on in the woods just outside their home. I'm a traveler, after all, and certainly not a familiar face.

I watch the older woman's expression change. "The very one. It's the only cottage in the forest. No one else would live there but Matilde, and that girl."

"Girl?" My interest is piqued, and suddenly, the back of my neck tingles with excitement. Perhaps there was a reason I was drawn to step inside this decrepit building. The smell surrounding me is unbearable. It is thick and heavy, but I can't seem to excuse myself to be on my way, not with the mention of the cottage and the possibility that the girl they speak of is the very one I'd met today.

The older woman eyes me curiously, and then seems pleased to tell me what I apparently don't know.

"The cottage has been there for years. If you're brave enough, you'll go there," she adds cryptically.

"And what might I go there for?" I ask. The bishop's words nag at the back of my mind, but it is the woman's reason I want to hear now.

"To know things, of course," she tells me. "To know whom you will love, or if you'll become rich."

At this I can see she eyes my clothing, and I realize I am more than an outsider to this village. She is wondering who I am, where I've come from, why I ask what I do, and why I do not know these things already. I can't help thinking how Eltz is so different from this place. The people here are dirty and starving, protected by a wall of green that is so deceiving. Then there is the seemingly lonesome cottage that sits away from it all, protected by stories to keep everyone away. Only a few who are eager to know the future cross the hedge for the chance to believe in something unreal. The girl who crossed the hedge today was surreal. Is Rune part of the illusion? I certainly felt under a spell the moment I looked into her face.

"Who exactly is Matilde?" I ask.

Anna clears her throat. "She's the crone who lives there."

"In my day," the older woman interrupts, "they called someone like her a Hedge Witch."

"Hedge Witch?"

"Mmm," she nods, reaching for an unlit pipe she stuffs into her near-toothless mouth. "She lives beyond the border to the village, some say beyond the border to the Other World."

"Mama!" Anna whispers harshly.

The older woman turns to her, "It's all right. No one else can hear us."

"But can we trust him?" Anna asks, her voice low and strained, and as soon as she does, she appears nervous.

"He just saved your life! Of course we can!" She turns back to me, "I was the fool who traded the handkerchief for the mushroom."

Handkerchief.

My neck is sweating and I swipe it with the palm of my hand.

"Are you all right, sir?" she asks me.

Am I?

The bishop's words are tumbling toward me like a stampede. It took only moments for me to become caught up in searching for a girl I never laid eyes on until today—one so beautiful, and interesting, and peculiar, with a skill I had never seen before...

Now, all I can think of is where I am, where I'm sitting, surrounded by filth and contagion. Pyrmont has most likely fallen by now. Eltz is next, and all I do is sit here. If I stay any longer, then surely I will be the one to carry the infection back with me. I will be responsible.

What have I done?

I watch the old woman slowly remove her pipe from her mouth. She holds it midair and assesses me, causing me to reach into my pocket and drop a number of coins into her hand. "Please, go on," I say.

"You've met the little thief, haven't you? The pretty thief who tried to kill my daughter?"

"Mama, you don't know that," Anna whispers from her thin little bed.

"But all the same, she could have." She turns her eyes to me and tilts her head, "You have, haven't you?"

I try not to touch my arm where Rune healed the deep scrape from the thorns. I don't want to bring any more attention to myself, or to her. Something tells me it will not do either of us any good. I swallow hard and stand, because as soon as I can, I will leave this place, where the living are as good as dead.

"I didn't recognize her before." The old woman's face is lost in thought as she holds the pipe between her trembling, aged fingers. "Something about her face, her hair."

Rune's face materializes in my thoughts—quiet, ethereal. Had I really been face to face with a witch? My instincts tell me no, but from my conversation with the bishop, and now this bitter old woman, I begin to wonder.

The old woman stares at me as a devilish grin spreads across her sunken cheeks. "The forest looks dead," she says. "But mark my words, it is very much alive. Today is the day the Hedge Witch conjures, for you and I have both been bewitched."

Chapter 8
Rune

*W*hen I return home my eye immediately notes the small patch of deadly mushrooms, and as I step closer to it, the sickness I felt earlier washes over me again. How could I have been so stupid? "Goddess, forgive me," I whisper, then I pull the entire cluster from the ground and look beneath the tops. If I'd only taken the time to see how they lack the blunt veins of true Chanterelles, I would have known what they were. I toss them behind the thick Hemlock, kicking dead needles over them to bury the mistake beneath, and open the door to the cottage.

I am prepared to tell Matilde of the misery I've caused in the short while I've been gone, but change my mind when I see her sitting alone at the table. Her head is in her hands and the rune stones are scattered about. Something is not right.

"What happened here?" I ask. "Why are the stones everywhere?" I squat down and begin to collect them from the floor, waiting for her to answer me, but she doesn't.

There is no sign of the distraught woman as I look around the otherwise tidy room. Matilde runs a hand through her hair, smoothing the shorter gray strands back into place. "I gave her a cup of Chamomile to settle her and sent her on her way."

The face of the fortune-hungry visitor is still vivid in my mind. It was hardly a cup of tea she was after, yet I bite my tongue.

"And what of her pain, her ailment?"

"She has no ailment, at least not that I can help with."

I'm confused. Surely the woman suffers from *something*. What else would have brought her to us today? Like earlier, Matilde is distracted, and I can't help feel the weight of the butcher's words ringing over and over again in my head. I need to tell her. I must. But now, it seems, I can't.

I try to change the subject. "Was she pleased with her fortune?"

I gently lay the gathered stones on top of the table. When she doesn't answer, I open my mouth to ask again, but the look she shoots me stops my words instantly.

"Her pain is in her heart."

"But you've always helped with—"

She grabs my hand fiercely, stopping what I am about to say.

"She has darker intentions than merely finding love."

With my free hand I lay the last stone beside the others and pretend all is normal.

"Why were you in the village today, Rune?"

It doesn't surprise me that she already knows. I can never hide anything from her. I am trembling, fearing I'll spill it all, and she will be so upset with me. It is no use to lie, either; she will surely find me out. It was bad enough I defied her and spoke back like an unruly child. It's unacceptable that I tricked an old woman out of something she worked very hard on, something she intended to sell for money, or medicine.

But no, I had to come along and talk her into trading it for a basket of murderous mushrooms.

Murder, I think to myself. *That's what it has come to. That's what I've done.*

I suddenly feel very ill again.

Regardless of the wrong I've done today, I've committed a greater offense. I'm sure I've angered the Sacred Mother. Something Matilde has taught me never to do.

The Sacred Mother will forgive you, child.

I pale at the voice that whispers gently in my ear, knowing it is the very one that spoke to me in the village, at the stream. Matilde gathers the stones I've just collected into a heap and spreads them with her palm, completely unaware that something, someone, has touched me. Matilde, of all people, has not heard the voice, and that frightens me. From her skirt Matilde pulls a small knife. I recognize it as the one we use to cut herbs and flowers, only she brings it dangerously close to my open hand. Before I can ask, she slices a steady line across my palm. It beads at first, then wells into a river of deep red.

"Mutti, what is this about?" I try to pull my hand to my side, wanting to cradle away the pain. She is never rough with me, and now she is squeezing my hand so tight it hurts. "Mutti, please! I'm sorry! I'll tell you!"

She does not free my hand, but rakes it over the stones. There is a searing heat beneath it that at first I believe is the combination of the deep gash and her grip, but I realize it's much more than that.

The stones are calling to me.

"You don't need the runes to tell you what happened today! I promise I'll tell you."

My hand grabs a stone, and I drop it onto the cloth. She doesn't bother to hide the etched symbol it holds, and I stare at the crude drawing of a triangle with a square inside and a straight line beneath it. From one of my earliest lessons, I know it is the rune that symbolizes Home.

My hand burns to choose another, and I reluctantly reach, choosing the one that is a stick with a triangle at the base of it. It represents a Woman, only I cannot take the time to wonder if it's symbolic of me or Matilde, as my hand is grabbed again.

More stones follow; the more the casting continues, the more my hand burns with the urgency of what the runes have to tell. The stone of Disordered Thoughts, the stone of Protection, the stone of a Man, the stone of War. The last stone—the rune of Poison—is chosen and laid upon the table with the others in an order I cannot follow. At long last, the runes no longer call to me.

This isn't the same casting Matilde used on the cloaked woman earlier this morning, nor is it one she has ever used in teaching me the Old Ways. Instead, it's intricate and confusing, and the symbols could be extremely volatile, depending on how Matilde interprets them. Right now, she is saying absolutely nothing.

My hand is left throbbing. I can't help staring at the etching that depicts Poison, and feel a sob form inside my chest. I am afraid to ask what this means. I am afraid to look at Matilde and see the answer on her face.

Minutes go by, and still Matilde reveals nothing to me. Is my fortune that horrible she can't speak of it? Does she regret the promise she made sixteen years ago? I've been nothing but a burden to her. She should have been left to live in peace in her little cottage in the woods. She's worked hard to sustain us, to protect us, while I've only ever been another mouth to feed, a person to worry over. The anger I feel over my birth mother wanting to hide me away like this comes in a wave. Did my own mother know the stones would someday reveal I'd be a terrible burden, or worse?

When I can no longer stand it, Matilde faces me with those soft gray eyes of hers and smiles that wonderful smile that's always felt like home. The sobs release and I fall into her arms, and she holds me tight.

"There, there, Schätzchen. It's all right. Everything will be all right."

I want to tell her I'm a horrid girl and she has every right to be angry with me, but the only sound that escapes me is a whimper.

"Come, my lovey. Dry your eyes. The moon is rising and I've something to show you."

"But the stones…"

"Leave them. They will still be here when we return, and when we do, I will tell you who you are."

I lean upright and feel dizzy.

Tell me who I am? She didn't say, "*I will tell you what the stones say.*"

No, she said something very, very different.

I don't ask this time, even though I want to more than anything. Instead, I rise to my feet, and although I am trembling, I follow Matilde outside into the night beneath the light of the full moon.

Chapter 9
Rune

"Come this way, Rune."

I follow Matilde's voice as it leads me out into the darkness, away from the reassuring warmth of the little cottage. For her age she walks briskly, and I find I'm the one lagging behind, my feet stumbling over roots and arms scraped by burrs. It's hard to see so I focus on the bobbing flame of the thick candle she carries, but the further we walk, the darker it seems. The moon peeks in and out through the treetops, making everything around me appear thick and wobbly. Things that shouldn't frighten me play tricks on my mind. What should be solid shifts and bends in the splattered light, and I begin to think that the stories that come from this place may hold a strange and terrifying truth.

We come to a stop and I am lost. This part of the forest looks foreign to me, though I am sure I would recognize it in the daylight. We stand in a small clearing; from where my feet are, it looks to be a complete circle swept clean of all woodland debris and underbrush.

"Where are we?" I ask.

"Some say this is the oldest part of the forest," Matilde says proudly, looking around. The wind makes the branches dance between the slices of moonlight, and she protects the small flame with her cupped hand. "Now take this for me and hold it tight."

She hands me the candle and pulls four more wax stubs from her apron pocket. One after another, they are lit and placed upon the ground. Framing the edge of our strange circle, their flames flicker to and fro, while the fifth sits at the center, shining enough light so that I can see. It's small and tight, and I am not sure where to place myself within it. I hold my skirt close to me so I don't accidently knock into the tiny fires and set myself ablaze. That chills me and brings a disturbing feeling to the edge of my senses.

For the first time in my life I am afraid of where I am. This place is my home. The boughs of green have always been comforting walls, but tonight I feel they are arms that stretch not only too far, but too close, and I am penned in. I used to think that living in the woods gave me an advantage over a girl my own age who might have grown up in the village. I've had room to roam, freedom. Tonight, I'm not so sure. Is it possible for a person's world to shrink before their eyes? To feel what was once comforting transform and become unrecognizable? The forest normally teems with life at this time of night. Wolves roam, owls hoot, mice scurry, but like earlier at the stream, all is dreadfully silent, as if the forest waits for something.

The knife Matilde used to cut my hand is now in the open air, circling high above her. She points it toward the sky, and then over each flame. I'm worried that she will use it on me again, so I begin to back away.

"You must stay within the circle, Rune," she tells me. "Don't step outside of it."

I will my feet to stay put, but the effort makes me sway.

"This is the altar to the Sacred Mother. As long as you remain within the circle during the invocation, you will be safe."

"Safe?" I am struck with fear that I've been found out in the village, and that I will forever be labeled a liar, a thief, a murderous girl.

"You are very special, Rune. Believe that." Matilde's hand coaxes my chin a little higher. I go to argue that point, but am stopped with a finger on my lips. "I know what happened today, Schätzchen. You don't have to relive it by telling me. Know that I love you still, as if you were my very own."

My heart breaks at this. Even after what I've done today, she still loves me. There is a place for me in her heart that promises to keep me safe. I want to reciprocate; I owe it to her to tell her what the butcher said to me on my way home. I want to warn her that I've done more than con an old woman at the market. I've brought death to the butcher's horse. I've brought death to an innocent woman and her child. I should take the blame for it, not her.

In a flash, the small silver knife is pointing and circling at the night.

"I call to the four corners of the earth and invoke the elements!" Matilde cries out. "Water, may you cleanse this girl of harm and wash away her fears. I invoke thee!"

She turns and points the tip of the knife over the next flame. "Earth, may you give solid footing to this girl. May she make choices that provide her with stability and wisdom. I invoke thee!"

Over the third flame, Matilde cries out, "Air, embrace this child and comfort her. Let harm blow away, and allow the power she must harness to stir within her. I invoke thee!"

At the fourth flame, where I stand, Matilde turns to me, and holds the knife upward toward the dark and endless sky. She appears to not notice me, although I'm sure she is aware that I am standing right in front of her.

"I call to Fire and ask that you give this girl, your servant, the power you possess. She will need you most of all. That by which her birth mother met her end, give her the flame of life to endure what is marked for her. Give her the power to fight fire with fire. I invoke thee!"

Matilde steps around the center flame and faces me over it. The light between us flickers and illuminates our features.

Where she is old and wise, I am young and naïve. I have no idea what she is doing or how she intends this to help me, but something inside feels right. There is a strength in me that was not present when I followed her here, and I hold my breath, waiting along with the rest of the forest.

With one hand she takes mine and wraps it over hers. Together, we hold the blade aloft.

"I invoke Spirit, the essence that is the Sacred Mother and the spirit that is Rune to join together. Keep this child steady. Never let her falter. Guide her, Mother. Keep her safe."

Matilde pulls her hand away, leaving mine the only one holding onto the hilt. I haven't been properly trained. I've had to leave the cottage on several occasions so that I did not witness certain ceremonies and words, and now I'm in the middle of something that seems so incredibly significant. I'm suddenly terrified of my place in it.

"Hold it steady, Rune." She urges me to keep my elbows locked to support the blade.

A warmth trembles through me from my fingertips to my shoulders. It spreads and warms its way down my back and chest, into my legs where it stretches out toward my feet, and then disappears.

When my skin has grown cold and my arms are trembling from holding the knife high for so long, Matilde guides my arms to my sides. She bids thanks to the Mother, as well as to each element, then blows out each flame and pulls my hand to follow her as we step to the edge of the small clearing. My feet feel useless. All I want to do is go home where, hopefully, Matilde will read the runes. Then, I want to lie down and sleep in my warm bed. But we aren't leaving the circle just yet, and I follow her around, and around, and around.

She senses that I am spent, but does not release my hand. "Widdershins," she says.

I think I've heard her wrong, because it's a word I don't recognize anyone ever saying. At last we stop, and my legs ache at the sudden stillness.

"Widdershins is when you walk against time to rid the circle of negative energy, before closing it."

"Oh," I say. I am too tired to try and understand it, and force myself to give a little smile.

Leaves and twigs crunch beneath our feet; the walk back to our cottage feels tremendously longer than the time it took venturing away.

"How did you learn to do that? The circle, I mean."

"I didn't know. I've heard of circles being drawn in the past, and the invoking of spirits. I've just never had the courage to try it until now. My guess is that it was you who allowed it."

"But I thought you were trained to do all this. Healing, circles, fortunes…didn't your own mother train you?"

Matilde chuckles a raspy chortle. "Oh goodness sakes, no, my grandmother was the one who taught me tricks to make money, to earn a little in order to survive. Folk remedies and intuition tend to skip a generation with peasant folk, with the exception of witches. _Real witches_. I'm no magick weaver like…"

I stop her then. "Like who, Mutti?"

She stares me in the eye and takes my hand. "Like _you_, Schätzchen. Like you."

I stare at her.

"Tell me, what did you feel?"

I know well what she is speaking of, but I don't know how to describe it. "It was very hot. In fact, it burned in the beginning, but then it just sort of tingled, like tiny butterflies fluttering beneath my skin."

"Then it was the Fire that spoke to you," Matilde says with a reflective smile. "I had a feeling it would be."

Fire. I've felt it before in dreams, only I was never too sure if they were dreams at all. They were more like memories.

Her memories.

My mother's.

"What did you mean when you said, _'that by which her birth mother met her end?'_"

Matilde is quiet.

"And you said something else too, about '*fighting fire with fire?*'" I ask. "And what do you mean, 'witches?'" I cast a glance into the dark trees around us, sensing eyes upon us, still hearing the old stories and feeling them come to life beneath my skin.

Matilde clucks her tongue against the roof of her mouth and wrings the hem of her dress. "Your mother's name has been included in several stories that have been told…along with the terrible things she was accused of."

"But you never told me what those terrible things were, Mutti. Won't you tell me now?" I pause quietly. "Especially since I'm just as terrible?"

"You are *not* terrible," she replies fiercely, and turns me around so that I am looking right at her. "You are *nothing* like her. There is no death tonight."

I'm speechless. Surely I am. Surely there is.

Suddenly, I'm filled with an absolute need to tell Matilde what has happened, what *will* happen, because of me. On top of it all, I'm filled with the overwhelming need to learn about the woman who was my mother—her life, her death, and, most of all, why she left me behind as her world fell apart. What terrible things could she have possibly done?

"Come, let the stones explain, child. But know that you are nothing like the woman who gave birth to you. You are far greater than she, in more ways than you will ever learn, and that is why you must be safe."

"Safe from what, Mutti?"

With a heavy sigh, she tells me, "Safe from *her.*"

There is lamp glow shining from within the window as we approach home. Matilde opens the door. I am trembling and wide awake. I am closer than ever to finding the answers. I must know. If I don't, I will be in pieces. The stones call to me from the doorway, as if I am holding my open hand over them at this very moment. The stones know the truth. They know why I must be protected from a mother who is dead.

They will tell Matilde, and she will tell me.

Only now, I'm fearful to find out *what* I am.

Chapter 10
Rune

"If you aren't prepared for this, you must tell me. Once we begin, there is no way of stopping her."

I nod my head. I understand what Matilde is telling me, but there is no way I can say no. Not now. No matter how it scares me.

"Rune, understand what I am saying." Her voice is urgent as she leans across the table to me. There are thirteen stones on the table between us, all upturned. I've been doing all I can not to lower my eyes and look at them. I don't know what they mean. I have no idea what they will say to her, or if she will be truthful in passing along their secrets. I hope she will. She's never lied to me before, but I guess there's always a first time for things. Like now, like piecing together who my mother was so I can understand who I am.

"I understand," I whisper, trying to sound strong. I *am* strong. *I am.*

And that's just it. Do I really understand? Do I understand the magnitude of what she is about to tell me?

I lift my chin. I'm ready.

Matilde takes a deep breath and steadies her hands against the wood. "We must begin at the beginning, then." She starts as she does with all her readings, by taking a deep breath and gazing upon the stones, then closing her eyes. I know the stones are speaking to her. I wish she would skip ahead to the important part, like telling me what they say, telling me who I really am, because, quite frankly, I really don't know. I know bits and pieces and fragments of what she's chosen to tell me all these years, never the whole story.

"Your blood chose the stones," she finally shares out loud, making me quite aware this is very important, not a fortune teller's trick. I've never witnessed her using someone's blood before, and it's disconcerting to see my own smeared across the top of each stone, marking a red streak over the black symbols.

"Blood is the strongest medium for revealing the future. Even more so for revealing the past. It calls to the soul and reveals only what is deep within."

The windows are wide open to invite the soul of my mother, yet despite the crisp breeze, I am sweating. My finger hovers above the rune stone that depicts a woman. "Is this my mother?" I ask.

She shushes me by placing a finger to her lips. "Rune, please, it must go in order."

I'm too anxious, though, and sitting still is a feat I cannot seem to master. I bite against the inside of my cheek in order to stop myself from speaking out again. No wonder I've never been included in secret readings, I have not the patience nor the ability to stay quiet or still. I'm not only a burden, but an annoyance.

"There will be a war," Matilde says at last, as she points to the first stone. "A war with many people, but it is a war with words and angry accusations." She points to the stone just above it, and says, "There is no war greater than the one you will find within your heart, and I fear it will be a long and treacherous journey you will make to finally be at peace with your decisions."

She takes her time touching the stones, reading them to herself first, much like I knew she would. I begin to think she's reluctant to tell me what they say. Her face changes through a multitude of expressions over the course of seconds, and I suspect there is something she is keeping to herself. I want to know what the Man stone means. I stare at it and cannot help thinking of the man at the hedge today—of Laurentz. A warm blush creeps beneath my cheeks, and I let my hair fall over my face to cover it, hoping she doesn't notice.

"You must watch your heart, Rune. Guard it closely," she warns, and I smile to myself that my dear Matilde has not lost her touch. "Decisions you make with your heart have the power to destroy not only you, but others as well."

I listen to her sigh. It is impossible to tell if she is tired or if the stone reveals something that is troubling. She picks up the smooth pebble that represents Disordered Thoughts, rolls it between her fingers, and then sets it down. It's a while before she speaks again, long enough that I pour water from the basin into the heavy kettle and set it over the flame. After I've busied myself long enough to not cause trouble, Matilde's voice breaks the silence.

"You must be wary of lies, Rune, lies strong enough to cause death. You will be the spark that sets these falsehoods ablaze." She gives me a knowing look, and in it, I know she is referring to the element of Fire. I notice how she grips the table until her knuckles turn white, and soon after, a strong wind blows into the room, upsetting the herbs above our heads, causing them to sway wildly until dried bits fall and float to the table. It is Rosemary that falls, nothing else, and the tiny leaves scatter between the stones, sticking to the blood that is not quite dry.

My very being bristles.

Rosemary is for remembrance… comes the whisper.

Matilde turns to me, her old eyes sharp and decisive. "She is here."

The wind whips throughout the room. Baskets overturn, linens rumple. Even the stones slide out of order across the table with the force that barges through the open windows. I try and help Matilde reach for the stones before they fall over the edge and onto the floor, but I'm too late. The fortune is ruined.

Matilde stops suddenly and thrusts her hand upon her heart. "There is something she doesn't wish you to know!"

But the wind has become a symphony of whispers, and is so loud that I cannot hear anything else she says. It fills my ears with a murmur reminiscent of my dreams. I try to listen, but it becomes too painful for me to bear. I cover my ears with my hands and sit on the floor, waiting for it to stop, only there seems no end to it.

I reach for Matilde's hand, and for one glimmer of a second we are face to face, and she presses her worn hands to my cheeks.

"You are stronger than she is, and she knows it. Don't let her know you are scared."

But how can I *not* be scared? What mother returns from the dead for her child? How can this not frighten me?

"She wants something, Rune. Whatever she tells you, always be aware it can mean something else entirely," says Matilde, as she covers her own ears with her hands against the noise that whirls around us.

I lean closer to her, "What does she want?"

Matilde shakes her head. Either she is saying she doesn't know or she won't tell me; I can't be sure.

The kettle's lid rattles and the hook falls over against the inside of the fireplace. The cupboard from the far end of the room swings open and the door flies off, splintering as it crashes to the floor.

Matilde's face is a horrified mask when I peek through the laced fingers that cover my eyes. She crawls along the floor, making her way toward the few stones left on the table.

"What are you doing?" I cry out to her, afraid she will get hurt, and I begin to crawl after her on my knees. She reaches for the tattered cloth, her gnarled fingers shaking and stretching.

"Mutti! Leave it!"

The little cottage begins to shake. My mother is angry.

"I'm sorry!" I cry out to the wind. "She's all you've given me!"

Matilde stands, white as a sheet, her mouth open as her hair whips about her face. Before either of us can speak, the wind stops and everything flying through the air falls to the floor with a clatter. It is followed by a deafening silence that steals our breath.

Somehow, the upturned stone that is Poison lies between us on the debris-scattered floor.

"That is your mother, Schätzchen." Matilde points to our feet. "She is the poison that threatens to destroy us all."

I open my hand, for there is something I have been holding, yet I do not remember what it is or how it has come to be in my grasp. I uncurl my fingers and suck in a deep breath seeing the single rune stone in my palm, its black-stabbed triangle smeared with my own blood. It is the symbol of Woman and I have no recollection of how it's come to be in my hand.

"Will you tell me now? Will you tell me who I am?" I ask, helping Matilde sink into the chair I've turned upright at the table's edge.

"You remember the stories, don't you, Schätzchen? Not just the ones I've told you, but the others?"

"Everyone knows those stories, Mutti, but they aren't true. They're make-believe."

"No, Rune, they are very real, especially one in particular—a story no one knows."

"And which one is that, Mutti?" I whisper against my will. The stone in my hand begins to wiggle and I hold it tight, confining it to a small space against my skin. My stomach clenches, as if knowing deep inside what she is about to say.

"The one about the witch from the forest," she gauges my reaction, "and the daughter she had."

At first I think the silence left behind by the wind is warping her words. I am not sure if I can trust my ears, because all along I've thought my mother to be a lost soul, someone worthy of pity. I've been saddened by the fact that she had to give me away as her life was cut short.

Matilde takes my hand and holds it steady.

"No she isn't, she wasn't." *I'm not.*

"Yes. It's all true," she nods slowly. "You, my dear, are the daughter of a great and powerful witch."

Chapter 11
Laurentz

I am relieved to find my horse still tethered outside the old woman's house. Dusk has fallen upon the village and the bleak square is a dark and dreary gray. The forest, as I see it, is blacker and more sinister still, and I am anxious to be on my way. I step over the crumbling stone threshold of the ailing house I've been inside for the last hour, glad I chose to do the unthinkable and intervene, for tonight could have ended very badly for the two women inside. Only now I am left feeling twisted and confused—about Rune, about what she did for my arm, and about what lies beyond the hedge, deep beneath the veil of the Black Forest.

"Hedge Witch," I say to myself. I'd never heard the term before. Aren't witches old, scraggly hags who spent their time concocting potions and spells? That's what I'd grown up to believe. Yet the girl I'd met today was young and beautiful, and yes, I was most pleasantly bewitched by her. Still, there is no explanation to what she did with my arm. A mossy bandage seems innocent enough, but healing the cut completely? It certainly seemed magickal.

I have no proof she is indeed the girl who lives with the old crone called Matilde; I am simply venturing a guess based on the word of an old woman from the village. I lead my horse to the far edge of the market square, near the wild growth that rises alongside the forest. The mushroom is in my pocket where it can do no harm, and I intend to throw the miserable thing into the trees, but something prevents me from going through with that plan. Instead, I leave it there and find myself staring off into the dark foliage, wondering about Rune and wanting to know more about who she is.

It will be dark soon and I know I should set out for Eltz now. Even on the brightest of days, the forest is like night and I've no doubt that the sounds and shadows I will encounter will play tricks on my mind, only I can't seem to mount the saddle and leave the village just yet. There are still a few traders along the street hoping to make some money before the end of the day, and walking slowly through the square toward them is the hooded woman I saw earlier in the forest. I crane my neck, wondering if she could be the famed Matilde I'd just learned about. I yank the bridle of my horse and follow her, making sure I stay at a distance, knowing that I'm still a stranger here, and it's best not to stand out.

There is just enough room between the hedge and the outer buildings to walk along without being directly within the market, and I follow the narrow path there, feeling anxious when I lose her from my view. At last, I round a corner, finding she has stopped by a craftsman's shop. She removes her hood and a crown of blonde hair falls around her face. She is neither old nor scraggly, and my heart sinks as I am convinced she cannot be the crone the old woman spoke of.

The glassblower she's facing holds up four fingers. He is standing near a pole, leaning heavily against it, sweating. A hot oven roars behind him; long metal poles protrude from its open mouth.

"Two," the woman tells him. "No higher." Her face is somewhat soft from this distance, but her voice indicates that she is determined and not willing to spend what he asks of her.

With a reluctant nod, the glassblower wipes his gloved hand across his heavy black apron and pulls on one of the poles, bringing it out of the furnace and onto a metal table, where he begins to roll it back and forth. Once cooled, he brings the end of the pole to his lips and blows into it, then covers the other end with his thumb. I am mesmerized, as are the others who've also stopped to watch. Slowly, the other end of the pole grows, and a beautifully colored bubble is formed. His gloved hands work quickly and he taps on the bubble with a block, shaping the molten glass before our eyes. It's a deep garnet. Out of the corner of my eye, I can see that the woman next to me is very pleased.

"Will it cool quickly enough?" she asks him with an irritating impatience, and he nods, pulling on the end of the bottle with a jack, elongating the neck of the bottle. "Make sure it's perfect. I don't want the face to be noticeable."

It is obvious the glassblower grows annoyed with her demands. He places a couple of drops of water where the glass meets the metal pipe. With a hiss, the glass disconnects from the metal and is set to cool while the woman next to me rummages beneath her sleeve and pulls out a beaded pouch that is connected to her wrist by a cord. She hands him two coins. It is not nearly enough for what he has created for her.

"It's beautiful," I comment, nodding toward the glass bottle that lies on the table cooling. "Is it to contain perfume?"

Her head turns slowly, assessing me. "No," she answers curtly, and offers no other purpose for which the newly made container will serve.

Her rudeness doesn't bother me. Her reaction would be different if she knew I was the Electorate's son, but that is something I am not willing to share simply because I want to be respected. I watch as she walks away with her purchase, but she pauses, pulls what appears to be thin strands of thread from her sleeve, and stuffs them into the bottle. She is soon on her way again, and I am left wondering.

"Not from around here, are you?" A burly man twice my size stares at me from beneath two thick eyebrows. He pulls his pants higher and spits on the ground as he approaches. "If you were, you'd recognize a bellermine when you see one."

"Bellermine?" I ask.

The man leans toward me, lowering his voice. "Bellermine, Bartmann, same difference."

When it's clear neither rings familiar, he steps even closer and bends his head toward mine. My horse shifts next to me, and I pat her neck to soothe her. The man reeks of ale and musky sweat, and I try not to cough, knowing it will insult him. Men like him have been known to hurl a man of like size clear across a town square for offenses like coughing at body odor, and I don't plan on having my bones broken today.

"Witch bottle," he says, enlightening me, and I nod, pretending I know what he's talking about.

"Usually they're stone, but the face she told the glassblower to imprint into the glass gave it away. Not to mention she just filled the glass with hair."

"I beg your pardon," I grimaced. "Did you just say 'hair?'"

The brawny man nods. "Seems she wants to protect herself."

"Protect herself? From a witch?"

"Now you're catching on!" he says with a throaty laugh.

"But why would she need to protect herself from a figment of one's imagination? Surely a big man like you doesn't believe in nonsense."

He stares at me, and so does his friend. I've said the wrong thing, apparently.

"Like I said before, you're not from around here, are you?"

"Sadly, no. Should I be worried? Should I ask the glassblower to create a…bellermine, as you call it, for myself?"

This earns me a scowl from the smaller man.

"Might not be a bad bit of advice. If you're visiting Württemberg for very long, you'll learn to sleep with one eye open."

Just as he's about to say more, a rickety cart pulls up to the tiny shop that fronts the slaughterhouse across the square, and it quickly becomes the center of attention.

"It's begun again!" a man shouts out loud. I presume he is the butcher, since he holds a long apron that is splattered in blood and gore. He's a rotund man with a bulbous nose and ruddy complexion, and he makes every effort to stand on the seat of his wagon. The people gathering take a step back, and I laugh a little, believing it's because of his size. They must be worried he'll topple himself out and crush his audience.

He holds up a withered slab, with bones and hooves intact. The gatherers furrow their brows at the sample their trusted butcher holds before them, realizing the telltale snout of the beast is the only way they can determine what hangs in front of them.

"This! This is what is happening! Tell me the crops aren't as deteriorated as this swine. Tell me you aren't running out of food and are scared of going hungry."

A murmur, like a rushing stream of water, begins to build among those standing closest to him, and crests as the villagers take in the enormity of his meaning.

"Tell me, when the landlord comes to collect his share of the harvest, as well as the rent from your stores, will your feet shake in your boots? I tell you this has happened before, and by God, it's happening again!"

The hum grows, and one by one, they all agree that something beyond their control is seemingly amiss, and that something that has the power to threaten their livelihood hasn't escaped this one man standing before them, urging them to open their eyes. One by one, they begin to recount the misfortunes that have otherwise gone unnoticed until this very moment. One has witnessed a burnt crop. Another claims a garden is overrun by grubs, leaving only a handful of potatoes to be harvested. The horses are growing thin, too thin to pull the plows, and the fields surrounding Württemberg are just too vast for animals who cannot keep up.

"Should we look to the forest for food?" a woman timidly asks, loud enough for the butcher to hear.

"We should not! This poison I speak of grows in the forest. My own horse is dead because of it!"

At this precise moment the door of the small home I had been in a short while ago creaks open, and out steps the old woman, her fist raised in alarm. "He speaks the truth! There is poison surrounding us all, and the hedge cannot keep us safe!" she intervenes, stepping closer toward the crowd as all eyes turn to her. "What was meant to keep evil spirits out of our village no longer protects us. It isn't enough to lock our doors at night, or hide the bellermines within our fireplaces, or bury them in our gardens."

"She's right." An elderly man to my left hobbles forward, leaning heavily upon his walking stick. It's obvious he is blind because he reaches out to find support and misses several times. "The witch is angry."

There is a tangible fear in the air that moments before did not exist. The skin beneath my sleeves prickles at the words they shout out. There are accusations, there is blame. One woman faints and falls to the street, but those standing closest to her are too afraid to help her to her feet, as if touching her will cause them harm. All at once their voices ring out, fists punch the sky, and before my eyes a frenzied retaliation against an unseen evil is born.

"She stole my eyes!" the blind man shouts. "She took all that I have seen in my life and boiled it in her kettle, then drank it!"

Another person caught up in the fury cries out, "She conjures while we sleep! I've seen the green smoke that coils from the trees at the Witching Hour!"

"Is it like before, Mama?" A young girl tugs at her mother's apron. "Did she really steal his eyes?"

The old woman across the way reaches inside the doorway and pulls with all her might. She produces an arm, then a shoulder, until the weak and wide-eyed Anna is standing outside for everyone to see.

"She nearly poisoned my daughter! She sent her apprentice to deliver the very evil I speak of, and tricked me into believing the lie that nearly killed my Anna! Look what she's done to her!"

She thrusts poor Anna forward, and the gathered crowd gasps at her fragile state. They see her sunken eyes, her sallow skin, the limp, lifeless hair. Never do they acknowledge that her clothes are as threadbare as the ones they wear themselves, that she is merely a victim of natural circumstances, starving and suffering as they all do.

I go to raise my voice, to argue that Anna suffers not from what her delusional mother claims, but my voice fails me. I don't know Anna. I don't know why she is so delicately ill other than overhearing of her pregnancy. Anna and her mother are strangers to me, and if I speak up then they might turn against me and reveal to everyone that I forced my way into their home.

I can't argue that.

I am guilty for entering their house, and the fact that I am indeed a stranger will work against me. Slowly, I begin to back away. Something tells me to turn and leave as fast as I possibly can.

Anna's eyes scan the group, and for the briefest of seconds I believe she notices me, but I see that she is staring beyond where I stand. There is no way to ignore the way Anna's face changes, how it registers alarm, then fear. I try to follow her line of vision, spying the cloaked woman in the distance. Their eyes meet, and soon, Anna is fleeing from our stares back inside her dilapidated home. This seems to please the peculiar woman, who stands away from the crowd. She doesn't seem to be interested in the fear brewing here, and she walks toward the road that will lead away from the village. I pull myself from the crowd and follow her, hiding behind a large brown barrel that leaks ale; my heart skips a beat as I see the bishop's red carriage waiting for her at the far end of the road. An arm extends from the coach window, producing a leather money pouch, and the woman takes it quickly. She opens it, but doesn't seem satisfied, and holds out her hand. Within seconds, more coins drop into her waiting hand, and the witch bottle is handed over.

Beside the coins, something shiny catches my eye as the arm retreats back inside the carriage. It is gold and glints in the sunlight before disappearing, and I am left watching, wondering, as the two depart in opposite directions, as if they'd never met at all.

Chapter 12
Rune

A faceless woman hovers over me. Her mouth moves quickly, like a violent wind, only I can't hear what it is she's telling me. Something warm touches me, and before my eyes, the face changes to a strong jaw, dark eyes, and chestnut hair. I feel myself smiling…

"Good dream, Schätzchen?"

My eyes open to see Matilde sitting on the edge of my bed, adjusting my quilt. I pull myself up and let the covers fall from me, chilled as the cool morning air touches my skin. I have a strong feeling she knows of the face that brought the smile to my lips. Suddenly, my senses are awakened as the most delectable smell fills the room. Floating on air is the delicious aroma of yeast, and citrus, and warmth.

Bread. She's made bread, I think to myself. *But not just any bread.*

I look at Matilde and raise my eyebrows. She knows what I'm about to ask and begins to laugh.

"Stollen? Today? Yule is months away!"

I am out of bed before she can answer, and am practically skipping to the table, where I stand over the most beautiful sight—a dense oblong bread filled with raisins and candied citrus she probably traded way too much for.

"You could eat it with your eyes, child!" She's pleased that she's done something to make me so happy. "There's fresh water in your room. Go wash up, and I'll slice you a thick piece," she says.

I can't help staring at her, and cannot help the smile forming at my lips.

"You went out this morning for water?" I rush to the window and peer outside, determined to make it up to her if I've slept the day away. After last night, I believe I could have, but the sky is still dark with only the faintest orange and yellow creeping between the trees. I do as she tells me, and in no time, I'm bathed and dressed, staring longingly at the Stollen again.

She cuts a thick piece as promised, and a slice of equal size for herself, then she settles into the chair by a fire that looks as if it's been burning for hours. The room has never felt so wonderful this early in the morning, except when we've celebrated Yule.

I take a bite and savor the taste on my tongue, marveling how the bits of dried fruit insist on sticking to my teeth long after I've swallowed. I am so lost in the wonder of this morning that it doesn't occur to me to ask why she's gone to all this trouble. Then last night comes tumbling through the sweet taste in my mouth and crashes into me with all the might of a hailstorm, forcing me to place the cake in my lap.

"What is it, Rune?"

She's gone through such trouble to make it up to me. Gone through the effort to hide what last night brought to us and make me forget, even if it's just for a little while. Do I even dare bring it all back again?

"What does she want, Mutti? Why does my mother come for me?" I pull the thick afghan from the end of her bed on top of me, wrapping it around my shoulders. The fire crackles while I wait for her, and I pick at the Stollen, no longer as ravenous as I was moments ago. I don't want to disappoint her. She worked so hard to make this morning special for me. And that's just it. Why has she done all this? What exactly is she making up to me?

"You should eat, Schätzchen." She points to the cake in my lap, but I am not listening.

The room holds no trace of last night's ordeal. Every stone picked up. Every last twig and broken dish swept away. A new cupboard door hangs where the loose one used to be, and it catches my eye.

"What's in the cupboard, Mutti?"

Without lifting her head she tells me, "Nothing. There's nothing in the cupboard."

I can't help myself and I cross the room to the whitewashed doors with little round knobs that hide everything from tea leaves to rune stones to soap. She doesn't stop me, not even when I reach up and pull the door toward me, and when I do, I step back, confused, because like Matilde said, there is nothing inside.

She takes an enormous bite of the cake and chews, intentionally ignoring the bewildered look on my face.

"I told you there was nothing in the cupboard."

"But where has it all gone?" My voice reaches an unnatural pitch. "It was all here yesterday. Where are the stones?"

Last night's fortune haunts me. There's no need to ask Matilde to read the future again, not to mention that I don't want to relive it any time soon, but this was how Matilde earns her living, by readings and tea leaves. Our lives have been shaped by predicting people's futures, and now, the most precious of her mediums is gone.

There is only one stone left, the tiny one that cleverly found its way into my hand last night. I was reluctant to relinquish it, so I slipped the rune into my pocket and placed it beneath my pillow before falling asleep. I didn't realize how powerful that single stone could be, and I remember feeling restless, not knowing what my dreams were until early this morning when Matilde woke me. I wonder if the stone of the Woman was the reason I dreamt of my mother. Perhaps she is represented by two stones, and not just Poison, like Matilde told me.

Still, Matilde offers no further explanation for the missing items in the cupboard and I cannot help but wonder. Did she trade them? Did she sell them to buy the ingredients for the cake?

"Mutti?"

"Sit down and eat, Rune." She rocks back and forth in her chair. I sit, but my mind is racing as I stare at the corner of the room where the cupboard door hangs open, empty. When I've given up all hope of hearing more, she whispers, "Years ago, terrible things happened in the village. The crops turned to dust; the livestock starved, and the people who lived there grew very sick. All fingers pointed to a small group of girls who seemed unaffected. Mind you, these girls were a bit older than you, some married, but they were young, vibrant, as close as sisters. They went on with their lives, taking no notice of the devastation that had begun around them, until one day, one came running into the village, hysterical and covered from head to toe in blood."

I walk over to the fire and drop to the floor at her feet, spellbound.

"The girl pointed toward the woods, claiming there had been a murder. When a group of men searched the forest, they found one of her friends hanging from a tree. Her heart had been cut out of her chest."

My hand is at my mouth and the mental picture her words are painting creates a horrifying scene in my head. If I look out the window I might see that girl hanging from the birch tree.

"The body of another was thrown across the stream, lying in a pile of leaves, and the last girl," Matilde continues, "couldn't be found. Many long days and nights of searching passed, and the town came to the conclusion that the missing girl had vanished into thin air. The truth finally came out, however. The missing girl was a witch, capable of causing unspeakable harm, and the cause of all the unfortunate experiences in the village.

"The hedge was planted soon after, strewn with Yew seedlings in order to keep her out. The last she was seen was in the Black Forest, and if she ever returned she would have to cross the barrier, and the town would know of it."

"What happened to the first girl?"

"Life wasn't easy for her, if that's what you're asking. She was taken into custody and placed on trial for involvement in witchcraft. The judges believed she was part of a coven, and that she and the other girls would sneak off to the forest at night to dance beneath the stars and practice spells. Some said they cavorted with dark and malevolent beings in order to maintain their youth, while the rest of the village suffered. Of course she denied this.

"She was accused of heresy and of creating a union with the devil himself. And when they found she was with child, they forced her to give the baby up, so they could destroy it."

"Mutti, no! Don't tell me she let them!"

"What choice did she have? By giving the life of her child, she was able to save her own."

"But—"

Matilde reaches out and cups my chin in her soft, papery hand. "You would have given your life for the child's, I know that. Just like your mother did for you."

I can't help bristling at the mention of my mother. After last night I have no idea what to think of her. Was she really a witch? Is she still? Is she good, or evil? And what will become of me should she ever manifest into my world and get ahold of me? Sheer terror runs through me and I am shaking because there is a connection I'm beginning to make here, only I don't want to give it life yet.

"Nearly a year later, a beautiful young woman wandered into the village, and someone recognized her," Matilde continues.

"Was she the missing girl?"

Matilde's cloudy eyes are wary, but I urge her on. "Yes," she whispers. "She was taken immediately and placed on trial for the murder of her friends."

Silence falls between us.

"She was my mother, wasn't she?"

Matilde nods slowly. "Yes, Schätzchen. She was."

I don't have to look at Matilde to know that she guards every second of silence passing between us. She knows me too well, knows how I absorb things, knows how I process my thoughts. The fire's dance is hypnotic, and I find it easy to lose myself while looking into the burning hearth. I am so captured by the flickering embers that I barely hear her.

"Be careful, Rune. I believe she will use you as her instrument against everyone who's crossed her. Against the entire village, if she can, for what they've done to her," says Matilde.

But the fire speaks too. The hiss from the flames is already a steady whisper, like a message it wishes for me to know. I am listening, caught somewhere between the truth Matilde reveals and the endless stream of secrets the fire has to tell me.

"What did they do, Mutti?"

Matilde is careful with her words. "They burned her at the stake, my child. In the center of the market square, they burned her until the devil was expelled from her soul and there was nothing left but ashes."

Chapter 13
Rune

By evening, Mutti is at it again, cooking and baking away. Encouraging me to eat more than my full stomach can hold.

"Eat, Schätzchen. You must fill up. You're too thin."

"Mutti, I can't eat any more. I'll burst if I do."

There is more food here than I've seen any other time of the year, even at Yule, or any of the other Sabbats. Matilde has yet to explain why the sudden extravagance, the sudden need to create each and every one of our favorite meals all on the same day, gorging ourselves until we practically burst at the seams.

"If I eat anything else, I'll be bigger than Rolf!" I half-joke, but at the rate she is insisting, I will surely pass him.

We are finishing up our day, lounging by the fire, quizzing each other about herbs and their medicinal properties. Now that night has fallen, Matilde is tired, but she is restless and hovers near the window more than usual, as if waiting for someone. I hope she doesn't open the sash. I have no desire to let the storm that is the spirit of my mother inside these walls again, nor do I wish to sweep the leaves off the floor.

"Why are you pacing so much?" I ask. She's done nothing but sit and eat, then pace the floor, for the last hour or so, and now she is at the window again, searching the darkening sky.

"Remember everything I've told you. All the herbs, what they mean, how they're used."

I nod my head. "Yes, Mutti, I know them inside and out."

She crosses the room and bends in front of me, creaking as she lowers her face to be level with my own. Her expression is grave, though I can see she tries to be soft. She tries to be the calm Mutti I've always known, but her eyes tell me something entirely different.

"I should have taught you so much more."

I begin to worry. She is acting so strange. Now I am the one rising to my feet and crossing the floorboards. She and I hear it at the same time. Rustling and snapping, footsteps coming closer. At first I think it's another person from the village approaching after dark and feel sour that the cupboard holds absolutely nothing to predict their future, that we will have to turn them away, but the look on Matilde's white face has me fearing the worst.

"Take this and go. Now!" She hands me a cloth sack, and I can smell the food it holds inside. Before I can object, she is pushing me from behind and into the doorway of my bedroom. "They won't find you if you are careful."

I realize the gravity of what she's saying. They've come for me—the bailiff, perhaps even Rolf. They are pounding on the door now, the light from their lanterns cutting beneath the seam, bleeding into our quiet home. With each fist that raps against the wood, I hear their voices yelling for Matilde to let them in.

She places her hands on both of my cheeks, leaning her forehead to mine. "Listen to the Sacred Mother. Follow the path she leads you on, no matter how frightening it might be. All steps we take make sense later. You'll see, Schätzchen."

I can barely focus on her words of wisdom, even though this might be the last solid piece of advice she ever gives me.

All I hear is the pounding at the door, the scuffle of boots outside, the angry voices. "I'm not going!" I tell her. "They're going to take you away for something I've done!"

"Not if I can help it." And with a final shove, she pushes me all the way in and shuts the door behind me.

"Öffnen Sie die Tür!"

I hear her cross the room and open the door as they've ordered. Low, disturbing voices quickly fill the room. I press my face to the door, hoping to catch a phrase, a fragment that will tell me what is happening—anything to let me know Mutti is safe on the other side of this door without me. I should be escaping through my window and into the trees, but I cannot move out of fear. Now I know what Matilde has done today. She's fattened me up because she knew they were coming. She knew all along she would force me to leave, perhaps never to come back. I want to cry and pound my fist against the door for what she is doing for me, but I'm resigned to staying hopelessly quiet.

I hear their boots scrape across the floor. I imagine they are staring around, scrutinizing the scarce belongings we have, trying to find fault that will jump out at them. Finally, one man speaks, and because his voice is so precisely calm, it is the one that scares me the most.

"Are you Matilde?" he asks.

If I close my eyes I can picture Matilde standing in front of him as she worries the ends of her apron.

"Yes. I am."

"You have been accused on good evidence of the crime of witchcraft. In the name of the Holy Empire, you are to come with us immediately."

There is silence, while on my side of the door there is disbelief.

"What 'good evidence' do you speak of, Sir?"

"Poison and murder, old woman," he spits the words into her face.

"I've neither poisoned nor murdered. You must have the wrong person. Now if you'll kindly leave my house, I'd like to go to bed."

Footsteps come closer to where I stand. I hold my breath, as if the person on the other side can hear me breathing. Dishes clink. Someone is going through our things.

"An old woman like you needs all this food? Are you a thief as well as a murderer?" another voice asks. He doesn't wait for her to answer, and I am shivering because that is exactly what I believe myself to be.

"Looks like a feast fit for the Prince Bishop himself."

Sounds of tasting what lies on the table are as clear as day, and I struggle not to fly out of this room, ready to yank our precious food from his vulgar mouth. They have no right to be inside our home, rummaging through our belongings, eating what is ours. There is a bit of laughter, dark and grimy-sounding, and something slides across the floor.

"Do you ride this at midnight, too?"

She doesn't answer him. A swishing noise strokes the floorboards again, and I know he speaks of the broom.

"We've been kind enough to allow you to live your life quietly for many years, old woman, but we haven't been blind to the sort of business you keep. You're a crone, a witch, telling fortunes for money…but you hide secrets, as all witches do, and for that reason alone you are being arrested."

"Is this where you keep your spells?" a voice interrupts, and the handle of the door jiggles near my waist. I step away from it. Every bone in my body quivers. There is a man in front of me. The door is the only thing between us, and when he opens it, he will find me.

I am light on my feet and cross the room until I am at the window, lifting my legs one after the other to climb through into the icy night. Just in time, I drop to the ground. Leaning my back against the house, I hear the door swing open inside my room.

"There's a bed in here, and a bed out there. Surely you sleep in only one," the man shouts loud enough for the others to hear, and just feet above me as I hide.

"Is the other for your demonic lover? Or is it for the girl you keep?"

Finally I hear Matilde's voice, and I want to cry and run to her, to pull her along with me while we make a run for it through the trees. The forest is haunted. They won't dare come after us.

"There is no girl, Sir." Her quiet, steady voice rings out against the gruff tones that chafe against all that is warm and comforting in our home.

"Tell us where she is. Or perhaps you conjured her to send along your magick, thus making you a witch in every sense of the word, which gravely changes matters. You are to come with us immediately."

There is no sound of struggle. In fact, Matilde goes along with them without argument. I peek around the corner of our cottage and watch with wide eyes as their lanterns shed a flickering path along the forest floor, leading them back to the village.

"Torch the house," the tall man says.

I press my hand to my mouth, careful not to let the scream I hold slip out, alerting them that I am only a few feet away.

A figure steps toward my home, tossing the lit torch he holds through the open door, and soon the main room is bright with a sinister orange glow. All we own is at the mercy of that brightness. It eats everything it touches—our food, our clothing…our memories. The look on Matilde's face is absolute devastation. I wonder if she fears I am still inside, trapped. I've already betrayed her today. Did she think I wouldn't listen again?

The men lead her away, and I am left with the smell of burning wood, the snapping of timber, and all I have ever known withering to a pile of ash. When they are a good distance ahead, I hug close to the sharp-needled trees that hide me, knowing I should run in the other direction, into the dark that is far away from them.

But I can't.

I know they are taking Matilde to the village. I know in my heart what they will do to her. The story she told of my mother comes to life behind my eyes, only it is Matilde's face I see. This is all my fault, and I cannot bear it. That is why I must follow them, and then, when I can stand it no more, I'll do as Matilde warned me to do. I'll run away from here, deep into the Black Forest to save myself.

A few yards ahead, Matilde struggles to push through the thick hedge. No one helps her. Instead, the men appear to be amused by her difficulty. Just past the cobbler's store, in the center of what was the market today, a large man keeps warm beneath his ankle-length cassock. The bishop greets the group, his eyes narrowing at Matilde as if she's a living contagion. The men push her along with a cattle prod, jabbing her in the back every so often.

If I follow too closely, I risk being seen. If I'm seen, then everything Matilde has done to protect me will have been in vain. There's a hollow space that nestles against the blacksmith's outpost, where he keeps wood for the furnace, and I curl myself into it. Since the blacksmith is a farmer most of his time, he isn't here to catch me. I can stay all night if I need to.

The break in the hedge along the village proper bends because of the stream, the very stream Matilde and I use daily. That stream, the Berg, runs its course, cutting in here and there, before spilling into the Danube. Württemberg's pretty, arched bridge sweeps over the moving water, and I see now that they are stopping beneath it instead of crossing to where the bishop's courthouse is.

One man holds the stool and a handful of rope, while another pulls a cart of heavy stones behind them. They bind Matilde's hands together and attach the rope to the bottom of the stool. Then they yank at her clothing and begin filling the front of her dress with the large, dirty stones. Her blouson is lumpy, making her body appear sinister and distorted in the candlelight, and she begins to wail. One by one, windows across the square fill with light, doors open, and people begin to pour out into the street to see what's going on. I crane my neck for a better view, wishing more than anything that I wasn't confined to this tiny hideaway.

There is shouting, which grows louder by the second, and soon peaks in a deafening uproar. I've never witnessed a riot before and stare wide-eyed at the disturbance.

"Witch!"

"Condemn her!"

Finally, the crowd hushes as the bishop at the top of the arched bridge speaks.

"You are accused of communing with souls, of manipulating the grace of God, and therefore we strip you of all rights. You are no longer a free citizen, having chosen to live your life beyond the protective borders of this village, allowing the curse of Satan to destroy your soul. Matilde of the Forest, you are hereby sentenced to death by dunking without trial and without jury."

The bishop motions to the man standing closest to Matilde, and I can see he wears a coat with dozens of tiny buttons that reflect the light.

"Admit you are a witch and renounce the devil; it will very well save your life," he tells her. I recognize his voice immediately as the composed man from our cottage, the one who spoke with such confidence that he scared me.

The crowd is silent, waiting for word that she will confess. They are wondering if she is indeed a witch, and I myself wonder if anyone standing there as witness feels remorse for having sought her out over the years. In private, Matilde was treated with kindness, yet tonight, the town gathers to scorn her, to see her suffer, as if she is their entertainment. My fists clench and I wish with all my heart that one of them, just one, would be brave enough to speak up for her, to tell the bishop there's been a grave mistake.

But no one says a word. Not even I, as I cower in the shadows and watch.

Her frail voice strains from the heavy stones upon her chest. "I am not a witch."

I close my eyes, knowing the truth cannot help her.

When I open my eyes against the tears I see the bishop making the sign of the cross over the crowd. Between two shoulders I see four men lift the stool Matilde is tied to, and for a second, my eyes connect with hers across the cobbled square. I know she sees me, as I see her. Her eyes from this distance are two shining orbs in the light. They flicker brilliantly, wildly, off the stones, off the man's buttoned waistcoat, off the open mouths of those yelling for her death.

Her lips part as if to tell me something, and then, with the fear of her own impending doom, she cries out, "Witches can't cross water! Witches can't cross water!"

She is telling me something. It is something important, but I don't understand. The men pull her and struggle against the cumbersome weight of the stool; then, with a heavy heaving motion, they thrust her into the stream. A tremendous splash surfaces, sending those standing closest to her recoiling backward. They pull her up, and she gasps for air. Over and over her body is dunked, plunging into the icy water.

Watch how they delight in her torture…

I am startled at the whisper that comes close to my ear, yet I don't allow it to fully frighten me. I'm too frightened by what I see with my eyes. I've heard this voice many times now. I know not to look for the lips that speak it—I won't find them. But the whisper is right, and I watch with growing rage at the terrible scene before me.

They live to see another die… They gain over another's loss… Tell me, daughter of mine. What will you do?

A man to the left of the bridge marks the number of times she is brought up and down, until at last, his hand is still. The stool is lowered one last time and quietly, the one person I ever loved, the one person who was my family, my world, sinks out of sight to the bottom of the black water.

I wait until the crowd thins and is gone altogether. Candles are snuffed. Windows grow dark. The water in the deepest part of the stream calms, its surface like a rippling window I can peer through, and if I were to, I would see the body of my beloved Mutti waiting patiently at the muddy bottom for someone to pull her up.

At last the rope is drawn. It is heavy and taut, and it takes seven men to lift her. I watch as her body is cut free and tossed upon the cart. The wheels scream as she is taken away from here, from this life, from me. I clasp my hand to my mouth to hold in my screams and squeeze my eyes shut, pushing the tears out and onto my cheeks.

And the voice comes again.

What will you do?

I break away from my hiding place and make a mad dash for the hedge.

You must make them pay for what they've done to the old woman, Rune. Make them pay for what they've done to you! my mother, the witch, whispers to me.

My hands cup my ears to keep her voice out of my head, but it does no good. I am distracted, confused, and I fall to the ground, tripping over roots and stones. Soon I am scrambling, up again, running faster, putting as much distance between myself and the horrific image of Matilde drowning, knowing no matter how far I run this night will haunt me forever.

If I had listened, done what Matilde told me to do, then I'd be far from here. I would have never witnessed what they did to her, and this night would haunt me in a different way, filling me with questions, the need to find out what became of her. I might even wonder if there was a chance she could still be alive. But now I know. I saw firsthand, and I can never rid myself of it.

With a burning ache in my chest, I try to catch my breath and realize I have run out of places to escape to. The cottage, my home, is in ruins, but I creep up to it hoping to find anything salvageable to get me through the night. There is nothing left.

Look what they've taken away from you, my daughter. You must seek revenge...

Her whisper is louder now, clearer.

"What good will it do?" I whisper back into the sooty darkness.

It will prove to them they cannot play with what they don't understand...

I raise my head, not quite knowing where to look. There is nothing but black around me—black smoke, black trees.

"Do you think I understand any better? Do you think I know what you're speaking of?"

I turn in circles, because when her whispers come, they come from all around. They are everywhere and nowhere, all at once.

"You entrusted Matilde to take care of me. You gave me away, and now I'm supposed to look to you for guidance and revenge?"

Soon you will understand, daughter of mine. You will understand that the power of a witch stretches beyond the human mind. Mark that day, dear one, for it will be the day you come into your own powers.

"When? When will it come?" I shout. "Because I will make sure I *never* understand it!"

Silence presses back against me in the dark. I've angered her. I know it.

You have no choice in that matter...

The day you were born is the day I died. My legacy passes to you...

I press my hands to my head in an effort to squeeze her voice out of it. There has to be a way to stop the whispers; there has to be a place I can run to and be safe. Matilde's last words come to me, pushing out the remainder of my mother's urgent declaration.

Witches can't cross water.

Matilde wasn't a witch. Not a true witch. I'm not even sure if *I* am. But I am sure she was telling me something. She must have known that I wouldn't listen to her, that I wouldn't run off into the forest, but would follow her instead.

"Of course," I say out loud to myself. I climb over the rubble, and cautiously walk into the trees. The stream greets me with its own whisper, and I reach into the frigid current, feeling around with my hand, not sure what it is I'm looking for, if anything at all. Minutes go by, and all I've got to show for my efforts are numb fingers. Even if I find something beneath the black water, I'd never be able to grip it tight enough to pull it up.

Just when I've about set my mind to giving up, my fingers brush against something soft. In the dark I believe I've touched the remains of a drowned animal, or that my fingers have brushed against the algae-covered rocks, but the texture is different, and I begin to clear away the heavy rocks holding it in place. The thought of what I'm doing shatters me. I could easily be freeing Matilde of her stony weights, helping her rise to the surface so she can breathe and live another day.

I force myself to keep at it, until at last I'm able to pull what is lodged beneath the water to the edge of the bank. I recognize it immediately. It's the bag of rune stones from the cupboard, safe like Matilde said it would be. I want to open the drawstring and make sure they are all there, knowing the stone I saved is still in my pocket waiting to join the others, but a low hiss that is almost human forms within the mist around the Berg stream. Through the trees from where I've come, I can make out the distinct shape of my still-smoldering home, feeling how it calls me back. I need to think. I need to plan what to do, because no matter how I look at it, I am absolutely alone in this world.

The whispering deepens, solidifying into words, but I tune them out and step into the icy water that moves as if it knows its place in this world. I, on the other hand, must discover what

Murgia

my place is. When I step further into the water I am greeted with blessed silence, but also an invisible force that stops me.

I cannot cross to the other side.

Chapter 14
Rune

"So I *am* a witch," I sigh.

Deep down, I'd hoped Matilde had created that fantastical story—a fairy tale like the others—and was not telling the story of my life. When she called out to me about the stream, I saw it as a way to escape the horror of this night, to escape the insisting whispers and flee to the other side, leaving my mother behind. But I'm the one who can't cross.

Dripping wet and shivering, I pull myself onto the muddy bank and stare at the other side. How far did Matilde believe I could go? How safe did she think I would be if I listened and ran away?

The voices in my head have grown eerily silent, leaving room for me to pay attention to all the other frightening sounds the night brings. My imagination stirs. Specters scream for my soul, ghosts come back from the dead to keep me company as the darkest hours begin to pass in slow sequential order. I wonder if they call out because I am one of them. I am a witch, and the ghost of a girl I used to be.

It is too dangerous to stay here. Every twig snap is a foot making its way closer. Every hoot from the owl is a secret call between the villagers signaling that they have found me. My heart beats strong, confined against my ribs. I imagine the men coming back for me. I imagine my fate much worse than Matilde's, for I am the thief and the poisoner. I am the one who has put everyone's lives in danger. I am the daughter of a witch they burned sixteen years ago.

A light breeze moves the treetops, revealing a waning moon. It offers enough light to make my way across the rubble, and I am able to see what I can find that will be help me survive. I scan the ground, but there is little for me to take. A button, a spoon, an acorn from the oak above the ruined cottage. I tuck it all in the precious bag of rune stones. It is all I have. It will have to be enough. I make my way back to the stream, intent on following it until my feet can carry me no further, praying that what frightens everyone else will welcome me and keep me safe.

Chapter 15
Laurentz

*P*ine needles fall from my coat as I shake out all evidence of the forest. I didn't realize how long I'd been gone. The sun has already set, and the aroma of the evening meal greets me as I step into the kitchen.

"Would you like to explain where you've been all day?" Cook smears her hands across her apron and stomps toward me. Her eyes are wide and anxious; now that I see her up close, I notice they are rather bloodshot, strangely matching her round, ruddy cheeks. "Your father's been worried."

"I doubt that." A bored sigh escapes me as a plate of butterbrot catches my eye. I reach for a slice, not realizing how starved I am, only to have my hand slapped with a wooden spoon.

"What is this?" Her voice reaches an octave short of explosion. She points the spoon handle at my arm, jabbing at my bloodstained sleeve. "Have you been fighting?"

Before I can make something up, she is in a full rant, sending the rest of the kitchen staff scurrying out of her way. "Don't let your father see this. You know as well as I do he doesn't condone fighting. You're supposed to be respectable."

This is Cook's usual speech—how I am an Electorate in training. I am a member of Eltz's regal Guard. I have no business exploring what lies beyond our land, no reason to venture out and show the world the man I am becoming, or try to prove anything else. Who I am should be plenty enough proof to anyone wishing to inquire.

"Well?" she asks, not taking silence for an answer. "Where were you?"

"I went to the village today. I was bored."

"Don't talk with your mouth full!" Cook is not in a good mood this evening. I shove a piece of the bread into my mouth and wipe my lips against my sleeve, earning myself another glare.

She clucks her tongue against her teeth as she inspects my arm, and I am silent, watching to see if I somehow missed a mark on my skin. Was the light in the forest dim enough that I only *believed* Rune had healed me? Cook finds nothing that will explain the blood, and she drops my arm in disgust.

"Someone else's, then? You'd better clean up and change your shirt. And be quick about it; your father is waiting for you."

"Is he...?"

"Angry with you?" Her eyes widen. "I would say he is, and mind you to be respectful for once. He's had some bad news." She begins to sniffle. "We all have."

The other servants avoid my eyes. Cook is on the verge of crying. She can be emotional; she can be overbearing, but breaking down in front of everyone is not like her, and my stomach sinks, wondering what I missed today while I was off in the village. I can't help thinking that my family has grown one less, and I peer around the corner into the neighboring room to see my father at the table with his head in his hands.

How he will handle another death in our family? How will it be with just the two of us now? I'm his only heir, his only company. Will it heal what's fallen apart between us, or drive a deeper wedge?

"Father," I say softly, approaching the table. The Weisswurst on his plate is untouched. It looks cold, and I wonder if he has been waiting for a son he thought would never return. He looks up at me, finally. I see how the lines around his eyes have deepened. I see the slump of his shoulders, and how he doesn't bother to hide it.

I kneel at his feet. "Is she…?"

My father pushes his chair out, and before I can rise, his hand comes crashing across my face. My eyes sting with the force of his slap.

"How dare you not call for me when the bishop arrived."

"Father, I didn't want to disturb you. I only thought…"

"You have no right to think, especially when it comes to business that is mine, not yours. You are not Electorate yet, merely a boy pretending to fill shoes that are much too large."

His words are cruel, lashing harder than the strike across my face. Words cannot describe the look in his eyes, yet I can't say I didn't expect it. I know I made a terrible mistake when I chose not to tell him of the bishop's visit. Even later, when I had the chance to, I didn't, wanting to let the bishop's words sit with me to try and understand what it was he was really telling me. I was surprised to learn the bishop believes a witch is at work, how he thinks it will cause the other half of society to fall. Does my father believe this as well? That is why I couldn't go to him. I have no idea what my father thinks, or what he wishes to hide from me.

I step away, out of his reach. "I was only thinking of sparing you one less concern. I planned on telling you about it at dinner tonight."

"For which you are late." The look on my father's face disturbs me. This is not the face of a man mourning a dead wife. My assumptions have been wrong.

He takes his finger and points, with an exaggerated flip, at my coat. "Burn these outside. Pyrmont is gone, and I don't want Eltz to be next. For all I know, you could have picked up every disease known to man in that despicable village."

"Despicable?" He's never spoken of Württemberg, or any other village for that matter, as despicable. "How do you know where I've been?"

My father looks at me and my cheek stings in anticipation of his hand.

"I make it a point to know *everything*. That's what it means to be Electorate—something you are far from understanding, it appears. I'm sure the people of Württemberg didn't appreciate your visit as much as you'd like to think they did. Can you imagine, the Electorate's son bringing contagion to their homes? Did you ever think what this could do to the alliances we've made?"

"I didn't. I couldn't have." But it's a possibility that I could be a carrier. I took it upon myself to step inside the small, rundown home of Anna and her mother. The inside was filthy. But I am certain the news of Plague hadn't spread yet. If it had, the entire village would have been hiding behind closed doors, not mulling around the streets.

"We are closer to Pyrmont than the village," my father says. "We are at a greater risk than they are. You don't think ahead, my son. You never have."

My father turns away from me, leaving me with angry words that bite and kick from the outside in.

"The Prince Bishop has been at the cathedral all day, praying for the souls that have fallen to this pestilence. He's in need of a messenger to spread word of the epidemic to Württemberg to warn them. Since it seems to be a place you're suddenly fond of, I've sent word that you will be his messenger."

I remember the bishop's carriage. If the town was already contagious, would the bishop chance being there? And what of the witch bottle? Is the bishop taking his own precautions?

"You have no choice but to honor me and do as I say. You will return to the village tomorrow, deliver the message, and leave immediately. And then you will promise me not to visit there again."

I stare down at my boots, knowing I cannot disobey him. Not now. "Yes, Father."

He tosses his napkin across the platter of untouched food and turns to leave. "One more thing." He faces me with a measured expression. "The bishop wishes to pray for your soul and a swift journey tomorrow. I suggest you repay the favor and pray tonight."

I draw a sharp breath into my lungs. "You know I don't pray, father."

"Then pray for your stepmother, and pray for us, that we make it through this dark time. Pray for your safety and quick return. The bishop believes the epidemic will spread to the village more quickly than we think. He seems to believe there is a distinct possibility it will bypass Eltz altogether."

The bishop's words are nonsense, but I can't reveal that to my father, who is more faithful than I am. The bishop believes the church saves souls only if they are noble and worthy. What of the others? Who calculates the worth of their souls? Must they be wealthy and high-born to deserve that chance?

Perhaps returning to Württemberg will prove to be worthwhile, because there I will be among those who have souls whose worth is in doubt, and I wonder if I will find mine among them.

Chapter 16
Rune

I am far from the boundaries of my home, but I am not far away enough yet, and though my muscles burn for rest, I will not stop.

"Please, Sacred Mother, please give me the strength to keep on."

I follow the stream weaving along the ground. It widens and narrows in places I have trouble following, twisting away from my feet as I shuffle behind its course, sometimes disappearing altogether. When that happens, I panic. I force myself to stand still and will it to come back to me. It always listens.

Until now.

The stream has vanished. It has faded into the deep, dark ground, and I cannot find where it surfaces again. I drop to my hands and knees, clawing at the earth, feeling the damp moss to see if my fingers drip with excess moisture. Perhaps the water has gone too far under for me to follow. Perhaps I am truly on my own. It hurts to pull myself to my feet, but I manage, and stand peering into the thick copse of trees that surrounds me, listening for the sound of trickling water. There is nothing but silence.

The forest is so dreadfully dark here as I pace, but I can see the large circular arc my footsteps have traced. It reminds me of the circle Matilde cast the night she told me about my mother. She asked the elements to guard me. Will they still do so, or have they left me?

I create a starting point with my eye, then begin walking to the left of it. *Widdershins.* The last thing I need is negative energy entering the circle. When I am through, I step inside, tracing a line in the dirt to close myself within.

I have nothing to offer the Sacred Mother, but hope the acorn will do. I pull it from the bag, placing it on a rock in the center of the circle, in a sliver of pale moonlight that cuts between the branches. I doubt very much the little acorn will do anything substantial, but if it is meant to nourish then I figure it might be of some value to give it up.

From my pocket, I pull out the remaining treasures I'd found by the cottage. I hold the little brown button up to the sky. "This is all I have to offer you—please accept it. May this button bind me to the earth and keep me steady. May this spoon carve a path for me to find safety."

I don't know what else to say, and fear I am not doing a very good job at my first witch circle. My voice sounds silly and trite. I feel very foolish holding the button and spoon. Even the acorn looks pathetic as I peer down at it from between my extended arms.

I am a witch, I am a witch, I am a witch, I think to myself.

I wait a few moments. Nothing happens. There is no spark of light. No feeling of tremendous warmth like the other night when Matilde invoked Fire. Maybe that's where I went wrong. Fire spoke to me that night, but I have no fire here, and no means to make one. Defeated, I settle myself to the ground, sulking.

"The Sacred Mother won't help me," I whisper out loud, hearing how my voice grates against the night. It echoes and surrounds me like a pulse that is much too loud for the stillness. "She's turned away from me."

You will never be alone, daughter of mine…

I am tempted to answer her, but that would mean I am accepting her, and I can't yet. I've grown up fearing her, much like I still do. When the air circles and stirs behind me, I know it's her. Dry leaves take flight and gather around me, rising into a tower, then falling to the ground just outside the circle. Even the wind will not enter it. I must have done something wrong.

"Why won't you let me be?" I ask into the darkness. "Why must it be *now* that you follow me?"

You need me, daughter...

"I will never need you."

Ah, but you do...

The walk has been so terribly exhausting and lonely—it's no wonder I am fighting with the voices inside my head. Strange—after living in the forest my entire life, it is here, alone, that my senses have become heightened. I can hear and feel more keenly than I ever have before. This is no longer the Black Forest I know. This is a strange new world waiting to engulf me, and I don't know if I am ready for it.

I kick at the ground and break the circle.

The tree boughs above me reach for one another, creating a thick impenetrable fence much denser than the hedge near the village. There is no wind, and I should be curious how the trees move without it, but I am sore. I am weary. It seems my legs will no longer cooperate with the rest of my body. Then there is a sound at my feet, and I am stunned to find the little stream has returned. It is no wider than my arm, and barely a trickle that seems content enough to disappear beneath the thick root of a tree just a few yards in front of me. I look behind me at my makeshift altar. The button and spoon are gone. Even the acorn.

Tired, I look up and rub my eyes. The wide trunk is gnarled in such a way it appears to have steps carved into it. I know I am seeing things that are not quite real or explainable, but I am in the Black Forest, and I have just made a bargain with the Sacred Mother. I am a witch.

I mutter a thank you to remain in the Mother's good graces and climb the trunk to a strange, flat platform made of wide branches. It is layered with fine needles that are soft to the touch, not prickly or pointy, and I settle myself upon them, resting within the crook of the great tree. Here I am completely hidden from the ground below, if someone were to come looking for me. I pray that if someone is searching, they'll assume I died in the fire that consumed the cottage. Where else would I be? Realistically, would a girl my age run off into the forest at nightfall? *This forest?* And would anyone really come after me?

My hand reaches out to separate the boughs, and I peek out into the vast darkness. Nothing that resembles a lantern or torch comes my way—nothing bobbing with light, no shouts from trackers. I am safe. For now. But for how long, I have no idea.

And then the tears come in waves, beginning in my chest, heaving their way up to my throat where they become stuck. I curl in on myself, missing Matilde, seeing her execution as vividly in my mind as if I were in the square watching it all over again. "I am a terrible girl," I say to myself. I half-hope I fall out of the tree. I half-hope the villagers come find me and whisk me away.

I deserve nothing less.

Chapter 17
Laurentz

*L*ast evening, after my father left the table, I wandered outside. I found myself at the mouth of the forest, looking intently on the ground for moss. All I could find were dead pine needles, brown lichen, and wild fern. At one point during the night I sat up in my bed and stared at my arm. I know the thorns had scraped it. I'd felt their sting. There'd been blood to prove it, yet there is no mark. It leaves me without explanation. Was the moss' cure medicinal, or was it more than that? Was this the work of a witch, such as the bishop had warned me of? Had I indeed been bewitched by Rune?

I suppose I invited these thoughts, for I did not heed my father's request. I did not pray. It isn't that I didn't believe God would hear my petition, but that my father told me to do it. As punishment, I'd spent the entire night looking for answers to the strange healing, seeing Rune's haunting eyes every time I tried.

When I awoke and ventured downstairs, Cook could barely speak. A timid boy, elbow-deep in brick dust as he scoured the stove irons, was the only person who could tell me what had happened. He'd just come from Pyrmont an hour before, sent to ask if all was well, but no one had answered the hail.

Through her sobs, I caught enough to understand that Cook's last remaining family, a cousin, had been a servant there. Last night she had not been weeping for my stepmother, who still clings to life this morning.

This is why I am here, saddled atop my horse overlooking the river at the foot of Eltz's land. My back is to the forest, something I have been told not to allow. I know I must go into the forest again, that I must make my way through the shadows and eerie pockets of cold, damp air to the village surrounded by the fence of green.

Let my father think I do this to honor his wish and appease the bishop, that I will warn this humble village of an imminent threat. The real reason is simple. I want to find Rune. I want answers. I want to see her do something else that will send chills up my spine and astound me. I want to look deep into her eyes and know that she holds something over me, a spell perhaps, and that what she is capable of isn't a figment of my imagination. Then, I want to bring her back to Eltz with me, her basket overflowing with herbs and stalks and a great big pile of spongy green moss. I will ask her to heal my stepmother. I will prove that the bishop is wrong, that what cannot be explained is not always a sign of evil. Eltz will have its protection against the Plague, and in the end, I will have won the respect of my father.

Chapter 18
Rune

*T*he night did not swallow me whole, much to my disappointment.

My face aches from crying. My jaw is stiff from clenching my teeth together. I do not need to peer into the flowing stream beneath the tree to see how red and swollen my eyes are. Last night was a nightmare, but still, I made it through. I am here. I am whole. The villagers did not follow me into the forest, and after all the terrible things I'd done, the Sacred Mother watched over me, and for that I am grateful.

I climb down from my woodland shelter and look around. It didn't rain during the night, yet the stream has indeed grown larger, making me wonder if magick forces were at work while I slept. Had I been purposely led to this spot to prevent me from wandering further away? The Black Forest is so disorienting, even during the day, that I surely would have walked in circles, perhaps even finding my way back to the village and into the arms of my enemies.

Strange, too, is that the ground is void of my footprints. The circle is gone, and I shudder, knowing well that which I do not understand is at work here. I feel it in the air, hear it in the trees. It waits for me to understand it, to welcome it, to beckon it. For the first time I wonder how long it will take me…or if I have, in fact, already begun to do so.

I drop to my knees and lean over the cool, glistening water, avoiding my reflection. The water is cold and satisfying on my parched tongue and it fills me so that I don't feel the empty space in my stomach. But I do make a mistake. It is one I cannot help. I open my eyes. Instead of looking at my face, I am staring back at another over my shoulder. She is gray and ghostlike, and the trees behind her show through her skin, as if she is nothing but a pane of glass.

I react, slipping from the loose pebbles that line the narrow bank and into the icy water up to my knees. When I look again, *he* is standing there. Not her.

"It's seems I am pulling you out of trouble again," Laurentz says to me.

He waits for an answer, and the pit of my stomach flutters. I cannot believe he is here. I am glad he is, yet I can't help feeling something else, and I stare at his hand, unsure if it is wise to take it and allow myself to be pulled from the stream. I don't like needing someone else's help, and honestly, I'm afraid. If he was able to find me so easily, will others come as well?

"You're far from home this morning," he tells me, ignoring the stretch of uncomfortable silence that pressures me to answer him. I bite the inside of my cheek. I don't have to tell him anything. I don't know him. I can't trust him, or anyone.

I nod toward the gold braid cording that adorns his uniform. "And you're dressed far too elegantly for a jaunt through the woods," I say in return.

He looks down at his chest, then back at me. "Yes, I suppose I am."

I've never seen these colors, nor the crest emblazoned upon his sash. It is a golden stag, and I wonder what it means. He looks devastatingly handsome, but in an official sort of way, and I wonder if he has anything to do with the men who took Matilde to the village square the night before. With all my heart, I don't want him to be. I want him to be the nice boy who helped me escape the clutches of the hedge, not a part of something so cruel.

I wring out the hem of my dress. It will take a while to dry. The sun doesn't seem to last very long over the forest, but it is something I'm used to.

"What did you say?" I ask, continuing to watch the steady trickle that falls from my skirt to the ground.

Laurentz has been looking around, but turns to me with a confused expression on his face. "I didn't speak."

"Yes, you did. You were wondering what I'm gathering today."

He takes a slow step in my direction, then pauses. "I've been quiet this entire time. I was…"

"You were what?" I ask him. My hand swipes at a loose hair that has fallen across my eye. I stand upright and look at him questioningly.

"I was wondering to myself what could have brought you so far away from the village. That perhaps the moss you used on my arm grows here. But I didn't say it. I *thought* it."

A strange smile creeps to the corner of my mouth, and I laugh a little at this. But my laugh is a nervous one, and he knows it. I can't pretend this into something else. What can I say to make him believe I made a mistake, that I heard a bird call and not his thoughts?

But I did. I must have. It was as clear as all the other times he's spoken to me; his voice has a silken quality to it. Nothing in the forest can replicate it. I shrug my shoulders convincingly. "Then it must have been my own thoughts I heard."

But I hear him again, and now, I watch him out of the corner of my eye because I am alarmed to the point of shaking. His lips don't move. They don't open; they don't even twitch so that he might be projecting his voice out to me, pretending not to speak when he really is. He must wonder why I am here. I have no basket, and the ground does not appear to be very fruitful.

I take a deep breath, astonished at what is happening between us. I can't help staring at his uniform because I am too afraid to look into his eyes. All I can think of is how he doesn't fit here. He is too formal to be standing in the forest with me. He is too perfect to blend in with the wild while I stand in a dirty, damp dress, my eyes swollen from my tears. We are as different as two worlds. But what is stranger still is how he doesn't appear to notice it as I do. In fact, he appears to be amused, even curious.

"You can hear me, can't you?"

His eyes light up at this preposterous, impossible idea, as he walks toward me. "Tell me you can hear what I'm thinking." It is clear this is amazing to him, while to me, it is practically horrifying. How will I talk my way out of it? Is this what he came for—proof that I am different? Proof that I am a witch's daughter, and maybe even a witch myself? Instantly my heart clenches.

Instead of grasping my wrists like I expect, he cautiously reaches out and lets his fingertips slide gently across my cheek. The eyes I look up into are soft, and then he asks, "Who are you?"

Who am I? Who am I? Echoes in my head. Do I even know? His mind is quiet while he waits, letting in another familiar voice, my mother's.

You know who you are…

I know my name is Rune. I grew up in the Black Forest, beyond the border of Württemberg. I was raised by Matilde, an old healing woman who peddled fortunes. I am the daughter of a woman who gave me away, who was then burned at the stake for being a witch.

Do I tell him this? Is there more to my story? Isn't this enough?

There is one thing I know for certain, and that is I feel so very alive at this moment as he touches my face and looks into my eyes. I am real. I am alive. My heartbeat tells me so, and it is beating so fast right now that I can't think straight.

Laurentz drops his hand and rolls up his sleeve without taking his eyes from mine. I break the gaze and look down, seeing the skin I healed with the moss is exposed.

"I've tried over and over again to come up with a logical explanation, and I simply can't," he whispers. "How did you do this? How can you hear what I'm thinking?"

"I don't know," I whisper back.

His face is so close to mine that it is nearly impossible to breathe. It seems the forest is covered in a veil that muffles the usual woodland sounds, as if it too waits for something magickal to happen. I have never felt my knees go weak before, except for when Rolf told me what the mushrooms had done to his horse, and when Matilde was taken away. Never have I felt this way because of someone *looking* at me.

"It's true then," Laurentz says softly. "You've bewitched me."

And then the spell is broken. I back away tensely, disturbed by what he has just said.

"I haven't bewitched you. I haven't bewitched anyone. You don't know who I am," I whisper back defensively, and then ask, "Why are you here?"

I look at his face, and for a moment I feel terrible for destroying the unexplainable magick felt between us. But I won't allow myself be blinded by a feeling I don't understand, not when it's crucial that I keep myself safe. I don't know who to trust. I want to trust Laurentz. I want to feel what I just did moments ago, again and again. It was so beautiful, so warm. I felt happy. But I don't know what the future holds for me. I am not a part of the world he belongs to. I am not even sure how I fit into the world that is meant to be mine.

He too seems to feel something is changed now. He holds himself straighter, stiffer, as if I've offended him. I watch as he rolls his sleeve back over his strong forearm, and I wish I had the courage to tell him what he wants to know. I wish I could tell him who my mother was, who I think I am. What would he say if I told him I hear her voice? That she wants to help me become like her? That the reason she's come back for me is because she wants me to destroy the village for what they did to her? Oh, yes, that would make him stay with me forever, wouldn't it?

"I'm on my way to the village. A favor to the bishop," Laurentz tells me.

My heart sinks. Now I know I must be careful around him. I can't help seeing the bishop in my mind, as he watched from the arched bridge and ordered the men to dunk Matilde over and over until she drowned.

"It's all right, Rune. I'm not contagious. I've only come to warn the others about the Plague."

He's mistaken my step back as indication that I know something terrible is possible. He still believes I live in the village, that he's doing me a favor by warning me, not that I am putting distance between us because he has anything to do with the terrible man who took Matilde away from me.

"Plague?" The word is foreign on my tongue.

"Have you and Matilde ever treated anyone with Plague before?" he asks, and it's like a knife thrusts into my heart.

"You know about Matilde?" I whisper so low that he moves toward me, bending his head to hear better.

"I know you and she help people—treat them for illness, as well as...other things."

Beneath his voice, I hear what he dares not say out loud. I hear his thoughts, and they twist and battle with themselves as he wonders if he should tell me what he really thinks. That I might be a witch. That I might be able to do the impossible and protect others from this illness he speaks of. That he wants me to trust him.

I take one more look at the uniform he wears, and all I can feel is fear. I turn and run as fast as my legs will carry me, deep into the forest where I know he will not follow. Even from this distance his thoughts reach me, and I know he is standing there watching me. I've hurt him, but he doesn't understand that I cannot be hurt. Not now. I've no more room for it. My lungs burn; when I feel I am far away enough, I force myself to slow down, leaning my back against the rough bark of a tree. I peer around the side, searching for Laurentz. His thoughts are quiet. It shouldn't surprise me that he is no longer there.

Chapter 19
Laurentz

My horse whinnies when we come to the hedge. I am sure she remembers nearly trampling Rune, and is worried we will attempt to jump over someone else today. I pat her neck and lead her along the border to where it splits open to a proper road stretching into the village.

Letting out an exhale of regret, I look over my shoulder toward the dense darkness behind me. I should have followed Rune when she ran off. She's out there somewhere, among the trees where no one will dare wander. I've upset her by mentioning Matilde's name and now I am here, while she is still out there, alone.

Now I am certain Rune is the girl who sold the mushrooms to the old woman. Perhaps that is why she ran away. She's afraid of being accused of a mistake. Or perhaps she is afraid of what I will think if her name is associated with Matilde's? If I settle things, Rune might understand I only meant to help her, that I was only trying to convince her to put whatever she and the old woman do for a living to good use and keep the sickness of the Plague at bay. That I would pay her back with kindness like that she had shown me.

Pleased with my idea, I strain to see the roof of the little cottage among the trees, knowing the height from my horse should make it easier than from the ground. But it isn't visible from here. Like the witch's house in a fairy tale, it has disappeared, swallowed whole by the evil forest. I laugh to myself and pull the reins to the left, venturing back into the trees, determined to find it. I will straighten this out with Matilde and put Rune's mind at ease.

I am both a little excited and nervous to meet the famed Hedge Witch, and as my horse steps across the forest floor, I picture what she might look like. I imagine her to be toothless and old, with a great big wart stuck to the side of an enormous pointy nose. *Silly.* This is how I've always thought a witch would look, and I know that I am creating quite a vivid picture that is most likely far-fetched. Rune, for example, is beautiful, and ethereal, and...

My eyes look at the path from which I've come, half-tempted to retrace my steps and find her.

The smell of charred wood floats toward me before the cottage ever comes into view. And then I realize that there is no cottage. I slip from my saddle and stand at the threshold of what I believe used to be Rune's home. It has completely burned to the ground. Nothing of it remains intact except the stone foundation.

"Rune," I whisper, remembering how her eyes shone with fear when I surprised her at the stream. "You have nothing to come home to." Everything is black and ruined, burnt beyond recognition. What was metal has melted; what was wood has burned to ash. A sudden chill comes over me as I place my hand in my pocket, my fingers touching the delicate stitches of the linen square. I forgot to return it to her. Now, as I feel the beautiful cloth and look at the remains of Rune's and Matilde's home, I wonder, was this an accident? I climb back onto my horse and hurry toward the village. If Rune's home was destroyed on purpose, I intend to find out why.

The village is bustling this morning and a group of women huddle a few feet away, whispering urgently. "It happened before my very eyes!" one woman says to the others in secret. "Over and over she was dunked in the stream until her lungs could hold no more air!"

"Whatever you do, don't visit the butcher. He's done for," comes the tattle of another woman. "Nearly all the animals have been slaughtered. They're either diseased or they are nothing but bags of bones, and I hear *she* was responsible."

"We've all visited her from time to time—how could we possibly know?"

This causes quite a stir among them, and a woman with a tight gray bun on top of her head leans in among them, quieting them all. "They say anyone who spoke with her or paid her for services shall be put on trial, so if I were you, I'd keep your good mouths shut!"

A well-dressed woman with a pinched face looks offended. "Well, I've done no such thing in all my life!"

One woman's face pales as she spots me; with a short nod to her friend, she switches their topic to the weather. I keep a straight face, but inside, a knot forms around my heart. I know they speak of Matilde, and there is no coincidence between her death and the burning of her house, nor the fact that Rune has run off into the woods. It hits me then. Rune is afraid for her life. The way she eyed my uniform, the way she stepped away when I mentioned Matilde's name. I hadn't known Matilde was dead. I take a deep breath and clench my jaw. *When I leave here, I will try to find Rune again. I will try to explain.*

In the center square I try to focus on the parchment I hold while the bell tolls for the village to gather. I see that I am recognized from yesterday, and the faces meeting mine are awash with questions about my presence and regal state of dress.

"By decree of his Holiness the Prince Bishop, I am to inform you of the fall of Pyrmont Castle."

There is an intake of breath from the crowd at the news, but I continue, "To protect the citizens of this village, Württemberg, from the destructive infection known as Plague, it is my duty to inform you to take heed."

Another collective gasp and several women cover their noses and mouths with their aprons, as if my warning has increased the risk of infection among them, my words making it airborne.

"How did the infection start?" a man calls out. The mutter of the crowd takes on a panicked edge.

I hold my hands up and cast a sharp glance to the bellman. "Regardless of how it started, I'm here, in the name of the bishop, to urge you to take every precaution."

Bits of what they think rise to my ears. I've created a frenzy by warning them of what has happened elsewhere. I only wanted to tell them to be aware, to take every precaution—to avoid spoiled food and to report any illness to the Bailiff. There is no way to tell if this little village will fall to what took down Pyrmont. There is no way to tell at all. The only person who may have been able to see that future, to warn and prepare us, has been put to her death.

"Surely the bishop knows the real reason behind our woes," comes a feminine voice through the din, causing the voices to fall silent. The crowd shuffles to make way for the woman, allowing her to stand directly in front of me, and I know her instantly. She is blonde-haired and older than me, closer to the age of my stepmother. Her hooded cloak lies against the back of her neck, instead of concealing her as it did when we watched the glassblower make the glass bottle.

"It's not only Plague we worry about, but everything else that allows our lives to be possible. What of the crops? Mice have overrun the fields to the north. Fleas infest our linens. Animals are starving and succumbing to disease, and we're supposed to ignore this? Perhaps this is God's way of purging the evil in this world. A way of ridding our town of something we all cringe to acknowledge."

"And what might that be, Madam?" I ask.

Her eyebrows lift playfully, but her eyes remain serious. "This village is plagued, but not by the illness you speak of, Sir. Not yet. Pyrmont is just a warning to us all."

The murmurs grow insistent among the crowd at the idea she has just given.

"Do you speak of the witch?" a faceless voice cries out.

She turns toward the anxious crowd, then slowly, returns her eyes to me. "Indeed, I do. Even in death does she find means to wreak havoc upon our village."

We stand and stare at one another while voices rise around us. It takes me a few moments to realize the panic has started.

The madness manifests out of one idea. One word spoken out loud creates a stir within the minds of every person present—just one word, so tainted, so blasphemous, so soaked in every dark possibility the human mind or soul could ever comprehend.

I say it in my head, just to feel how powerful it really is. *Witch.*

And indeed, it sends a chill up my spine.

"Executed or not, the witch wields her power!" The woman continues, knowing she holds the attention of the crowd. "You must be wary of whom you trust, for the cunning crone's dead eyes see among the living. Mind you, she cloaks herself in the skin of our neighbors."

Murmurs fill the square and soon argument replaces the woman's warning. The man who wears a bloodied butcher's apron climbs upon a sturdy barrel and clenches his fist above his head. "They must take the devil's maidens to the Drudenhaus and lock them behind prison doors!"

Heads bob in agreement. Shouts fill the air. "Only then will we be safe!"

Mention of the Drudenhaus chills me, for I've heard it is more than a prison. It is a place of torture and death—its new walls already stained with blood.

Murgia

From where I stand I can see the little house where the old woman and Anna live. The door stands wide open, askew on its hinges. I look away and focus on my hands, folding the parchment no one wants to hear, and then push my way through the throngs of people to where my horse is hitched to the fence. I have only a small window of time before they remember there is another person they can blame. I mount my horse, making sure I keep her steps slow, so that we don't draw extra attention. Once I am at the hedge, we make a break for it—trot, canter, gallop—until the only sound in my ears is the heavy pounding of hooves.

The forest is deep and foreboding. It might be the only place Rune stands a chance at surviving, and I realize she must already know this. Although the townspeople's tongues are cruel and hateful, they only speak that way because they are frightened. They will not search for Rune in the haunted forest.

The stream dwindles considerably until I find myself at the base of a great thick tree. I am sure this is where I found her earlier, but she is not here now.

"Rune!" I shout, turning in all directions so that my voice can be heard. "Rune!"

She doesn't answer. The forest is silent. My heart beats hard in my chest. All I want is to find her, to say how sorry I am, to warn her, but she is gone without a trace into the fairy-tale forest where only witches are safe.

Chapter 20
Rune

I awake to my name carried on the wind and sit up stiffly. I don't remember falling asleep, but I do remember seeing Laurentz's face behind my eyes. It fills me with the strangest feeling, and I don't know whether to be wary of him or to allow myself to smile at the warmth I feel when I think of him, when I try to recall the way his hand touched my face.

The day has slipped away, and I rise to my feet, knowing much of the walk back to the tree will be in darkness. My stomach is tight and rumbles like thunder. At my feet is a cluster of mushrooms and I shake my head, stepping over them. "I won't make that mistake twice," I say out loud.

I begin searching for food as I make my way back, spying shiny blackish-blue berries. They look inviting, but I remember Matilde once warned me never to eat them. "Tollkirsche," she called them. I thought the other name she sometimes used was by far prettier, and I would have fun saying it over and over. *Belladonna, Belladonna.* I cup the tiny bunch in the palm of my hand and take a closer look. *Pretty little things*, I think. I hear they are sweet, but I know one taste will stop my heart, and I release them, wiping my hands across the front of my dress.

A few yards away I see wild tomatoes, and I know they will tide me over. They are small—the pink-purplish fruit fits into the palm of my hand. Gathering a few, I walk slowly back to the tree and the tiny stream.

Darkness fully hushes the forest by the time I have finished my little meal, and I feel an exhaustion I have never known spread through my limbs, into my bones, making me long for sleep. All day, I had hoped Laurentz would come back, but he never did. He went to the village, and I wonder if he is still there. I'm afraid of going back home to where the cottage stood, but for a strange reason, it pulls me.

I take the drawstring bag into my lap and tug at the bottlenecked opening. A soft cloth inside holds Matilde's precious rune stones. My name came from these. A sad smile comes to my lips. With trembling fingers I carefully unfold the cloth, finding its softness comforting. I'd watched Matilde read the runes many times, and she kept this cloth as pristine as age would allow, but here in the dark I feel a marking in the center of it. I panic, hoping I haven't torn it, but as I run my fingers over it, I feel tiny pinpricks clustered near the same spot. The feeling reminds me of an old piece of stitchery someone had changed their mind about, the old threads removed so it could be reworked. Matilde must have taken it as payment long ago, thinking she could turn it into something else.

This is the first time I've been able to hold the runes for any length of time, and I run my fingertips along them, wishing Matilde had taken the time to teach me what they mean. I miss her more than anything, and without her, I wonder what's to become of me. Before I allow the sadness to consume me all over again, I spill the stones over my legs, keeping very still so they don't tumble out of the tree. By touch I feel each stone faces downward, and even though it is nearly impossible to see in the dark, I close my eyes and let my open hand hover over them, waiting to feel the familiar tickle against my skin.

To my surprise, it happens, and I am so overjoyed I nearly spill them. Eyes still closed, I choose stones, one after the other, until the peculiar warmth in my hand fades and disappears. I've chosen five stones, and slowly, I turn them over just as the moon pokes its light overhead, allowing me to see. But I don't know what they mean.

Try, my child... Listen to what they tell you...

I wish it were Matilde's voice and not my mother's, but I do as she tells me and I listen hard. The fortune does not come to me in words, or a voice, but as an odd feeling that speaks clearly to me, as if I've understood all along. The first stone, hagalaz, looks like two pillars connected by a slanting line. I remember this stone in many of the fortunes Matilde read, and although destructive, it means something new will arise from my loss, and it fills me with hope. I look over the others, which promise protection and change, as well as hardships to be overcome, but in the end, there is happiness.

The fortune washes over me like flowing water, and I know instantly what I am supposed to do. I am to follow the stream, not further into the forest, but back... Widdershins... Away from the unknown and back to my home. That even though there is food and water here in the forest, I cannot stay here any longer by myself. I have to go back. I must face fears in order to become strong. Matilde would want me to do that. She wouldn't want me to cower.

I carefully collect the stones and place them back into the bag, tying the cord to keep them safe. My mother is silent. I can feel how she relishes that I've decided to return. I will go back for myself. I will go back to make things right, not because the witch seeks revenge. I will go back because facing what I've run from is the only way to fight, to survive, not because witch blood runs through my veins.

Chapter 21
Rune

*T*he hedge looks easy to cross as I approach it, crouching low. The morning is still new. Fog covers me. I am hidden. I pretend I am invisible as each footstep I take lands with silence upon the ground. No one beyond the green border stirs. The square is empty; it is too early for vendors to be setting up for Market Day. I only hope my stomach is quiet enough not to draw attention to me.

I walk through the village, head down, palms sweating. Fear overtakes me; in an instant, all changes. My resolve has vanished, leaving me with the blinding fear that I'll be recognized, taken, imprisoned…executed. The enormity of what I'm doing crashes into me and suddenly, the unthinkable happens, and I find myself asking, "Mother, are you there?"

I'm always here…

"I feel so alone."

You are never alone…

I want to believe it.

Be careful who you speak to…

This unseen force that is my mother sounds completely authentic—telling me what to do, warning me against harm. It frightens me to wonder how long she has been with me, yet I can't help appreciating the reassurance I just asked for. I coil the drawstring of the rune stone bag around my fingers until I am left with a numb ache that travels up my arm. The contents are the only valuable thing I have, and I cannot bear to lose them. They remind me of why I am here, why I've chosen to leave the protection of the forest to make my way through the streets, where I run the risk of getting caught.

Bright red apples spill from a basket outside a baker's door. They will meet their doom to become pies today, and my stomach growls fiercely at the sight of them. I am so hungry despite Matilde's attempt to stuff me like a sausage. It stretched my stomach and now works against me, instead of keeping me full. I have nothing to trade, but can't help spying the reddest, plumpest apple in the bunch. My hunger and ideas of wagering are interrupted by a flurry of movement. Voices. Legs. Arms. They zero in on me from all directions, and I am surrounded by a group of people, with only two faces that I recognize. Rolf, the butcher, and the old woman I gave the mushrooms to.

I thought I had been so careful not to be seen. The village was empty! But now, arms grab at me and pull me in one direction, then another, like a leaf caught in an angry storm.

"She's the one!" the old woman cries out. Her eyes carry a crazed, determined look, which makes me believe my worst fear has come true, that I am responsible for the deaths of her daughter and grandchild.

"Rolf, please!" I try to plea. "You know me!"

His eyes are dark little beads that won't acknowledge my helpless state. With or without his help, I try to break free from the hands that grasp me, but I find his grip is the tightest one of all.

"You," he grumbles.

"I had nothing to do with your horse."

"I couldn't care less about my horse," Rolf says, "Stupid animal."

I stare at him, astonished, and then the glimmer of recognition in his eyes sets off a series of alarms deep inside me.

"You look like *her.*"

I swallow hard.

"*Her,*" he says, and I follow his eyes that dart toward the forest. "*The witch.*"

I shake my head. *No. No, I don't. You don't recognize me. I am no one.*

All the trips to the market, all the times I spent watching my shoes instead of looking around, all those efforts to make sure I was safe, are melting into this one moment.

The old woman pinches my arm, and I cry out in pain.

"She welts!" Her eyes nearly glow with glee. "She's a witch!"

"I am not a witch!" I try to convince them, but it's useless. Even lying does nothing to save me.

Let them take you. Make them pay…

The whisper cuts through the riot. No one else hears the voice that chimes against my ear. No one can hear my mother but me—and she wants them to take me. I was a fool to call out to her, to allow the slightest bit of trust, the thinnest bit of hope.

They drag me past storefronts and houses toward buildings I've never seen before. I turn my head for one last glimpse of the trees, my home, hoping to see even a tiny portion of the hedge, but I've gone too far. We pass the cobbler, the bakery, but everything else is unrecognizable. Everything is dismal and on the verge of deteriorating. How could I think this was a thriving, wonderful place to be? We hurry along and I see the real Württemberg—how poorly constructed the buildings are, how the horses' bones are rivets just beneath their girths, how the smell of this place nearly chokes me.

We trudge up a slope like a slow-moving horde. At the crest should be a painstakingly beautiful view of the land surrounding the village. It's the only time I've been able to see it in all my life, but instead of appreciating the lush farmland that allows the village to thrive, I see it with large, fearful eyes. Fields stretch far and wide like an ocean keeping me confined to this place, where all around me are shouting voices and hateful eyes. The more I take in of the countryside, the more it sinks in that I am far from where I belong, and in a most terrible predicament.

The townspeople continue to pinch and swear at me. A little girl half my age spits at me, and instead of scolding her, the adults surrounding us encourage her and congratulate her for being so brave.

There is a large, regal building looming just up ahead, and although I have never seen it before, I know it must be the bishop's courthouse. No other building would demand such honor. Instead of climbing the steps to the front door, I am handed over to two angry-looking guards who wait at a large wooden door near the lower part of the building.

The arms of my new captors are covered in gold-corded rope, entirely different from the uniform Laurentz wore. The sashes knotted at their hips do not have stags emblazoned upon them. The guards serve the Prince Bishop, and once my arms are in their grasp, they yank me mercilessly toward the darkness that waits below.

Inside, it is dreadfully gloomy. I stand still, waiting, as the two men lock the door behind us. The heavy scraping of the iron bolt slides into place just as my heart drops into my stomach. There is no escape. Soon enough, I am being led further away from the outside world. I cannot see well inside this hall, but I am able to make out the distinct outlines of two doors. Before I can slow my feet to try and see where they might lead, I am whisked past, my arms aching with every pull.

I think there are people behind those doors. Noises creep beneath them, and those noises follow us—whimpering voices that tell me I am not the only person these two armed guards have locked away here. But I've heard too many voices today— voices that told me I will never be alone, voices that happily accused me and inflicted pain. I have no desire to hear another human voice right now, except one that will tell me this is a terrible mistake and allow me to go home to the remains of my cottage in the woods and be left alone.

"Why am I here? Please?"

The guards will not look at me, but lead me deeper into the dark. At last we stop and I am facing a big, wooden door that is open, revealing an empty space inside. I realize this is for me. A calloused hand grips my elbow and thrusts me inside.

"Please tell me what I've done," I ask the man closest to me. He refuses to meet my eyes.

So it has come to this after all, despite Matilde's efforts to keep me safe, despite my misinterpretation of the rune stones last night.

"You will await your trial here," the guard says. Then he turns the key in the lock and walks away.

I take in the sight of the cell. Its interior is cold stone, and it reeks with a musty smell that clings to the inside of my nose. Straw covers a small portion of the floor in one corner. I suppose that is where I am meant to sleep. I walk slowly toward it and, seeing that it appears to be somewhat clean, I settle myself on top of it, hugging my knees to my chest. Something rustles beneath the pile, causing me to jump, but I am too devastated to move to another spot.

"Why am I here, Mother?" I ask quietly, knowing if anyone were to hear me, my sanity would most definitely be questioned. They would be convinced I am a witch and put me to death immediately.

You must bide your time.

"Is this what they did to you? Did they take you away and put you in a place like this?"

You will be luckier than I was, my daughter. Bide your time and wait. It won't be long now.

I shiver, and pull myself into a little ball to keep warm. "Wait for what?"

There is silence. I count the breaths that flow in and out of my mouth while I wait, and then, I hear the whisper.

Revenge.

Hours later, there are footsteps outside my door. Before I am fully awake, I hear the key slip into the lock and watch with sleep-filled eyes as the door swings open.

"Come," the guard says gruffly. His face is not one I recognize, and the lines surrounding his eyes are deep, giving him an almost terrifying appearance. I rise from the makeshift bed of straw and find that I can barely move. My bones feel splintered, and the slightest motion, such as straightening my skirt, brings dull pain to my arms and back.

"I said come, you lazy girl!" he yells at me and sets a foot just inside the door, making it clear that that he'll come fetch me himself if I don't hurry.

I scramble toward him quickly and feel his fingers pinch my arm where I'm already bruised. From the corner of my eye I see this amuses him, so he does it repeatedly before yanking me into the dark hallway, and then we begin to walk. I want to ask where he's taking me, but to speak to him could be a decision I might regret making, especially since I can only assume it's to stand before the judges who will decide my fate.

"I hear you're trouble," he whispers harshly behind my ear, gripping my elbow until it twists painfully behind my back. "Girls like you shouldn't cause trouble."

I don't answer him. It will only promote more taunting if I do, and I can hear the sneer in his voice as clearly as if I were facing him. This is apparently the part of his job he enjoys best, and I almost find myself wishing the other guards had come for me instead of this one, who is not nearly as quiet and much more egotistical.

The fingers of his other hand twirl my hair at the nape of my neck, and I feel sickened. Between the pain he inflicts in my arm and the almost tender exploring of my skin, it's somewhat of a relief when we approach the stairs at the end of the hall. I climb the steps fully aware that he is behind me, probably enjoying the view, and pray this will lead me out of this suffocating darkness with this stranger. When we reach the top, sunlight streams through the long windows, blinding me, and I have to blink several times. My head is kept down as he leads me toward another door, and I begin to think what awaits me can't be much worse than spending another moment alone with this brute.

Four men in tall black hats and buttoned coats are seated at a long table at the far end of the room, and I freeze. They are ones who took Matilde, the very ones who tied her to the dunking stool, killing her for a crime she did not commit. The guard behind me senses my fear. With a low, evil chuckle he pushes my back, and I am sent stumbling into the room.

"State your name, girl," one of the men orders me.

I tell them who I am, but their faces tell me I haven't spoken loud enough, so I say it again, hearing the unmistakable tremble in my voice. "My name is Rune." I say it louder this time, determined to hide how scared I really am.

Their eyes see right through me, and I can't figure out which is more demoralizing, the expression in them, or the lingering touch of the guard who still stands behind me. His fingers play with my back and I am sure he means to irritate me.

"You were apprentice to the old woman who lived in the forest, were you not?" The man who asks stares at me with such ferocity that I am forced to look down at my feet.

"Yes," I answer hesitantly.

It is clear he must be the one in charge of my interrogation, and I hear him rise out of his chair. The table creaks as he leans his weight upon it. When I find the courage to look up, they all stare at me as if I am a dangerous thing.

"Tell me, child. What services would you and your employer provide to the good people of Württemberg?"

I frown in confusion. "Matilde was not my employer, Sir."

"It's a simple question," he says, smirking. "Surely you don't mean to begin your trial with a lie."

"What do you mean?" my palms are sweating but I am afraid to let them see that.

"You have already testified that you were an apprentice to the old woman. I assume she paid you like any other indentured servant, did she not?"

His eyes sear through me, waiting, relishing how I might explain myself.

"Matilde did not employ me, Sir, or hold papers for me. She raised me as a daughter. We tended the sick—the usual ailments."

"'Ailments.' I see." He comes to the front of the table and slowly paces, his dark, polished boots echoing off the floorboards.

"And what else, child, tell me. Did she entrust in you the skills of midwifery? Did she teach you to read the future, or perhaps to accept money for lies?" He steps closer until I can smell the tobacco on his breath, and my head begins to spin. His face is inches from mine. "Did she train you to become a witch?"

My heart thuds unevenly within my chest. I can feel my mother with me and I hope with all my might she does not whisper to me. This is not a good time to be hearing two voices, not when my life is perched so precariously on the decision of these men.

"Are you a witch, Rune? Answer the question."

"No," I tell them adamantly, but already there is a deep-rooted fear that I've answered too quickly, or perhaps I've taken too long. They all stare a while longer, as if picking me apart to see the lies I might hide beneath my clothes, my skin.

You must lie to them…

"Say you are, and this trial will be easy for you."

Lie, my daughter. You must lie!

There is a vicious tone in her whisper that matches the gleam in the man's eyes. It is contagious and I want to yell and scream at the men sitting at the table for what they've done. I want to tell them they've destroyed the life of a simple woman who'd only kept to herself, that they took away the only family I've ever known, destroying my life as well.

He stares straight into my eyes, and asks, "Will you not confess to heresy, girl? On the Holy Bible itself, will you not admit you are a witch?"

"I am not a witch." My words disintegrate into the air between us.

"You have given us just proof. By associating yourself with witchcraft, telling fortunes by means of sorcery, and offering the devil's payment, you *are* indeed a witch."

"I've told you nothing!" I watch as the others finally rise from their seats at my indignant reply. I am not meek, nor reverent, and it's clearly a display of trouble that I even respond at all, but I don't care. I'm being accused for something I am not. I am not a witch—despite the whispers. I am not. Then, I realize something he has said.

"Devil's payment?"

"The gold you offered the woman in the market for the handkerchief." He looks at me as if I'm crazed that I don't remember, or that he's appalled that I'm lying to his face. "The gold the devil himself gave you for his favors, the coins that turned to poisonous mushrooms hours later so you might offer a sacrifice to the evil god you worship in exchange for your beauty."

I am fully aware my mouth hangs open, and my legs threaten to buckle beneath me. The ludicrous lies that come from him, that must have come from the old woman in the square, are too much for me to bear. The room spins as one of the men walks to a table nestled in the far-right corner of the room. A number of iron tools and instruments lie across the white cloth. I watch as he slowly chooses one before turning back toward me.

Make them pay, my daughter! Make them pay and you shall live!

But my mother's voice becomes tangled with the horror I feel as the man approaches me, and my eyes are filled with the image of the metal grips he holds in his hands. He reaches for my wrist and I jerk backwards to avoid him touching me with those dreadful things, but I've moved too quickly, and the cord of the drawstring pouch hidden beneath my skirt comes loose, letting the entire bag fall to the floor.

"What do we have here?" He bends to scoop the little sack into his hands.

"It's mine. Give it back."

All he gives me is a sarcastic little laugh. "Indignant little thing, aren't you? Nothing belongs to you anymore. What was once yours is now the property of the Prince Bishop."

I tremble as his hands roughly pull at the cording. He yanks at the cloth, pulling it out and handling it with such disrespect, then emptying it into his open hand. My heart sinks as I see the first stone.

"How interesting." His eyes meet mine. They are so filled with anger and evil that I can hardly stand to hold his gaze. "These will go into custody immediately."

He folds them back up into a disheveled bundle and hands it over to the man next to him. "They are marked with the sign of the devil, which I'm sure the bishop will be especially interested in. The Prince Bishop has long suspected heresy in these parts, especially the forest. He'll be quite pleased to hear his suspicions have been proven correct."

I stare after the rune bag, watching the man toss it onto the table with disgust. That was all I had left of home, all that was left to remind me of Mutti. All too soon, I feel the cold, hard metal close around my wrists. Grips are placed around my ankles. They squeeze my skin until I am sure I can feel my bones crunching beneath the pressure. My wrists are bound behind me, bringing liquid pain to my arms.

"Do you repent?" the man asks.

I don't know what to say, or how to answer. I am so absolutely petrified that there is nothing I can do but stay as quiet and still as my body will allow me.

"Do you repent?" His voice is booming now at my hesitancy, which he probably assumes I'm doing on purpose, just to be troublesome.

"Forgive me, but I don't understand. What should I repent, exactly?"

I hope he understands that I don't know what it is he wants me to say. His hand comes down hard, and I hear it crack across my cheekbone, leaving the violent sting behind once he takes it away.

"You should atone for your sins, girl. Do you not see the church that stands in this village? Do you not see the statues of the saints surrounding it? Do you attend the Mass? Because if not, I suggest you pray that the Virgin takes pity on your soul."

His breath beats down on me, but his hands are holding my arms so tight I can't look away.

I wish with all my might that I'd spent my time with Matilde learning spells, casting…anything that might save me now, instead of wasting my time on silly things. I wish the stories of the forest were true, and that I might find a way to conjure and disappear altogether, or fly high into the sky, away from this place. Desperately, I try to remember anything Matilde could have told me to use to protect myself. And then it comes to me, as my eyes find the little bag of runes lying on the table across the room.

The runes. My fortune. She *did* see this coming.

Quickly, I try to remember the symbols. The woman, the man, the war that would be with words, and angry accusations, and lies cruel enough to cause death.

Make them pay!

My mother's voice startles me, and I let out a little shriek.

I'm just a girl. I don't know how! I whisper back to the voice inside myself, only I haven't been as quiet as I thought. The men have heard me.

"Whom do you speak to?" the man in the tall hat demands. I say nothing.

Tell them. Make them fear you, my mother urges me. Her anger boils inside me, and I fear her as much as I fear the men who wait for an answer in front of me.

The vice screws tighten, and I can bear it no longer.

"Who do you speak to? Is it the devil you worship, witch?"

My arms bend further behind me, twisting, threatening to snap…until finally against my will I open my mouth.

There is a terrible ringing in my ears, and for a moment, it is like I float away. A name I have never heard of comes to me. *Liese.* I think I am losing consciousness, or already have, and then I focus on the man's face. The ringing slowly fades, and I realize to my horror the voice produced from my throat was not my own.

The men step back, wide-eyed, confused, silent, and then they begin to whisper in secret among themselves.

"You will be taken to the Drudenhaus immediately to await your execution, Witch. May God have mercy upon your soul!" the man in the black hat tells me.

The ropes slacken, and I am lifted beneath my arms and taken away to a place that is dark and blissfully quiet—a place where there are no accusations, a place where even the whispers cannot follow, and I slip away inside myself and dream of nightmarish things.

Chapter 22
Laurentz

The next morning I return to the tree in the forest, hoping to find her, but now, I am about to follow my instinct that perhaps Rune has returned to the cottage, or what's left of it. When I arrive, I see that it is as empty and lonely as the other day. I turn and look toward the village. Could she have gone there? Was that wise of her, I wonder, and just as I'm about to head along the path that will take me to the hedge, I spy a dark-haired girl on the other side of the green. I cannot get to the border fast enough, tearing along, hoping it's her. When I round the corner, there is no one but an approaching wagon and driver and I am convinced my mind has once again been tricked by the elusive Rune.

"Wait! You there!" I rush along the cobbled street, urging him to slow his pace. He pulls the reins toward his chest while skillfully shooting me a look that tells me I've annoyed him.

"What is this?" I ask, pointing to the cart he pulls behind him, seeing it is full of people, not animals.

"Prisoners, My Lord." He answers as if the load he pulls is simple bales of hay on the way to the stables, and eyes me as if I am quite the fool for asking.

The cart holds about eight women, each crammed into the tiny space and equally wide-eyed and frightened. The ones closest reach their arms through the bars, begging me with their eyes to help them, while the others cower silently.

"For what crimes have they been arrested?"

The driver sticks a piece of wheat between his two front teeth. "Treason, I s'pose. I'm just following orders, Sir. I've been told to collect them from the guards and take them to the courthouse." He gives a nod, silently conveying I'm done wasting his time, and with a snap of the reins, he and the cart roll off again. I follow at a distance and begin the slow climb up the road, ignoring those who eye me curiously. Once at the top, a large building of white limestone greets me, its grand staircase rising to where two of the Prince Bishop's guards stand watch in front of a double set of heavy wooden doors. They don't question me as I approach, and we nod to one another as they let me pass.

Inside, a long-mustached man greets me with surprise. "Welcome, My Lord," he says with a curt nod. "It's so rare the Electorate's son pays us a visit."

I follow behind him along a whitewashed corridor, past framed paintings of the Prince Bishop and others ordained before him. There is one painting in particular that moves me, and I find myself falling behind the man, slowing my pace to take a closer look. I am drawn to the lower portion of the canvas, where a gold and garnet ring gleams. It seems so real it appears to leap from the painting into the very hall I stand.

This is a ring I've been familiar with my whole life. My lips have kissed it in reverence on many occasions, and as a child, I struggled with the concept of being taught not only to trust it, but to also fear it. Something unnerves me, and I cannot figure out what it is.

"His Council will see you now, My Lord."

I nod, overwhelmed by an intense feeling that I may not understand all that is going on around me.

"Lord Mayor." My boots tap along the floor as I make my way toward the council table at the end of the room.

The Burgermeister, tall and impeccably dressed, stands and extends his hand. "Laurentz, you were a boy the last time I saw you," he nods. "How is your father?"

"He's well," I answer.

"Ah, good to hear," he says with a cool smile. "And the Countess?"

I don't tell him she has been on the brink of death since the loss of her baby, how each day spirals into the next, dragging my father along with her. It isn't any of his concern. Instead, I nod and give a curt smile, allowing him to assume all is well at Eltz. My life after I fill my father's shoes will be filled with moments like this. My father may think I have much to learn about the duties of being Electorate, but I know more than I am given credit for. I've learned that, while you keep allies close, you should always keep enemies closer.

"My father has sent me as favor to our Prince Bishop. I've already taken the liberty of addressing the village."

"Yes, it's a pity what's become of Pyrmont," he says. "But I have the upmost faith that we will be spared."

Ringing through my mind are the bishop's words from our meeting in the chapel—the precautions, the purging of evil that is the root of all disease, an ill-fated society, all at the hands of a witch. The people in the village placed blame on Matilde, and like a wildfire, the accusations spread fiercely. This is why I fear for Rune. Will the fingers point to her? I know I am treading where I should not, but I can't keep what I learned earlier to myself any longer.

"I hear there has been a recent execution."

I don't miss the way his face blanches.

"If this town had fallen to the whims of a witch," I continue, "then surely all order should have been restored upon the moment of her death."

"Then you too believe this village is suffering at the hands of witchcraft?" His eyebrows knit together as he waits for me to agree. When I am too quiet for too long, he simply says, "Perhaps that was her plan. That her curse outlives her death."

I give a shrug, letting him believe what he wants. "I passed a wagon of prisoners today." My eyes survey the room. "Tell me of that. Is it coincidence that not a single male was among them?"

My attention diverts to the men working at a table in the far corner while I wait for an answer. The table is filled with strange devices I cannot help staring at. The Burgermeister notices what has me so captured and clears his throat in a way that makes me realize I've overstepped a boundary he has left loosely guarded. As the Electorate's son, I should be free to ask what I want and demand an answer. But his sudden offense to my question proves otherwise; it proves that this is none of my business, and even though the bishop has asked me to relay a message to the people, I should not go digging into affairs that are not mine.

"They have been arrested for suspicious behavior, My Lord. It has come to my attention that the crone from the forest was responsible for corrupting the souls of some of the people of our town. We are simply removing something she so skillfully put in place."

"What have these women done?"

"I am not at liberty to tell you, but perhaps your father might, if it is something he wishes to discuss with you." He narrows dark eyes at me. "But take my word, this is for the best interest of the people. Once we have removed the threat of witchcraft, all shall be normal again."

I lean across the table and stare straight into his eyes. "I'll ask again, Lord Mayor. What have these prisoners done?"

"If you must know the details, each has displayed hostile behavior, and oddities, marking them as…not average citizens. One woman, for instance, has six toes. Another was in the presence of the tavern keeper and fresh milk curdled before his eyes. Trust me when I tell you all is not normal here, despite the old woman's death. I assure you, each prisoner will be tried in the court, and we shall determine if they are fit to live freely among the rest of us."

"You realize there may very well be explanations for what you hold them responsible for?"

"You are the Electorate's son. Because I am employed by your father, who is a man I deeply respect and trust, I won't argue with you. However, I do believe we may have found the cause for all that has gone wrong lately. One can't be too careful, though, which is why we've made every effort to increase our search."

"And what cause might that be?" I ask. I try to remain calm, but my eyes will not leave the table across the room. The men there are oiling iron gadgets of all shapes and sizes, making sure each instrument is in good working order—finger vices with nails, wrist and ankle constraints, rope, keys of various sizes. This table set in the middle of a courtroom is horrifying in and of itself, yet there is one item that sets itself apart from all the rest, and the men seem to find it of particular interest.

"You seem to disagree with our methods for finding justice, Sir. If you insist on knowing, I believe we have a most vile prisoner in our captivity, and we shall see a distinct improvement in things once she is destroyed."

His voice tunnels out of my ears as I watch the men spill tiny stones from a cloth sack onto the table. They look at the contents curiously, trying to decipher what they could possibly be used for, and take turns stacking them and knocking them down.

I've seen stones like those before in the kitchen of Eltz, long ago. Two young serving girls played at reading each other's fortune. Cook walked in and nearly fainted on the spot, telling them to bury the stones deep in the ground at the far end of the garden. She said she wouldn't have the devil's work tainting the food she worked so hard to make, and I remember how ashen her red face had turned at the sight of them. When I had the courage to ask what they were, she told me they were rune stones, and I'd do best to stay far away from them, if I knew what was good for me.

Rune...

At once I realize why I'm standing here—the *real* reason I've come. There is only one person those little marked stones could have been confiscated from. I break the force I've been mesmerized by and look at the man who waits impatiently across from me.

"May I see this prisoner you speak of?"

"Are you sure you know what you're asking? She's a very powerful witch."

"If you can lay eyes on her, then I suppose I am up for the challenge," I say brusquely.

"The burning shouldn't have occurred yet. I suppose you have time."

I stare at him. "Burning?"

"Why, yes. She's guilty of witchcraft."

"Are you to tell me you have no idea if a prisoner's been sent to execution, even though all orders to do so would be given by you?"

He gives a tight, even laugh, despite the fact that I've come just short of insulting him.

"That's because she is not being held here. We can't run the risk of someone like her corrupting our other prisoners." The Burgermeister holds a smug look upon his face now, one that is entirely different from the welcoming mask he first greeted me with. Quickly, my brain sifts through questions. I must know where this "witch" has been taken. I need to know if it's Rune.

"Well then, if she's as dangerous as you seem to think," I say, "both my father and the bishop will be quite pleased to find you are indeed ensuring the safety of the village. Where exactly did you say she was sent?"

He eyes me suspiciously, but I know he won't refuse me, not if it will reassure his status and control to the Electorate. A malicious grin of delight tinged with caution flares across his face. I pace nonchalantly to the window and look out onto the lawn, pretending his answer isn't very important. The macabre sight below is mesmerizing and disturbing all the same. Nooses are being slung and tested in the gallows. I watch as four men build the stake and pyre, filling the spaces beneath the boards with bone-dry hay that will catch the instant a flame touches it.

Somewhere, someone is doing this for Rune, I think to myself. I could very well be standing in another window, in another building, witnessing the preparations for her death.

"I suggest you pay the city of Bamberg a visit. Now if you'll excuse me, My Lord, you can see there is much to be done." His voice booms behind me, and I don't miss the implication that he means to return to more important matters.

Rune is in Bamberg—taken to the Drudenhaus, the witch prison. Anyone taken there is as good as dead.

The look on his face is cold when I turn around, and the Burgermeister nods my way, excusing himself, while the other men from the table rise to follow him out.

"Did you give her a fair trial, then?" I ask heatedly, crossing to stand in front of him. "One that suggests she is not guilty until she is fully examined?"

"The inquiry we gave her took all of five minutes— enough time to prove to us she is indeed guilty and extremely dangerous."

"So minutes are all it takes to determine if a girl should be put to death, in the most violent of ways?" I am sure he wonders why I am so interested, why this affects me so, but I can't be bothered with covering up my emotions. I need to know before he walks out of this room and I lose my chance.

"Tell me, what exactly has she done?" I doubt trading mushrooms is enough to prove oneself of being a witch.

"It's not a matter of what she has done, but more who she is, that greatly concerns us."

The door swings open, and the man who greeted me when I first came is standing there. "Sir, the prisoners have arrived." He delivers his message flatly. If Rune isn't here, then the stakes and gallows being built are for them. I look the Burgermeister in the eye, knowing he doesn't plan to give trials to the newly arrested. He plans on killing them all, and I am angered by the atrocity of it.

The Burgermeister mutters to himself and avoids my gaze as he leaves the room with the others, and I'm left alone in the massive meeting room. The witch prison in Bamberg has already earned a dark reputation. I cannot imagine anyone surviving it. It is a place of horror, I hear, with screams that leach from the walls in the middle of the night and float away among the darkened streets. And poor Rune is there.

I waste no time and rush toward the table, collecting the rune stones and pushing them into the little bag. I toss the last one in, giving the old cord a firm tug, but a lumpy cloth sticks out, preventing me from closing it all the way. I pull it out and look it over in the graying light of the room, tracing my thumb over the impression of old stitchery holes that dot it. I fumble inside my coat, knowing the bishop's parchment is still there, read and forgotten. I am sure its words mean nothing to this village. They show no fear or concern about an illness; all they see is that a witch still lives among them and must be destroyed. I uncurl the scroll and exhale a stunned breath, then hold it up to the cloth. The parchment bears the Prince Bishop's insignia at the top, of course, but halfway down the decree is the Pyrmont shield. It is practically an exact replica of the design made by the missing stitches on the cloth.

How did this cloth ever come to be in Rune's possession, I wonder? And why has only Pyrmont fallen to the illness? Perhaps Plague is not the monster here, but something else entirely, something that will undoubtedly continue to fill the hearts and minds of everyone with a dread so terrible they will be willing to turn on one another to escape it. They'll be willing to blame neighbors, even their own families, for an invisible evil, just to save themselves.

A wave of sickness hits me. The cleansing of this village has nothing to do with an epidemic that has claimed the lives of those just miles away, but an invisible disease that I fear is far more volatile. I spare a second to glance out the window one last time and hope I am wrong, but I'm not. It's happening, just like the bishop more or less warned me the other day.

An inquisition.

A stage in which the real monster is set, and the clever characters who will act it all out are ones who wouldn't dare be questioned—the Burgermeister, the council, even the Prince Bishop himself.

And from what I've learned here today, Rune could very well be caught in the middle of it.

Chapter 23
Rune

*T*he cart's wheels hit every rock and hole in the road on purpose, just to torment us. We've been traveling for hours along the Regnitz River, and I long to stretch my limbs, only there isn't any room.

I sit on a bed of straw in this tiny wagon, along with four other women. Three girls are about my age, while the fourth is much older. She reminds me of Matilde, and for that reason I turn my head. I cannot look at her without feeling myself fall apart.

The girl closest to me is crying. Our shoulders bump one another, and despite the many times I've tried to give her room, she ends up leaning against me, drenching my shoulder with her tears. The sour-looking girl sits with her back to us and has spent the entire trip looking out at the moving trees, clearly mesmerized by the endless green scrolling past us. She would be pretty if she didn't have awful teeth, and every time she curls her lips back at what she sees during our ride, the muddy stain of brown pokes out. It sickens me, and I turn away.

"My son will come for me." The old woman chants to herself, as if convincing us, rather than herself, that she will escape the horror of where they are taking us.

"No one leaves the Drudenhaus, old woman. At least not alive." The girl with the bad teeth pulls herself away from watching the road and pitilessly acknowledges the old woman's declaration. I feel sorry for the woman. She was just trying to be hopeful, and now, she is not even allowed that.

My hand presses against the girl whose head lolls back and forth on me. She's cried herself to sleep, I think, although I can't understand how she's managed to do that under these circumstances. She begins to shift a little, and I've just enough room to twist myself around and peer out the bars myself, but what I see, I cannot believe.

We have reached Bamberg. From between the bars of the wagon, I count the seven hills that dot the city, using the steeples of the churches that sit atop each one as landmarks. I think of the stories Matilde told me. This is the city whose red rooftops cover the buildings like a sunset blazing across them at all hours of the day. It's almost easy to forget what's happening and see the beauty in it, but it's as if this town mimics the one I've just come from and it has turned on itself overnight.

Stores have been pillaged, and cries and screams leak out from the shadows, which seem to be everywhere. Those who stray from the safety of their homes walk along the street with quick steps and disappear as they retreat behind closed doors.

"Is this it?" the girl beside me asks softly. She's woken, probably because the cart moves differently along the cobbled road.

I stare up at the large stone structure in front of us and watch the clock that hangs below the bell tower, waiting for a chance to see the hands move, but the wagon moves too quickly and we pass beneath the massive archway without giving me the chance.

There are more guards than I have ever seen in one place before. Dressed in the regal red and gold of the Prince Bishop, they move like a giant wave from house to house. The stocks that line the street are full, which is something I've never seen in all the times I've visited my own village. From what I can see, the prisoners are mostly women.

"Look at all of them," the older girl says. "They are all being taken for something they haven't done. Just like us."

I watch her closely, noting how she is angry while the others are silenced by shock and fear.

"What have they taken you for?" I ask.

She looks at me, and something in her eyes turns vile.

"Because they think I'm just like you."

"Me? You don't even know who I am."

She looks at me as if I am every bit as clueless as I feel at this moment. "If it weren't for you and the old woman, I'd be safe in my bed right now. But no, now they accuse each and every woman, here, in Baden and Württemberg, as if we are all responsible for some means of sorcery. Those men came and broke into my home. They hit my mother and told her she was a witch, just like the old woman who lived in the woods, just like *you*."

I am frozen by the fierceness of her words. It seems all the efforts I'd spent staying quiet and invisible have been worthless. I want to ask what became of her mother, but I don't dare. How can it be that absolute strangers seem to know me, and believe that this, all of this, is my fault? I turn away, unable to answer her, because it *is* my fault. Even though I was never taught to cast a circle or a single spell, or dance beneath the light of a full moon, as they say witches do...

Even though I have never done any of those things, I am every bit a witch.

What good did it do that Matilde tried to protect me, by teaching me the very basics of what I should know—how to survive, how to respect the Sacred Mother and all she gives to the world? I begged and begged for her to teach me the Old Ways, to learn what she learned at my age, and she refused. Her protection failed because I am still the one responsible. It is my veins that are tainted. The true blood of a spellcaster runs through my body. The whispers in my head remind me who I am. I cannot escape it, and now I fear I must face it, no matter what the price.

My back presses tightly against the bars. I don't wince as they dig into my shoulder blades when the wheels catch and rise along the uneven road. I can't look beyond the interior of the wagon anymore. I close my eyes and picture the forest instead—the shelter of the shady branches, the coolness of the air that is trapped between the shadows, the moss-covered slopes that find their way down to the hum of the little stream. If I pretend I'm there, I can escape all this, because when we finally reach the Drudenhaus, the witch prison, I fear I never will.

It looks like an ordinary building, with cream walls and timbered beams running the length of it; only what lies behind the doors, I am sure, is anything but commonplace. We are not slowing as we approach the massive front doors, but instead are taken around back, where the wagon heaves before finally coming to a rest. The lock is released, and the metal door swings open. My first instinct is to leap through the little hinged gate of the cart, throw myself out and run—run anywhere, with all the strength my legs can endure. But I cannot. As terrifying as the ride was, it's the wagon that feels safe now, compared to the building that looms over us.

We move inch by inch, pushing against one another to the edge, where we are grabbed by the wrists and yanked to the ground. The guards lead us through a larger gate, and I am surprised to find we are now in a little courtyard, contained by a high stone wall that surrounds it. But the prison casts its grim shadow across the moist, green grass as we approach, leaving me to stare up at its tall sides. I can't help think how the cheery garden disguises what must be inside, waiting for me. Before I have the chance to glance up at the blue sky one last time, I am inside the witch house, submerged in darkness, watching with dread as the door closes, swallowing away the sun's warmth.

New faces look us over and grunt at us as if we are livestock headed for slaughter. We are sized up, poked, and prodded as if we were things, not people.

"This has to go." The guard grabs a long strand of hair belonging to the girl who slept beside me. He shoves her toward a much quieter man, who stands against the wall waiting for orders. "Shave it."

This makes her cry all over again, but the man nods, and soon he and the girl disappear down a hall too dark for me to see the end.

My hair is still wrapped at the nape of my neck, and I pray no one wants to take it from me. Instead, we are separated and taken to individual rooms which are really tiny dungeons lined with crossed metal bars separating one from the other. Like the other prison, there is straw on the floor, and it smells of urine. The acidity burns my nostrils, and I choose to sit on the bare floor against the wall once I am locked in. I try to calm myself, but I am shaking too hard, trying to make sense of how this has all happened so quickly. Just when I'm allowed the littlest bit of peace today, the voices begin again, pestering me. I press my hands to my ears to shut them out, until I realize it is not whispering I hear, but an actual voice.

"Will you speak to me?" The thin tone comes from between the bars at the far end of my cell.

I raise my head and see that I am not as alone as I thought, that there is a girl on the other side of the partition.

"You want to speak with me?" After the accusations from the brown-haired girl in the wagon earlier, why would anyone wish to even be near me?

She doesn't seem to be much older than me, but she is horribly weak and sickly looking. If it weren't for my enormous dinner the night before last, I suspect I'd be as frail as her.

"You're the girl from the market. The one with the mushrooms, aren't you?"

I flinch.

"You sold them to my mother," she says, and I feel my legs turn to jelly. It's her, the girl with the broken heart. My eyes automatically fall to her abdomen, where, despite her state, I can see the swelling of what she holds inside her.

"I told my mother that perhaps you didn't know the mushrooms were toxic. It's an easy mistake to make. Even she didn't catch that they weren't Chanterelles."

I've lived my whole life in the forest, and still I couldn't tell the difference between a mushroom that is safe to eat and one that could end a person's life with one nibble. I am at a loss for words to tell her how relieved I am—the idea of causing such harm to her and her baby was almost too much to bear. And yet, I can't help feel the crushing weight of what it means that she's alive, while Matilde is dead.

"I'm so sorry." I want to say more, but can't find the words. So much has happened today, and the relief that this girl is speaking with me is overwhelming.

"My name is Anna."

"And mine is Rune," I answer back, so pleased that not only is she alive, but she has offered her name.

Anna ponders for a minute, "Rune. That's an unusual name. My mother once visited Matilde for a reading. Is that how your mother named you, from those tiny little stones?"

I hesitate, feeling the effects of her question catching me off-guard. "Matilde wasn't my mother. My real mother is dead."

"Oh," she whispers. "I have no idea what's happened to my own mother. I have no idea if she is alive or dead."

I haven't the heart to divulge how her mother helped lead me to the courthouse with the others. That she was partly to blame for my arrest. Instead, I squeeze my hand between the little openings that divide our cells and feel her place her cold, clammy hand in mine.

I'm about to ask why she's here in this dreadful place when a shrill scream comes coursing down the hall outside the door. Anna closes her eyes tight, as if she can block it out of her head.

"Every now and then the screams come," she says. "They must be doing horrible things."

The image of the table full of tools in the bishop's courthouse flashes through my mind.

"How long have you been here?" I ask her. She speaks as if she's been here for days. I wonder how many other wagons have come and gone, bringing girls and women to this terrible place.

"Since last night," she answers. "They've taken most of the girls from our village, said we were all witches. I didn't realize they would move me so early."

I look at her questioningly. "Because of your condition?"

After I say it, I realize she hadn't known I was aware of the state she is in. She turns away from me and fiddles with the ratty hem of her dress. I'm certain I've upset her, but it doesn't matter much. I'm not here to make friends. My eyes follow the stones that cover the wall, using the mortar between them like a tiny road that eventually leads to a small window, strangely placed where the metal bars divide my side from hers. There is barely enough room to place one's head to peer outside, let alone manage to squeeze a body through. But all I can think of is escape, and because of that, I feel as if someone is pressing my lungs together.

"I shared a cell with another girl from our village. She, too, was with child." Anna's voice is small and vacant. "After they took her baby, they told me I would be moved here."

Matilde's ghostly words assault me—how the baby of the girl who knew my mother was taken.

"They *took* the baby?"

Her eyes are wide and wet, and there is a slight nod of her head. I watch as her fingers stretch protectively across her stomach. I cannot help but stare, and yes, I am certain she appears thick around the middle, though slightly. When is her time? All those wonderful days in the cottage with Matilde come rushing back to me—the days when a knock would come and a woman ready to become a mother would be taken to Matilde's bed to rest, while I boiled the water in the kettle and fetched buckets more from the stream until my legs burned.

"Did they at least allow her a midwife?"

I'm a foolish girl to think that. Why would the same men who thought it nothing to kill an innocent woman in an icy stream come to the aid of a woman giving birth?

"They told us midwives are the devil's handmaidens, and the guards waited outside the door while she delivered. They laughed while she screamed, and then, when the baby cried, the door flew open. She barely had time to see it was a daughter before they took her out of her arms."

We are both driven to an almost unbearable silence.

I try to place myself in the moment she'd just described and feel sick. How agonizing to be alone during such a time as giving birth. And then afterwards, to have your child taken from you, as if your very soul is being ripped from your being. My own mother gave me away, but it was by choice, not by the hands of vicious men. Or *was* it her choice? Had she known others would take me away?

"Have they no respect for women?" I whisper out loud. Her empty eyes answer me.

"They don't know about me," she says quietly, leaning wearily against the cold metal. Anna wraps her arms over her stomach and looks at me with worry etched in her face. I can't process the fact that she's managed to hide her condition from the guards, or from the men who sat at the long table back home in the bishop's courthouse.

"You won't tell them, will you?" she asks again. I motion that I'll keep her secret, and then I stare at the hole in the wall, knowing our freedom is just beyond it, laughing at us. If there is no hope for us, then surely, there is no hope for the child that sleeps innocently inside her.

I realize what a terrible position I am in. Not only am I female, I am the daughter of someone who, supposedly, was much worse. The longer I can keep that to myself, the better my chances of buying time to find a way out of here.

Chapter 24
Rune

Anna and I wake stiffly to a thin wedge of sunlight pushing its way into the chamber.

"Do you suppose this is on purpose? That they give us a glimpse of a freedom they don't intend for us to ever enjoy?" Anna's pale face is pressed against the black metal bars that divide our areas. She peers between the thin opening in the mortar, while the lush patch of green I admired yesterday lies on the other side, teasing us. It's so close we can smell the grass, and it makes me angry and frightened—angry at how they taunt us this way, and frightened I will never get out of here.

"Of course it is. It's just another form of torture." I sigh heavily. "Like dangling a meaty bone in front of a dog that hasn't eaten for days."

Already the few hours I've been here have been full of indescribable terror. We were woken in the middle of the night and taken to confession. I'm not sure what Anna went through, but I was nearly drowned. Over and over, buckets of water were poured down my throat while the men demanded I admit my crimes. All I could think of was Matilde—as if they chose this particular punishment on purpose. As if it were not meant to garner a confession out of me, but to deeply instill something else. My throat and lungs burn from choking for nearly half the night, and I'm chilled to the bone in my wet dress. The funny thing is, after all that water, I'm dying of thirst, and there is nothing to drink.

Anna won't talk about what happened. She was already in her cell when I returned, curled up in a tight little ball. She tries to hide the way her arm dangles limply behind her as she attempts to catch a warm ray of sunlight on her face. After last night, a strange word is stuck in my head—*strappado*. I can only imagine what it means, because whenever it was mentioned by the guards, a short while later I would hear agonizing screams.

"What was it like growing up in the forest, Rune? Weren't you scared?" She asks this quietly, turning her head away from the scant sunlight to face me.

"I never had anything to be scared of, really. Not until now. Matilde told me stories, but I always thought of them as fairy tales. The forest I knew was nothing like the dark tales the others told about it."

Her eyes are large, glassy orbs as she focuses on me now instead of the elusive courtyard outside the window. "You didn't hear noises at night, then? You never heard the banshees screaming, or the witches flying through the treetops?"

I nearly choke at how ridiculous she sounds. If it weren't for the searing pain in my throat, I would laugh. "Of course not," I say to her, smiling. "I'm sure the wind or a wild animal was someone's way of preventing their child from running off where they couldn't be seen. The forest was a wonderland; the pines were giant castle towers and the moss-covered hills were the soft waves of a deep green ocean. I could be who I wanted, when I wanted, with no one to stop me."

She gives me this moment, and then asks, "Were you lonely?"

The pit of my stomach gives way and plummets through the ground. I've never missed anything so deeply in all my life. I never had the reason to. Before the emptiness has the chance to take me under, I hear Anna's voice. It buffers my heart against revisiting the past.

"I was always lonely," she admits.

"In the village, with tons of children to keep you company?"

"Children in the village don't play like the ones from landed gentry. We're too busy helping our families put food on the table."

All along I'd assumed the ones from the other side of the hedge lived better than the meager life Matilde and I had. While I ran through the forest and waded in the cool stream, just beyond the line of green in the bustling village, children my age were already experienced at manual labor.

"You never had a close friend, someone to talk to, or share secrets with?" I ask her.

She meets me with a tired expression, and shakes her head. "This is the closest I've ever gotten." She gives a little laugh. "I'm a fool to think of this now, under these circumstances, aren't I? But, at least, I think we _could_ be friends."

There is something bittersweet in how she tentatively tests the waters between us.

"But Anna," I whisper. "I almost killed you."

"I know you didn't mean it."

She says it with such certainty that I believe her.

"I didn't, and I'd like to be friends. I'd like that very much."

Soon enough, her attention is back at the little window. The light fades as the sun moves higher and the angle of our little window can no longer catch the rays.

"Do you think we'll die here?"

"Don't speak of such things, of course not," I tell her, although I've begun to wonder that myself. I can't imagine living in this tiny room any longer, feeling this sentence stretch for weeks, or months. I've heard people can been imprisoned for years. Here I imagine we _could_ die, depending on how long it takes for us to tell them the words they want us to say. I doubt very much that even confessing to witchcraft would help us. They would find that reason enough to put an end to us. Why say we are guilty and expect to live? Even a fool knows it won't work that way.

I shuffle my way over to where she is curled up on her side and stretch my hand through the opening. I am clammy from my damp clothing, but her hands feel strangely hot to me. Feverish.

"Are you all right, Anna? Do you not feel well?"

"I'm just tired, that's all."

I nod once, giving in to her, but if there is anything Matilde ever taught me, it was how to read the signs of illness.

"How far along are you?" It's difficult to tell when the baby might be born. Anna's frame is slight, and she's bone-thin.

"My mother told me sometime around the first planting of the fields, but I don't really know. I only feel it move now and then."

She keeps her eyes closed, and I can't help but wonder if perhaps losing the child would be best for her. Slowly, I let the back of my hand glide across her forehead, feeling beads of perspiration form beneath my touch. Her breath is sour, and I see purplish swellings beneath her eyes that I didn't notice from across the room.

"You won't let them take the baby, will you, Rune? Promise me you won't."

I open my mouth to tell her I can't make a promise like that. What does she expect me to do if they come for the child she carries? I am nothing against these guards, and Anna is practically a stranger to me. My answer sits on my tongue but refuses to come out, and it's for the best, because Anna is soon drowsy.

"The father…he never loved me, but this baby is mine. It doesn't matter."

My skirt is wet enough to work as a compress; I find a spot along the hem where the fibers have thinned and rip off a strip the length of my arm. Wadding it up, I press it to her forehead, then stand to inspect the bowl of food that was delivered earlier.

"Do you suppose it's safe?" I ask, knowing my voice is too low for her to hear.

We were reluctant to taste it when it first came, even though our stomachs burned and growled mercilessly. They slid it beneath the bars before the sun came up, and we couldn't see what it was. I lift the tray to my nose and smell it. There is a watery gruel, with a small chunk of bread that is more than a day old, and the unrecognizable meaty fat of an animal.

My finger dips into the gruel. I carefully touch it to my tongue. It seems to taste fine, so I consider it safe. The fat has seen its day, but Anna needs her strength, and I know the little bits of meat I can pull from it will be good for her. My greasy fingers scrape along my dress, and I am actually grateful for the wetness to clean them. I carry the bowl to her sleeping form.

"Anna, please try to eat this."

She rolls over and murmurs words that are incoherent, but manages to pull herself up enough to lean against the metal. From here I can do the rest. I wiggle my arm between the bars, up to my elbow, and grip her sleeve so she doesn't slip back down to the straw.

"Just open your mouth," I say, coaxing her.

She begins to giggle, but in a dark strange way that I have trouble understanding. "This is how my mother tried to get me to eat those mushrooms of yours."

"Well, this is much better, I can assure you. Now just try it," I say back. "If we're going to get out of here, you'll need to be strong."

I can tell the fever is taking hold of her. When she looks up at me, her eyes cannot focus on my face, but she opens her mouth, and despite the unpleasant appearance of the meal, she takes the gruel.

"That's it, Anna. Just a little more, and then you can sleep."

But she hasn't the appetite for more than a mouthful and immediately lies back upon the rank straw.

"It's not that bad, is it?" I try to convince her. "If I were home I'd add some herbs to it, something to give it life."

This stirs her somewhat, but she won't take another bite, so I give her imagery to entice her, hoping it will make her hungry enough to eat a little more.

"I'd add sage to it. That would be almost perfect," I tell her. "Or maybe a little apple cut up inside it, with fennel. Matilde would cure our sausage with fennel, and on cold winter nights, we'd sit by the fire and eat bowlfuls of it until our stomachs burst."

But my words do nothing to help her, and before long, her chest rises rhythmically and she begins the fight against the fever in her sleep.

You can help her, Rune. You have the power to make her well again... You didn't need Matilde to teach what you already hold within you.

"Matilde taught me the bare bones of survival. Not witchcraft," I whisper back to the voice in my head. How on earth can she say I didn't need Matilde?

Yes, but some crafts are not learned. They are passed down...

"Passed down by a mother who was never there for me?" There's a bitterness inside me that is slowly taking shape. I'm not used to being confined, not after having grown up as a wild wraith, and all I can think of is how I might never get out of here. This room echoes every movement I make. It's growing smaller by the minute, and the voice in my head makes it feel ten times worse.

I look at Anna's inert form and breathe in the filth that surrounds us. What will become of her baby when it is born? What will become of us? There's a part of me that believes if her child does survive it will be better off knowing it was taken, not that Anna gave it away.

I did it so you would live... Everything I did was for you...

"Was it, Mother? Was it really for me?"

I don't understand what I am asking, only that I'm feeling something tremendously powerful build inside me. It has no name, for no words describe it, but if I try to harness the tiniest taste of it, I fear it will explode.

And it scares me.

I've never known a force so strong—never felt a power so untapped, like a bottle begging to be uncorked.

Do this for her, my child, and you will unleash all the power you need to set yourself free...

"What is it that you are asking me to do? There is no medicine. There are no herbs for me to use."

You know...

"No, Mother. I don't understand."

She will be better off...

"Better off? How?"

Kill her...

I grip the iron bar that separates me from my quiescent neighbor and pull myself up, bringing my face to the edge of the window. A turbulent stream of energy rides on the wind, and it blows toward me, kissing my cheeks, urging me to listen, urging me to set myself free, as my mother wants. I look at my hands, speechless, and see the air quiver at my fingertips, like heat stretching to the sky in mid-summer.

This is what my mother wants me to see.

This is who I am.

I am no longer the simple girl hidden behind the safety of a make-believe forest. I am the story. I am the tall tale.

I am the witch.

What she asks is so horrendous and against everything taught to me—against everything the Sacred Mother wants for her children. I can't take Anna's life, or her child's, no matter what future this dreaded place holds for them. I can't bring myself to cast.

"I won't do it!" I shut my eyes tight. "This won't set me free! This will condemn me!"

Ah, daughter of mine, this will save her from a life of misery and pain. This will save you both...

Finally, I know what my mother wants from me. I understand why she has come, after all these years. Tomorrow I will turn sixteen. I will come into my own.

Murgia

And her greatest wish is that, through me, *she* will be set free.

Chapter 25
Laurentz

The sound is deafening as my horse tears through the forest, its hooves grinding the pulpy mulch floor, churning it into bits that spray behind us. I have only a day to reach Bamberg, perhaps only hours. In the distance, Eltz's rooftops poke through the trees, and I'm suddenly aware that I've made it through the forest unscathed. Gone are the prospects of ghostly specters and spirits to charm me, or worse, the wrath of a witch to turn me into a toad, or a stone, or whatever witches do. Perhaps it's because the witch is now dead, and the only one to follow in her place has been taken away, where she waits for her own death—one that I must stop.

I am filled with something I haven't felt in a long time—a mission to find answers. A mission to put a stop to something horrible, and to reverse it. I hadn't felt this way since the day my brother died, when all I had wanted was to turn back time and make that day never happen. I asked "why" a million times, cursed God for taking away my only friend—and the one person who should have been there to comfort me, to give me answers, turned away from me. But this isn't about my brother. This is about someone else now. I don't expect my father to side with me against the bishop, but I can only hope he sees how important this is to me. That this time, I can stop something senseless from happening.

I jump from the saddle, my feet landing hard on the gravel, and I march inside. There is little time to waste and I am every bit determined to put an end to the events I witnessed earlier. My fist closes around the decree from the bishop, crumpling it. I am like a storm blown in from the south, causing the servants in the entry hall to stop and gape at me, their mouths hanging open in silence. Every door I barge through hangs wide open; every polished stone I step on rings with the heel of my boot, announcing I've come for an answer. And I will get one.

"Where is he?" My voice startles the maid who polishes the silver at the top of the stairs. She motions with her head that my father is at his wife's bedside, and I charge down the hall, not bothering to announce myself at the door, which I thrust open—and then I stop.

The room I enter is a tomb closed off from the rest of the world. The air, thick and dark, hangs profoundly around me. In the corner I see my father, who leans heavily upon the mattress where my stepmother lies deathly still, his head buried within her covers.

I watch for a moment. When he doesn't acknowledge me, I bring myself to ask what we've all feared for weeks.

"Is she…?"

"No, just sleeping," he replies thickly as he lifts his head and rubs his eyes.

It has been this way for months, with no sign of her recovering. Any day now, she will be gone. I will be all he has, but he will only see what he has lost.

Seeing his devotion sends an overwhelming determination coursing through me. I can't let his emotional state stamp out what's going on, and the balled-up paper in my fist reminds me I've come for something equally important that cannot wait.

"Father, there are…"

He turns ever so slightly my way, keeping his face from being fully exposed. "Yes, I know. There are people dying in the village."

He must think the Plague has finally hit Württemberg and will be furious when he finds out I didn't leave as soon as I'd delivered the message. I throw the paper to the floor at his feet, knowing what I am about to tell him comes at a terrible price, but I am willing to do so in order to save Rune's life.

"Yes, there are people dying, but not from disease." I keep my voice low for my stepmother's sake, but it still sounds coarse and urgent, no matter how quiet I keep it. "They are being murdered, and I was sent to deliver a diversion."

My father smoothes the crumpled covers over the still bed.

"Have you nothing to say about this?" I bend down to retrieve the parchment, holding it out to him so that he cannot ignore it.

"And you believe these people are being murdered because you've seen it with your own eyes? You lingered in Württemberg, even after I told you not to."

"I…"

"You've deliberately disobeyed me," my father says coldly.

I pause, knowing I must own up to the truth. "Yes."

Then, much to my surprise, he utters, "I know well of the tyranny that has started." He continues to fuss about, making sure the draperies are closed against draft, stuffing warm rocks from the fire at the foot of the bed, everything a servant should be doing, instead of telling me more. I suppose my honesty has prompted him to be frank with me as well, but I can't help the anger that rises in me and am having trouble keeping it at bay inside me.

"You know?"

The muscle in his jaw twitches, and all that fills the air for a sequence of agonizing minutes are the crackle of the fire and the raspy breaths coming from the bed.

Finally, he looks me square in the eye. "You'd do best to avoid the village, like I told you."

He says nothing more of this "tyranny," nothing more of what is really happening around us, as if pretending I am still a little boy he cannot trust with important issues. I begin pacing. I'd never planned on returning home. I'd planned on riding all the way to Bamberg, but I'd hoped to find answers, or at least an alliance. What I have found instead is a brick wall, much like all the other times I've tried to converse with him on a level other than what he wants me to know, and I am running out of time. *Rune* is running out of time. I turn to leave, realizing I've made a grave mistake in coming here.

"I disagree with it." His voice comes from behind me, stopping me. "I've worked too hard to restore peace to the village. It will take too many years to build it again."

"Why did you have to restore peace?" I ask, stepping back into the room. "What happened there?"

"There was a girl—beautiful, dark hair, the color of night. Her face was like a porcelain angel." My father's eyes are cautious, and I want to believe I see a glint of sadness in them, but I blame it on the glow from the fire. "Her heart was a wicked thing, though, and she was put to death before she could do any more harm—burned at the stake in the center of the village, where the market is now."

A long sigh escapes my father's lips. He presses his hands to his thighs and stands. "It was a long time ago, and I had hoped the village would learn from that day, but I see now that there is never any insurance that all will be right with the world. The village cannot let the past go, replacing their fear with a witch hunt."

"The witch who burned… Do you believe she was guilty?"

"I was never quite sure." He looks at the sleeping body on the bed. "But witch or not, I do believe there's a power a woman holds over a man."

My mind turns to Rune. She has definitely cast a spell over me. I watch as he walks slowly toward the bedside and gingerly places his hand on top of my stepmother's. "I'd give anything," he whispers.

"But the doctor…"

"No doctor can help her."

I am certain my father has given up all hope, for even after the doctor's daily trips to Eltz, it is quite evident she continues to fail. His hand moves from hers to the edge of the coverlet, and quietly lifts its corner, revealing the delicate ankle beneath. The skin is mottled with color, sickly, and while the rest of her body lies incredibly still, her leg twitches as if moved by an unseen hand.

"The Prince Bishop comes each morning now to bless her. It was he who alerted me to this new symptom, not the doctor. See how she convulses, how she moves erratically, as if a mere puppet to Death's dark hand."

A low moan escapes her lips, followed by a shallow breath, and then a string of strange phrases that I have trouble deciphering. My father tenses beside me.

"Father?"

My reaction is quick, and I am eager to see his face—surely it is a sign from God himself that she will be cured. But my father shakes his head.

"She speaks in tongues."

"Yes, but she *speaks*." I stress, "which is better than lying as still and pale as death, is it not?"

My father pulls the covers back over my stepmother's legs. "She speaks, but not to us."

When my father sees that I do not follow him he tries to explain.

"It is the language of death. She speaks to those who have gathered, waiting for her to succumb." His face is a pale mask of sorrow. I have not seen him in such a state since the day my own mother's lifeless body emerged from the forest on the back of a cart. "Her illness astounds us all. I thought we lost her the moment the child slipped from her womb, but this game that plays us bewilders me. One moment she is tranquil, and then her body is seized by uncontrollable tremors so fierce I fear she will break in two."

I watch him sigh deeply and rake his fingers through his grayed hair. "The bishop has expressed his fears to me…"

"Which are?"

He does not continue for many breaths.

"He believes something unholy works amongst us all, and the people trust him and his word."

"Trust him, or fear him?" I ask.

"Both," my father agrees. "They will go along with his little witch hunt and believe they are doing it in the name of God— that it will save their souls."

"And will it? Do you believe this as they do?"

His sigh is long and weary, "I don't know."

My thumb grazes the soft linen lying deep within my pocket, searching for something hopeful as I leave my father and pull the heavy door closed behind me. I pray against what the village fears. I pray that Rune *is* a witch, and that her power is strong, strong enough to turn against death and find the life that still flows through my stepmother's veins—for my father's sake.

Bounding down the steps and out the door, I climb up onto my horse. I should reach Bamberg by noon. I want to believe this is a sign that God has forgiven me for all I've done wrong in the past. That saving Rune will save others, and that perhaps I do have a soul after all.

Chapter 26
Rune

*T*oday I am sixteen.

I haven't told Anna. Instead, I've set myself to fussing over her in order to keep myself occupied.

It isn't working.

I find myself remembering the mornings Matilde would wake me with something new to mark the year—the tiny crystal bead she threaded for a necklace, the warm cake she baked early before sunrise. Today, I find new bruises upon my flesh and a searing pain across my back from my jailor's strap. Today there is only stale bread and gruel that is more water than meal. It is the same as yesterday, and the day before that— pain and starvation. My mind wanders as I stare beyond the tiny window, for it is easy to imagine I have been a prisoner for weeks rather than three hopeless days.

I'd like to lose myself in thoughts of birthdays past, but then I look around at the reality the breaking dawn reveals. It's clear those days are gone, replaced by this day, which is unbearably monumental over all the others. I have given up trying to resist what I am. The truth is, I am a witch—one who unfortunately is capable of wielding poor judgment, not spells, and not one whose very being is made up of a strange, dark substance. What happened yesterday, the breaking point I reached, the way my fingers nearly sparked with a terrifying power, was an illusion. I have to believe that. It will not happen again. It is not who I want to be.

Anna lets out a moan, and I make my way to the bars, kneeling next to her. Her skin is shiny and waxen. I try to encourage her to take the thin slice of bread from my hand, but she ignores my coaxing. It's clear she won't eat, so I place the bread back on the tray and reach between the bars, giving a gentle tug to the knot beneath her dress, tucking it as flat as I can possibly get it. Last night, in a feverish panic, she told me she's certain the next time the guards come for her they'll be able to notice the swelling in her stomach. By the light of the low moon pouring through the window, we tied a ripped piece of my underskirt tightly around her middle, in hopes of hiding it.

I suck my breath in sharply as I notice the deep bloom of crimson that soaks through her skirt.

"Anna," I whisper softly, not wanting to alarm her. "Are you in pain?"

She moans and rolls away from me.

I've seen this before. Matilde told me not every pregnancy comes to fruition, that the Sacred Mother will take a child she feels is not ready for the world. It's no wonder the Mother intervenes now.

In a matter of moments blood is everywhere. I can't help staring at it as it fans further out, staining the strands of straw beneath her. *Hemorrhaging*, Matilde called it. My pulse thrums a steady beat in my temple. Without Matilde, I cannot think of what to do. I can't remember the steps to take to prevent the loss of a mother, and suddenly, I'm desperately afraid.

"Anna, it will be okay," I whisper, trying to hide the worry in my voice.

She leans her head against the cool hand I place on her cheek, and I'm almost grateful she isn't conscious enough to understand.

You know how to help her, daughter... It is time...

The words are easy to ignore as I watch as Anna's life slowly bleed from her.

"I won't take her life. I'll give it back, if I'm able." Insistent, I push myself away from her and begin smoothing the surface of the dirt floor with my hand. I have no idea what I'm doing, what I'm thinking of attempting. I only know that something deep inside drives me to do what I can to save her.

End this and she will not suffer... Save her, and they will know what you are...

"Isn't that what you want, Mother? Don't you want them to know I'm a witch? If she dies by my hand it will give them more reason to take my life!"

If you save her it will be a miracle, an act of grace they will not be able to explain... It will seal the sentence they have given you...

"I'm already dead," I say out loud. There is no hope within these walls, and the truth is devastatingly painful.

All at once, the symbols of Matilde's rune stones take shape behind my eyes. The words she used in the forest as she beckoned to the elements, invoking their power within the circle, form on my lips. I mark four points, tracing my finger on the dusty ground. I don't know how, but the words come to me, as if they are alive. There is the deepest need to let my soul free for the sake of the child that struggles to live in Anna's womb.

I reach between the metal bars that divide me from her weak body and take a bundle of red straw in my fist, pressing it between my hands before placing it in the center of the floor. The rocks of the window's edge are rough as I drag my hand across them.

"My blood for the baby's... Let this child live... Let it live... No more death... Let me do something good..."

But death is everywhere. Against my words, hammering resonates from the little patch of green outside. Guards have begun to assemble the gallows and pyres that will send us to our deaths. Branches and bales of hay wait to be stacked against tall stakes, and nails are driven into coffins for those who will meet a different end.

A scream meets my ears. It does nothing to shake me until I realize it comes from Anna. I'm at her side, reaching for her as far as my arms are allowed between the dividers.

"Just breathe, Anna. The baby's coming." I try to soothe her, reassure her that all will be fine, but she fights against me.

"It can't come! Not here!"

"Anna, you must do this."

Her eyes are feral and she holds onto my fingers so tightly, I fear she will snap them off. "You promised you wouldn't let them take my baby. Keep your promise, Rune."

Fear prickles at the back of my neck that it may be beyond my power to keep that promise, but I tell her what she needs to hear. Anna's face contorts as she is seized by a vice of pain, taking every ounce of control to not scream out, which will ultimately bring the guards.

"Look at me," I urge. "It's all right. You're not alone. I'm with you."

This calms her somehow, even for just a moment, and she's able to concentrate on the breaths she draws in and out of her lungs. I pry her hands from mine, placing her fingers around the cold metal to hold onto as I push as much straw beneath her as I can.

"It's time, Anna."

She doesn't wait for me to tell her what to do. The straw is drenched in red. If I concentrate I can feel Matilde with me, knowing she'd be proud. And she is with me. Matilde is everywhere today.

I catch something that feels small and slippery in both hands, but it's warm and alive, and although Anna's face is bone-white, she is smiling.

"It's a daughter! Anna, you have a daughter!" I stretch my hands toward her so she can see the beautiful baby in them.

"Not yet, Rune." Her breath is labored behind her relief. "Give me a minute."

The baby is so small she fits between the bars, and soon, I'm holding her in my arms, watching her tiny mouth open and close, watching her arms and legs extend, moving this way and that.

"Anna, she's wonderful." I say, in awe of the tiny thing. I take a layer of my dress and wrap it about the miniature body to keep her warm, covering her bare skin from the chilly dampness of the room. There is a tiny raised blemish beneath her arm that I notice instantly. A birthmark. A normal thing. Only whoever sees it, a guard, or anyone searching for such a flaw, will determine it's a witch mark—an imperfection upon her tiny soul, as opposed to a sign that she struggled to be born. *Poor thing*, I think.

The only sounds are the baby's tiny mews and the sucking motions she makes with her mouth. I gently lay the baby on the floor. Anna is silent. I've never seen such a grey tone to a person before.

"Anna?" Her chest rises and falls slightly. "Your baby needs you." I whisper urgently, willing her to open her eyes.

The baby squirms behind me, but I can't turn away just yet. I can't leave Anna. I hold her hand in mine, rubbing it until the skin glows a deep, raw pink, but all she does is bleed, her life flowing out of her in a steady stream.

The door scrapes open on her side of the divider and guards step into the room, their eyes wide at the sight of her still body. They peer across the partition to where I crouch beside her, and suddenly, there are shouts ringing through the two spaces, and into the hall. Footsteps pound closer until my door opens. Automatically, I rise to my feet and when I do, I turn, taking in the extent of what they see, and I too am horror-struck.

Before us, the room is awash with red. A squirming newborn cries in the middle of a makeshift circle, surrounded by strange, inhuman symbols etched upon the floor. One guard reaches to take my hand, but he is wary, afraid to touch me. I watch the leather straps encircle my wrists, pulling against my skin, and notice the blood caked beneath my fingernails.

Anna lies still and pale on the floor in the other chamber. I'm too far away to see if her chest still moves. I want to tell the guards to save her.

"I'm sorry, Anna," I whisper, knowing her child lies on the floor, unprotected. "I couldn't keep my promise." Before I pass through the opening to the hall, I force myself to look back, my eyes tracing the ground and the markings that confuse me. I drew them, yet they are not familiar to me, not at all.

Chapter 27
Rune

No one speaks.

I'm led away quickly, leaving behind a girl who, for the briefest time, was my friend, and a hysterical infant lying on a dirt floor surrounded by what clearly looks like the work of a witch.

I did it. I made the markings.

But I did it to save the baby, not to harm it.

Only that's not how it looks. Even I am astonished at the impression it leaves. A baby lying in the middle of a strangely drawn circle of rune glyphs looks like...

...*a sacrifice*.

I was a fool to believe I had a chance, that if I played my cards in a smart, calculated sort of way, they would set me free and I'd be returned home to the Black Forest. All the times the guards shoved me in front of the long table before the judges, I repeated the same answer. *I am not a witch*. Today I have proven that wrong. Today I have shown them that I am capable of lying, and that I am capable of much more than meets the eye. They will accuse me of everything and anything now. Today, I am as good as dead.

Craning my neck, I look back from where I've just walked. The baby no longer cries. I hear a soft voice offering comforting words, even though no one else is in this stretch of hall but the guards and myself. The voices come from the chamber and only I can hear them. Someone is holding Anna's baby, telling her that she will be all right. A cloaked figure steals from the chamber, arms wrapped around a precious package, and melts into the darkness. Soon after, two guards emerge carrying Anna's lifeless body. One arm hangs down and her fingers slide along the floor. I turn my head, feeling the scream build in my throat, and then I swallow it. She's better off now.

A door scrapes open ahead of me and my eyes ache. They are not used to such brilliant light.

The cool air rushes against my skin, and I know where I am, finally in the tiny courtyard. It is green with a clear blue sky overhead, and it is real. All the sounds and smells come to me, and I'm instantly transfixed as I am heartbroken. It has been so long since I've been outside. All I can think of is home.

Gone are the sounds of mallets pounding iron into wooden planks. Gone is the commotion of preparing. As if the bright day before me is a magickal new reality, I am inexpressibly aware of the illusion that it hides. It is one that marks it is time. I am the center of it. All of this has been for me.

How long have the people been standing there watching? I didn't notice them when I was brought out, and now, I see there are dozens. They wait and watch as I am led toward a small riser of three steps. To the back of the little landing, a wooden pole stands straight and tall, reaching into the air. I should be trembling at the sight of it, but I can't help stare up its length toward the sky it nearly touches. My bound hands ache to come loose from their binds, that I too might raise my hand high, feeling the coolness of freedom between my fingers.

I never confessed, yet I am here.

If I had given in, told them what they wanted from me, I would still be standing in this very place, cringing beneath the stares of those who have come to be entertained. They are here for one reason—to see a witch die.

My back is shoved gruffly, and I'm forced to take a step closer to the riser. A symphony of noise rises around me, and I try to concentrate on the dark brown knots in the wood, saddened that this tree died for my own death. But I can't shut them out. Shouts. Questions. Cries. It is overwhelming. I notice how the guard who has brought me lingers a few feet away, how he looks at me with something unspeakable in his eyes.

After all, I am dangerous.

The voice in my head is quiet for now, but she is here. She sees what I see, hears what I hear, and I wonder if it reminds her of that day, and if that is why she has been reduced to silence.

Or perhaps it is because someone new stands to watch.

My heart races when I see how elegantly dressed he is, how the folds of his sleeves swallow his arms, how the glinting ring on his finger shines in the brilliant sunlight that shimmers overhead. I've grown up secluded, but I know well the person I face.

His balding head is covered with a white, skin-tight caplet. He is robust in size as well as shape, a sign of wealth and prosperity, and he reminds me of Rolf, which makes me feel angry. I notice he keeps his distance from me. Perhaps he believes the idea of heresy is a contagious one.

"You're a difficult one, they tell me."

Quickly, I think how to answer him. Sweat beads down the center of my back.

"Tell me, witch, do you confess to your crime?"

I am silent. After what I've done, I don't attempt to defend myself.

"Your silence tells me you truly believe you've done no wrong."

My mind is a flurry of questions. All I can focus on is his ring. It's by far easier to look at than his face. From the corner of my eye I see him nod, and soon after, I feel the touch of someone taking hold of my wrists, leading me up those little steps. One foot after the other, I reach the top. I'm turned to face the courtyard and everyone in it. What I see are dark eyes and still mouths stretched into harsh lines. They hold their breath, as do I. The stake behind me has been shaved smooth. I feel it with my fingertips. Rising within my chest is a steady beat that threatens to burst. I cannot breathe. I cannot think. If it were not for the tight binds fixing me to the pole at my back, I'd have fallen to the floor of the riser by now; my knees no longer know how to hold me up.

I think of Matilde. I think of the Sacred Mother.

I try to be strong.

And then, it comes—the fierce whisper I've been dreading. *Let them burn. Let them all burn…*

My eyes are filled with the man who walks closer, torch in hand, flames bouncing in the same gentle breeze that kisses my cheeks. I want to scream out. I want to tell the voice that is my mother she doesn't make sense. That it's I who will burn, not them.

The flame is closer, hovering over the wisps of straw that poke out from beneath the branches. It has not been lit yet, but I already feel the heat beneath my feet. I am already stamping out an invisible fire that feels so real because my fear has made it so.

The town will burn from the flame that takes you. I will breathe life into the air that will carry it to our home and beyond, to any village that has wrongly accused, wrongly condemned, a woman for what she has not done. And then, my daughter, then you and I will be together… This is how it ends. We will all burn. We will all burn. We will all burn.

The bishop steps closer, a sneer stretched across his wide face as he looks into my own, anxious to taste my panic— but to my surprise his expression changes, and his eyes reflect something close to the fear I hold inside me. He shakes his head to and fro, then closes his eyes. When they open, he takes a deep, long look at me.

"Wait," he says, holding up his hand.

The man with the torch stops.

I bite the inside of my cheek for fear of speaking out loud. *Look closer, and you will see me...* My mother's voice stirs.

As if commanded to do so, he leans in inches from my face, close enough that I smell the ale and meat from his lunch souring his breath, and then he draws back, like an animal sensing what humans cannot.

A woman's voice floats invisibly between us.

And all I hear is laughter.

Chapter 28
Laurentz

I round my horse along the exterior wall of the Drudenhaus courtyard, where a good portion of the city has gathered, their murmurs heard from the street. The height my horse elevates me to is ample to peer overhead without drawing attention to myself, and I see a good number of empty wooden stocks and containments.

The bishop's carriage is at the gate. It is easy to recognize, and I look at it in disgust, understanding now that what he has set in motion will result in the deaths of many innocent women. I am not defying him out of spite. I am not choosing to save Rune because I want to play with fire.

I am doing it because the bishop is wrong.

My anger motivates me, as does my conversation with my father nearly two hours ago. My horse enters the gate and I see Rune at the far end.

"Now! Do it now!" The bishop orders a guard to light the straw and timber, but the guard is distracted. The sound of a crying infant slices the gathered silence. A woman in a hooded cloak carrying a small bundle to her chest creeps along the wall of the prison. Her previously inconspicuous escape is now the center of attention, and people begin to whisper among themselves.

The wind picks up and her hood is thrown back. It is the woman from Württemberg—the witch bottle woman, the very one who had accepted payment from the bishop's carriage. Her eyes meet the bishop's in a moment of steely acknowledgment. There is a slight gesture across the courtyard, and in a matter of seconds, she is gone. When the bishop turns to resume the burning, the wind has unpredictably turned stormy, and the guard's torch now lies at the base of the pyre Rune is fixed to.

Screams rise as the sudden gale fuels the flames, sending spectators to flee in panic for the open gate. The small flame has managed to ignite the entire courtyard, and there is nothing but an orange inferno surrounding us.

A shriek of terror has me running and I stop short to see the bishop's robe has caught. He and the guard are swatting with all their might to extinguish it, leaving the flames to creep upon the elevated stand toward Rune.

She is more beautiful than I remember—dark hair against light skin, strong against what should be her most fragile moment. Her hands work at the knot that holds her arms behind her, but she can't concentrate. Her eyes are filled with what is happening around her, so I slip behind the stake, knowing the thick smoke conceals me, and yank my dagger from my boot. I slice the thick rope, and she crumples down.

Chapter 29
Rune

Laurentz whispers to me, and my heart leaps at the sound of his voice.

"Trust me," he says softly with a strange calm, though the deep timbre of his voice clearly conveys urgency.

Before us lies an orange world that appears to have split open in mayhem. Flames eat away at the flags that line the Drudenhaus walls. Blurred bodies press against one another, screaming in unison, fleeing for the gate that will spill them out onto the street.

Laurentz too is covered in red, but when a hot breeze sweeps past us I see it is his uniform, red and gold, the colors of the Prince Bishop, the colors he wore in the forest.

"Hurry!" he urges me. I thrust my hand into his, and we are running. The heat from the courtyard is unbearable, and the steady rush of air brings a relief to my skin. We run in the opposite direction of the screams and I try to pull my hand back, knowing the other way is the only way out, but Laurentz will not let me go until we've reached a high wall on one end of the yard. He holds his entwined fingers inverted, motioning for me to climb onto them so he can hoist me up.

"Why? Why should I trust you?"

The muscle in his strong jaw contracts, and I watch his throat move as he swallows before answering me.

"Because I know who you are."

Immediately, I pull my hand back. If I try, I might be able to run into the crowd that pushes past the gate. I might be able to slip away unseen.

"No, Rune," he says, leaning a little closer. "That's a good thing."

I want to trust him. I want to trust something, and I know I must make a most crucial decision. If I run toward the gate, there is a good chance I will be caught or killed by the fire. If I stay here, I'm as good as dead. I don't think. I don't let it process, I only trust in the most blinding sort of way, and I find my hand reaching for his arm for support. I place my foot in his open hands, and soon I am being lifted up and over the stone wall that for days has held me prisoner. My legs dangle over the side and I drop, landing a little crooked, but otherwise unhurt. Alive. Free.

Laurentz follows me, scaling the wall and landing on his feet more gracefully than I. He brings his fingers to the sides of his mouth and blows, and I am stunned by the shrill whistle that flies from his lips, more stunned to see the dark brown mare with wild black eyes charge upon us and stop at our feet.

The city of Bamberg flies past us at breakneck speed. The red rooftops and cream buildings are a blur out of the corner of my eye. I cling to the back of Laurentz's coat so tightly I fear I may pull the stitching, and then we are in a flurry of green that is breathtakingly familiar. We are in the Black Forest.

I breathe in the pine, the pleasant damp, the sweet moss as the horse's hooves land faster and faster. It is not the same part of the forest I grew up in, but it is connected, and therefore I am home.

Trees careen past, and all I hear is the rush of the boughs and the deep breaths of the horse who, like Pegasus, has given us invisible wings to fly. Gone is the smell of burning timber. Gone is the frightened girl. I've left her behind, and they will think she is dead. She *is* dead, and I am alive. I test my bravery and lift my chin, peering over the shoulder in front of me. The trees thin in the distance, and nestled within the dips of the mossy mounds, the ground sparkles like moving diamonds. Just as I'm about to warn him, we are in the stream with spray rising, drenching us. The horse reaches the far bank; with the power of hitting a stone wall at full speed, it rears, and we are thrown back, landing in a heap in the water, our lungs sucking at the air.

Laurentz is up well before I am, brushing moss and mud from his waistcoat. He holds his hand out to help me. "Are you all right?"

I'm soaked, but I'm fine, and I nod to answer him.

He grabs the reins that hang from the shaken animal. He is in the saddle, ready to try it again, when I figure it's time to tell him the truth.

"You go on ahead," I motion with my hand. "I can make my way back from here."

"Absolutely not. I've gotten you this far. I'm not going to leave you on your own."

I have no idea how far I am from the little ruined cottage, but my heart tells me to walk toward the darker part of the forest, the part where the trees bend as if speaking.

"Oh, no you don't, you're not going back there." His hand is out again, waiting to pull me up behind him. "Besides, there's someone who needs your gifts, your skills—someone who is very close to me. Will you help me?"

My heart stutters, and then plummets. There is someone else. A betrothed? A wife? I swallow the strange feeling that has hit me and hide it away. Fine. He seems to be aware that I'm capable of doing *something*, yet he doesn't run.

"Didn't you just see what happened? You can't go very far with me. Witches can't..." I stumble with my words. "Witches can't cross water."

I've said it. It's out now. I stare at the muddy bank knowing I should hear hooves by now. He should be leaving, but all I hear is the lapping water as the stream settles into its natural rhythm again.

When I look up, he's staring right at me, a crooked smile lighting his face. "I suppose we'll have to walk *in* the water then. The stream leads to the river, and the river leads to Burg Eltz. We should reach home by sundown."

"Home?"

"Yes, my home," Laurentz replies. "Now come on." He extends his hand once again, and this time I take it. I've admitted I'm a witch. He's seen the proof, yet he doesn't blow the whistle, alerting those who are surely looking for me that I've escaped with him into the forest. I climb up onto the horse's back and resume my position behind him, and soon we are off, trotting steadily through the water.

"Did you say Burg Eltz?"

"Yes, do you know it?" he asks me.

"No. Is it an important place?"

I feel his back shake with laughter, but I don't see what's so amusing, unless he laughs at my ignorance.

"Burg Eltz is my home. It's been my father's home for years, as it was his father's before him. My father is the Electorate."

I've heard that word before and know I should feel impressed. In the market, snippets of a great man with as much power as the Prince Bishop would come to my ears. I'd noticed how the people in the village spoke of him, using the word "Electorate" with genuine respect and kindness. If this man is Laurentz's father, then I suppose I might be in safe company, although I can't help peering behind me. Surely I will hear hooves or see the flames from the prison following me. I watch the trees move past us, knowing that with each step I'm moving further away from my home.

I want to ask who it is I'm supposed to help, and how, but the steady swaying of the horse lulls me. Without thinking, I allow my cheek to lean against the back of this man who seems to know where we're headed. In the back of my mind I think of how smooth his jacket feels, not like the itchy wool Matilde

Murgia

would sew into cloaks for us in winter. My head seems to find a spot that fits perfectly, and I see the turn of his head, looking back at me. He doesn't lean forward, doesn't tell me not to rest against him even though his back is to me, despite what I am. This boy is brave. He stepped through fire to save me. He is not afraid of what I am. I let myself think about this, feeling the smile tickle my mouth.

Today, I feel safe.

Chapter 30
Rune

*W*e have stopped moving. Instead of the cool damp of the forest upon my skin, I feel the warmth of the sun. I open my eyes to find that we are on a narrow bridge. It hovers over a deep ravine and we face the entrance to a large stone castle. The very size of the shadow it casts steals my breath. I can't help feeling frightened, because what I see before me looks like another prison—carefully and skillfully disguised as something appealing.

"There she is, Burg Eltz," the boy I am holding onto announces proudly. "She's the finest castle in all of Germany." The horse responds to the pressure he places against her sides with his legs and resumes her steady trot forward.

On either side of us the ground drops steeply, making it feel like the bridge is magickally suspended in the air, and I cling to Laurentz tightly. Around us are trees and sky; below, more trees, and a rushing stream at the very bottom. From what I can see, this is the one and only entrance in and out of the castle that towers over us, and I already feel closed in.

"You'll be safe here," Laurentz whispers encouragingly. "I wouldn't have brought you here if I didn't believe so."

I fear my head will fall straight off my neck if I bend it any higher, but I can't help trying to take it all in. The stones are enormous; each one is the size of a man's head, or larger. The windows and turrets reach as far as my eyes can see and become lost in the low, hovering clouds. I take Laurentz's hand, and soon I am settling my feet on solid ground. I am stiff from riding and am grateful he is here to help hold me steady.

Inside the castle, I am surprised to find a cold, sterile atmosphere. I suppose I expected it to be warm and homey, much like my old home, and I am disappointed in a way. Laurentz seemed to speak of it with such fondness, but perhaps he was only reassuring me that my safety was a matter I needn't concern myself with—that Burg Eltz would protect me with the mighty arms of the fortress she is, and that is all I need right now.

The room we enter is full of tapestries and paintings that cover nearly every square inch of the walls. There are vases on tables, and the smell of freshly cut flowers fills the air with a heady sweetness. That alone reminds me of home. There are tall, polished men of armor and shields—and eyes.

Of course I should have realized a castle would have a staff to run it, only I didn't prepare myself for how they would react when they saw me.

"Pay no mind to them," his reassuring voice comes to my ear. "You're simply something new to look at."

I nod and tilt my face but am caught by the light catching his eyes, and find myself off-balance. In a swift movement, his hand steadies me.

"I'm just tired from the ride," I say, convincing both of us that what I've gone through today is taking its toll. At least, that is what I tell myself.

"I'll have a room prepared for you," he tells me. In response to a wave of his hand, a girl my age crosses the hall. "Draw a bath, Elsie, and prepare a room in the left wing for our guest."

I watch as he gives the girl the instructions. He is neither bossy nor commanding, but instead it's as if he is genuinely pleased to ask her to do this for me, as if he is happy I am here. And when the maid obliges, I too manage a little smile for her, just to show how appreciative I am.

"Go ahead, you're in good hands." Laurentz nods that I am supposed to follow the girl. "I'll come for you in a while, after I've spoken to my father."

The wonder of Eltz has me mesmerized, and I've forgotten that I will soon meet the Electorate. Suddenly, I am a bundle of nerves again, but I follow Elsie, who stands patiently at the foot of a tall and winding staircase for me. Soon I am in an endless hallway with doors and oil paintings in between. She opens one but waits just outside of it, expecting me to enter first. It is a bath with a large porcelain basin in the center of the room. Everything is white. Stark. Clean. A fire heats a kettle in the corner of the room, and I watch as she begins to pour it into the tub. She adds flowers and oil to the bath, creating a lovely aroma that permeates the room as the steam rises; then, she motions for me to undress.

With trembling hands I begin to loosen the ties of my dress and am relieved when she leaves the room. If I undress quickly I can step into the water before she returns. I dip a toe into the swirling water, hastily testing its incredible warmth while hoping I can be fully submerged by the time I hear her on the other side of the door. Just as I bend my knee and am lifting my other leg to step into the tub, Elsie returns. I don't know which sound shocks me most—her gasp, or the pitcher shattering when it is dropped, smashing to pieces across the stone floor.

"Gnädig! Gracious!"

I sink into the tub, but I've moved too quickly and water sloshes over the sides, spilling onto the floor. I stare down at my bare legs beneath the water and wait for her to ask me, but what I expect does not come. A few minutes perhaps, and her curiosity will win out and she will ask to know what the gashes and bruises are from. I can tell her I fell from a horse, which I imagine is very easy to do. Or I can say I was running through the forest, that I was lost and tripped, that Laurentz was kind enough to help me.

Her head down, she collects the broken pieces of the ruined pitcher, and the floor is as tidy as it was when we arrived. She places a soft-looking pile of towels on the vanity and leaves without saying another word.

I can't help myself. I can't stop it. The tears come without warning, and when they've left me feeling spent and worn, I splash the water to my face with my hands, hoping any trace of them is gone.

I cannot survive if I am weak. I cannot cry for what I've lost, because that will not bring any of it back.

I pull myself up and let the water run from my limbs, back into the tub with the bits of flowers. The sound reminds me of when the rain would drip into the stream from the trees overhead after a rain shower, and it calms me, until I realize I am not alone. There is a strange girl staring at me, reflected in a large gilt-framed looking glass. Her wet hair clings to her head and trails down her bony shoulders. I stare and she stares back. I turn and she turns, and when she does I see the marks that sent the poor servant girl fleeing from the room.

My back is a canvas of criss-crossed lashes that match the purple circles on my arms. My skin is marked and tender, like the hides that are treated by the tanner in the village back home.

I am hideous. I am vile.

I stare until the lines bleed into a map that travels across my skin, telling my tale, telling all who might step into this room what I've endured, what I am.

And though my skin screams, my head is blissfully quiet. The silly notion that it's because I am standing in water crosses my mind, but I dismiss that. I know the truth. My mother, the witch, is mad. Not because of what they've done to me.

She is furious because I'm still alive.

Chapter 31
Laurentz

J've left Rune in the care of our quietest maid, hoping not only to put her at ease in an unfamiliar place, but also to avoid the gossip I know will eventually surface. I venture downstairs in search of my father. Behind my back I know Eltz's servants are speculating who she is, where she's come from, and most of all, why she is here. They will just have to wonder for now.

I probably should have told my father of my intention to ride to Bamberg, but he would have stopped me before I reached the door, and I couldn't take the risk of not going at all. I hope he understands. I hope he can see the plan I have brewing inside me—the plan that includes Rune.

But any hope of that happening quickly deteriorates as he looks upon me with cold eyes from across the dining hall when I enter.

"What have you done?" His knuckles are white against the edge of the table.

I am not a fool to entertain the fact that I left earlier believing my father and I reached an understanding. What transpired between us was more of a door creaking open ever so slightly, letting in the notion of possibility, and I don't intend to let that door slam shut, not when I've come this far.

He doesn't wait for me to begin, but draws in a deep sigh. "It's unethical..." he begins.

"And so is what they've done to her." I approach the table calmly, ready to state my plea. "You yourself said that you don't agree with the bishop's actions. Look at what is happening. Look at what he has caused. Women, even children, everywhere, are being accused simply because there is something about them the bishop does not like."

My father's jaw is set tight. "Still, you never should have interfered. Why? Because she's pleasing to the eye? Has she offered you anything?"

"No." I shake my head. "I've interfered because they'd nearly destroyed her life."

My father runs a hand through his salted hair. "Laurentz," he says, voice tight with anger. "You aided someone who is accused of witchcraft."

"Yes, I have," I admit. "And do you realize the Plague has spread no further than Pyrmont? If she is a witch, then why hasn't it affected her own village? Why do they believe she is to blame?"

I know well that I cannot take back what I have just said. My words have decisively piqued interest in my father's eyes. I also know that Cook and the scullery staff listen to us from behind the kitchen door, but it's too late to talk my father into discussing this elsewhere. What's done is done. They will all know who and what Rune is soon enough.

"What do you know, Laurentz? Have you witnessed anything that resembles sorcery?"

I step closer until I too am leaning across the table. "All who inhabit Württemberg seem to thrive on the idea that the 'witch-proof' hedge growing around them will keep out a true witch, yet she has crossed it, time and time again. I nearly trampled her with my horse while she was doing so, and my arm ended up cut and bleeding. Father," I take a deep breath, "she *healed* it."

He offers nothing, so I go on.

"They burned her home to the ground. They executed her guardian. All because the bishop placed the seeds in everyone's minds that she was a witch. Father, this girl is not evil. Yes, I do believe she is magickal, but she is *not* what the bishop makes her out to be."

"And what makes you so sure she is not capable of causing harm?"

"Because she would have done so by now," I tell him.

He sighs deeply and stares down at his hands. "And you've brought her here because you assume my position will grant her security."

"I brought her here because of what she can do."

I have his full attention now. He knows what I am getting at. In my head I hear the door between us opening a little more, because my father has grown so very desperate not to lose someone else he loves.

"This girl shines with a light I've only ever seen once in my life."

He's skeptical, and I don't blame him for his disapproving frown, as if I am nothing but a hopeless dreamer.

"You used to be married to it, Father," I say carefully.

"That light is a memory, Laurentz. You were three when your mother died, and I doubt very much you can recall anything about her that the oil painting in the library cannot give you."

"You're wrong—I do remember. I remember she meant everything to me, and you, and right now there are two women upstairs—one whose life was nearly extinguished, who is capable of doing the impossible, and the other who has only moments left to hold onto hers."

The nod is barely perceptible, but he seems to agree.

"There's more." I pull at the small cloth bag fixed to my belt and spill its contents across the table, praying Cook isn't eavesdropping too closely.

My father carefully extends a hand to pick up one of the small, rounded stones, then cautiously recoils. With guarded eyes, he asks me, "Do you have any idea who you are dealing with here?"

"Actually," I unfold the cloth and lay it flat across the wood. "I was hoping you might."

He studies the aged cloth closely and before long his face registers with the same gleam of recognition I felt when I first saw it. "Pyrmont's coat of arms. Where did you get this?"

"The runes were wrapped in it. It was confiscated by the Burgermeister of Württemberg shortly after Rune's arrest."

"Rune?"

"The girl," I explain.

My father stares at the stones, knowing the coincidence is too great. He carefully lifts the cloth by the corners and carries it to the brighter light at the window.

"The stitches were removed on purpose," I offer.

"Yes, I see that. If the threads had fallen out naturally from age or overuse, the holes would have been ripped larger; the cloth would be thin. These holes are just as small as the day the sampler was stitched. The embroidery must have been removed shortly after."

"Are you familiar with the type of cloth that is?"

"Of course I am," he replies. "It's a portion of an infant's mantle. You were wrapped in one just like it when you were born. But look here." He walks the cloth back to the table so I can see it. "This is a little different than the coat of arms Pyrmont has now." He shows me the way a line of stitching would have extended up, rather than over, as the Pyrmont shield appears now.

"This is the original coat of arms." My father's finger traces past the stitchery holes to show me, then looks at me, realizing I know nothing about our neighbor's past. "A family's crest is only ever changed when there is a threat to the ruling heir."

"But Pyrmont had no heirs."

"Exactly," my father agrees.

I stare at the cloth, wishing its secret to jump out of it. "Was it to protect the Electorate of Pyrmont when he was a child?"

"The crest was altered just after you were born," my father explains. "That would have been too late to protect the Electorate. It was obviously changed for another reason."

I shake my head. There is something here, I'm sure of it. I lean my chin into my hand as I think of all I know about Pyrmont, about witches and plagues, and everything else in between, trying to find some way to allow it all to make sense.

"Tell me, Father, is there a reason why Pyrmont is the only castle to succumb to Plague? There is no word of the infection amongst the villages."

"Then it is a witch's farce—an illusion. Laurentz, it's possible she stole this," my father says, holding up the old scrap. "The girl could be a lying thief for all we know."

I understand what he's trying to do, only I'm in too deep now. "And what would a girl accused of sorcery want with an old castle—going as far as casting a spell of Black Death within its walls, killing all who remain there, and instilling fear along its borders?"

"We know nothing of this girl."

"And apparently, we don't know everything about Pyrmont," I argue back. "Should Rune be found guilty, what will become of the estate? What will become of the castle and the land?"

"It would be legally inherited by the Prince Bishop, of course. He is the former Electorate's younger brother, but any territory found without descendants automatically falls to the hands of the Church. And since Pyrmont is within the Prince Bishop's province, then I suppose it comes full circle that he ends up its rightful owner."

I shake my head at the ideas that come crashing all at once into it, where nothing and everything begin to make sense. "And so, we are back to the bishop, aren't we?"

Murgia

"Laurentz, any remaining descendent of Pyrmont is gone. They are *all* gone."

Steadily, I raise my eyes to his as I let my hand touch the strange old cloth, and ask, "Are you sure?"

Chapter 32
Rune

I step out of the tub and onto the cool floor wondering when Laurentz will come for me. My soiled clothing lies in a heap at my feet, reminding me that it hadn't even occurred to me what I would change into once I stepped out of the water, but nestled between the towels Elsie left is a simple blue dress, and the thoughtfulness brings a smile to my lips.

Despite the bath, shame clings to me that I walked into this grand house wearing the filth that I did. I'm embarrassed to have clung to Laurentz's back. He must have found me revolting. Even the water is a pale, gruesome gray with tiny bits of color floating in it, and I wish I could dispose of it before anyone sees it, but don't know where, and I'm afraid of making a mess like I did before.

The dress is exquisite and finer than anything I've ever owned. I touch it carefully, certain that, while I have been scrubbed clean, there is a film that will rub off of me onto it. I make sure my skin is dry and slip the delicate fabric over my head, eager, yet scared, to peer into the looking glass to see. It fits well, and the softness of it is like a cloud that sways around me as I lean across the vanity.

Murgia

My appearance has never mattered, except when the villagers seemed to take marked interest in me. It shouldn't matter now, only there's a certain boy—a man, really—waiting for me somewhere in this enormous place. Perhaps he hopes to see if the clean water and soap has transformed me. Has it erased not only the dirt and grime, but the terrifying stigma that has attached itself to me? Can a bit of flowers and oil do that? Can it wipe clean what someone is?

I'd like to think so.

I don't look into the looking glass because I am afraid of the girl I've already seen reflected in it. She will be there still, wearing blue now. And this time, she will speak and tell me what I don't want to hear. She will tell me I am a thief. I am a murderer. I am a witch.

I should find Laurentz and tell him I'm grateful for what he's done. I'm grateful for the new start—the chance for a new life. But he's done enough, and I'll leave immediately and find my way, somehow.

The hall is empty when I open the door and step into it. There is no sign of Elsie or Laurentz, and certainly no rhyme or reason to the direction it takes me as I walk along, knowing one way or another will lead me to an exit.

My legs have longed to stretch. Living in a tiny stone room for days has made me all but crawl out of my skin. The corridor runs long and far, bending around corner after corner, leaving me eager to find its end. It's almost easy to ignore the closed doors I pass, and I am glad I do, because they remind me of the prison. They remind me of walking to confession, passing door after endless door, hearing the screams and cries of those locked behind them.

There are no screams behind these doors. There is only a gentle hum that blows in and out of my head, allowing me to forget the hideous girl in the mirror. Its pull is magnetic, and I find I'm following an unseen force along the corridor that makes me wonder if I'm headed in the right direction or further into the depths of the castle. I am not imagining things.

It is not my mother but the pull of someone else entirely, and it crosses my mind that the witch is playing with me, disguising herself, so I am tempted to be led elsewhere.

There is a window at the far end of the hall through which the sunlight casts a yellow rectangle upon the floor. For all the ornate beauty that surrounds me, I cannot help but be reminded of when I was led out of the dark prison and into the bright sunlight of the courtyard. And with this, I am reminded of the day before that, and the week before that. It seems my mind holds only terrible memories—Matilde, the prison, fire, death. I wish I could forget them all, but I force them to stay. If I choose to forget them, what will I have to push me onward? These terrible memories are all I have left to remind me who I am, that I can only rely on myself, that I am the only one I can trust. That is why I must leave.

I tiptoe toward the deep sill and peer out, but the height of the window is tremendous, and I quickly back away, feeling dizzy. I will never make it if I'm frightened by silly things, so I step closer to the glass and force myself to look out at where I am. Off in the distance is an emerald sea of pointed trees. If I were to throw a pebble from this height I imagine the giant ripple it would make, stretching out further and further. Beyond where the ripple calms lies my freedom. It will take forever to get there.

From the corner of my eye I notice the tall tower of smoke where the trees are not so thick. Possibly it is the prison burning. I briefly wonder if Laurentz will really come for me, or if he's in fact disposed of me here. I've gone from one prison to the next, a low dungeon to a high tower, both fortresses to hold me in. Like the tiny window in the prison cell, I see a freedom that calls to me and laughs that I cannot touch it.

When I turn away an enormous door faces me. The pull to open it is more powerful than anything I've ever felt. My hand reaches out for the latch…

"You don't belong here."

The voice startles me, because it is not in my head but behind me. It is Elsie, and another woman standing by her side who is older and very stern-looking.

"The guest chambers are this way," the gray-haired woman says, making sure I know I've explored a part of the castle where I am not welcome. "You will remain there until you are called for."

I follow her and leave behind the fading whisper, which has disappeared beneath the strange and beautiful door.

Chapter 33
Laurentz

"There you are. Have you rested?" I smile when I see how transformed she has become in the blue dress she wears. I had asked Elsie to lay something nice out for her, and the quiet servant girl has indeed chosen well. If ever before I have felt that Rune has bewitched me, it is certainly now. I am practically speechless at the sight of her.

"You look lovely," I bend closer to her ear and extend my elbow, satisfied she has at least a small amount of faith in me to take it and let me lead her to dinner. "I've asked Cook to prepare a wonderful surprise for you. It's one of her finest desserts, and she's a master at it." This brings a polite smile to her lips, so I feel confident in what I tell her next. "And I've already informed my father that you are here. He's anxious to meet you," I say, eager to put her mind to rest.

She suddenly tilts her head to the side and slows her pace beside me.

"Is there something wrong?"

Rune bites her bottom lip and looks around. "It's just that I thought I heard someone else speaking just now. Like a whisper."

I slow us to a stop, and I too listen.

"I'm sure it's probably one of the servants," I tell her, although I don't hear a thing. "You'll be surprised to find the softest noises travel the farthest here."

It is best I don't tell her the staff will find means to know of every possible thing that goes on within these walls. That there are too many spies among them, and that they are most likely looking at Rune's presence as an excuse to follow her around instead of attending to the duties they should be concerning themselves with.

"My stepmother's chamber is down the hall from yours. You'll most likely hear the servants attending to her."

"Is she the reason I'm here?" Rune asks me.

"I see you're reading my mind again." I smile a little, hoping it softens the reason I've brought her here. "She's dying. You've been surrounded by a lot of that, it seems—dying. I'm afraid I've brought you to a place that can't seem to escape it, much like everywhere else in Bavaria."

We are walking again and her arm is light against the crook of my own as I hold it to me.

"I've seen my fair share, I suppose."

I take a deep breath. "I don't suppose you can work a miracle, can you? My father isn't convinced that magick will help her."

She stiffens involuntarily, and it appears I've gone and stuck my foot in my mouth again.

"What they've accused you of doesn't scare me," I say to reassure her. "There are men more terrifying than a girl accused of sorcery."

"Yes, I believe I've met him," she replies.

I know all too well who she speaks of, and all the other tyrants she's run into in the days before today. "You're safe here, you know that. Whatever happened to you in the village, or in Bamberg, will not happen here."

I want to touch her cheek like I did in the forest, but I don't know that displaying such affection is a good idea. She is frightened, and I can't help being frightened for her. I've brought her here to keep her safe, to gain her trust, and the last thing I want to do is give her the impression that she owes me, that she must save my stepmother's life in exchange for my saving hers. This amazing girl by my side can do the impossible; I've seen it. I can't explain it, but I believe in it, and if my father sees it too, then I will gain his respect—even though part of me still fears that is impossible in its own right.

She takes my hand and places it back upon her cheek, as if my thoughts are obvious to her again, and it is like we are in the forest surrounded by the trees and the gentle breeze—surrounded by everything she is familiar with, and everything that dares to reveal who she really is.

"Why do you fear me?" she asks. "Is it because you believe the silly tales that a person like me can end your existence with a flick of my finger, or turn you into a toad?"

I reach into my pocket and pull out the delicate linen handkerchief, then hand it to her.

"Someone who appreciates something so beautiful couldn't possibly have a heart as dark as gossip says."

Her eyes light up at the sight of it, and I know holding onto it all this time has been a good idea. "Thank you, but something so beautiful has gotten me into a lot of trouble."

"Yes, I know the feeling."

I don't miss the way her cheeks blush at what I've just said.

"I don't fear you, Rune. I'm enamored by you."

"And your father? Will he be enamored too?" she asks, the worry returning to her eyes. "Will he sit at the head of a long table staring me down, trying to pick apart what I am? Am I a witch capable of doing damage? Or simply a girl mistakenly accused of being everyone's nightmare?"

The tender moment between us has changed to something very sad, and Rune looks down at the floor.

"How can you have small talk with someone accused of something so enormous?" she asks. "Can you take a person who has witnessed unspeakable horror and put them in a pretty dress and expect them to behave the way you want them to?"

"No, you can't." I lift her chin with my thumb and make her look into my face so she can see I am not just saying words that don't mean anything, just to make her feel better. "That isn't the girl I intend to take to dinner tonight, or to introduce to my father. I don't want you to fill a role that isn't yours. I only want you to be you."

The girl I want to know, *need* to know, is someone surviving just like I am, faced with a stain upon her soul, the way I am. We're standing outside of the door to the dining room. Inside is a long table of sumptuous food and a man I am more terrified of than anything, perhaps even a little more than this girl who stands by my side.

"You're afraid of him," she whispers.

I look into her beautiful eyes, and suddenly, the world has changed again. I nod, admitting to what she asks because there is no way to say it isn't true. Then I take her hand in mine. "I suppose we'll be frightened of him together then, won't we?" And the only thing left to do is open the door.

Chapter 34
Rune

*T*he door opens to a beautiful room where windows fills an entire wall and a table, longer than any I've ever seen, sits at the center of the room, adorned with crystal goblets of all shapes and sizes filled with colorful liquids. The man who stands alongside the bejeweled banquet table, though, bears an expression that is not quite as inviting at first glance.

"Rune, this is my father, the Electorate of Burg Eltz," Laurentz tells me.

I am not accustomed to meeting someone so formally, and do what I think is appropriate, giving a demure curtsy. Once again, I am grateful for the dress, doubting very much that my own tattered frock would have made a very good first impression. By the look on Laurentz's face, I've done well.

The Electorate steps closer and takes my hand, placing his lips to it, a gesture that stuns me because I know he does not really want to touch me. His eyes are not as warm as his son's, and yet I am struck with a need to make this man approve of me. Perhaps if I do, it will help erase the terrible ideas he holds in his head about who and what I am.

"I hope you'll find our home comfortable while you're here." The Electorate gestures to the chair that will be mine for the duration of our dinner.

In one swift motion, he is behind me, adjusting my chair so I am now penned in at the enormous table. I can't help feeling that familiar dread that I am to be interrogated. The chair I sit in is made from a heavy wood. It would take a few tries to push myself away from the table to free myself. With all my heart I want to believe that this is just a simple meeting—a dinner that we will share, not a trial conducted by a judge who will sit at the far end of the table, dissecting me until he reaches a verdict that I am guilty.

My eyes follow him as he walks back to his own chair at the opposite end, while Laurentz takes a seat along the length between us. The look on Laurentz's face tells me he notices I'm uncomfortable. He must have told his father who I am, but I wonder if he has told him the extent of it. Will he hand me over to the guards? The bishop? Will my stay here, as well as Laurentz's kind intentions, be short-lived? Just before my mind can wander to darker places, I notice the Electorate staring at me from the opposite length of the great table, and my hands automatically grip the chair's arms, ready to push myself away, preparing myself for whatever should come next.

"My son has told me you've been wrongly accused. That with his help, you've managed to escape the Drudenhaus in Bamberg. I am sure I don't have to tell you that alone puts an even greater price on your head."

I look from him to Laurentz, not knowing if I should answer. All the times I've been pressed to confess, I've chosen to stay quiet, admitting to nothing.

"Everyone in the villages is being accused, Father…"

The Electorate cuts him off by raising his hand in the air. "I'd like to hear *her* story, Laurentz, not your interpretation of it." He looks at me again, attempting a smile that he must believe will calm my nerves and make me more willing to comply. "After all, if she's to be under our protection and a guest in our home, I should know everything there is to know about her."

Laurentz sends a silent message my way with his eyes. This is the role I am supposed to play. The real one. Just like he told me to. Only, I am not comfortable with the legacy that has been handed to me, and I wonder if it's safe to show that, or if playing along with the game my mother has initiated is a strong card I must hold onto in order to survive. I self-consciously pull at the handkerchief hidden inside the sleeve of my dress and think of how to answer.

It seems the silence that has fallen over the room is a tangible thing. I am shaking, wondering what I should give away about myself. What is safe to reveal? Everything up until now has been a nightmare to me; my world has disappeared, and I have found myself in one hellish predicament after another. Could I have been brought into the beauty and apparent safety of this grand house under false pretenses?

Finally, I opt for the truth.

"I made a mistake," I say, hoping my meek voice travels across the length of the table so that I don't have to repeat myself. "I traded mushrooms for a linen handkerchief in the square. I had no idea the mushrooms were toxic, Sir." I am startled at how good it feels to finally be able to speak my side. "But if you're asking if I'm a witch, then I'm not quite sure what to tell you."

"Well, only tell the truth," the Electorate prompts me. "Let's start with the beginning, then, shall we? What do you know of your parentage?"

"Nothing, really. My mother was…" I pause, trembling. Whatever I say now will forever give proof that I am what they fear me to be. I hold my chin high, and go on. "I never knew my mother. She sought the help of Matilde in the forest and gave me away."

The Electorate leans forward on his elbows as a strange desire to hear my story lights his eyes, and I know that there is no turning back now. I swallow hard, grip the arms of the chair, and say it.

"She was burned at the stake in the square of Württemberg."

An odd exchange passes between the two men after I tell them of my mother's death, as if they know something I do not. I wait without breathing for the next question to come. A movement to my right startles me, and I catch my gaunt reflection shining back at me in the silver dome the serving girl lifts from a platter, revealing a selection of meats lying in a savory sauce. The Electorate opens a folded cloth and settles it beneath the table, out of view. It is clear he won't ask anything else until the girl has left us.

As if there isn't enough on the table already, the serving staff brings more dishes from the kitchen. Round and round like the ticking of a clock, they present a feast, then disappear in a swift orderly fashion. The last to leave is the gray-haired woman from the hall, her eyes settling on me sharply as if she is the only one here who has figured me out—that although I am clean, in a change of fine clothing, I can never cover up the witch inside.

I see that Laurentz watches his father closely. He too is waiting for what will come next. Suddenly, the Electorate stands, pushing his chair out behind him, the dinner on his plate ignored.

"Father?" Laurentz asks after him.

My heart is hammering in my chest, and I know with every beat it signifies the end of the little comfort I've had since my escape from the prison. There is a feeling of crazed panic building inside me that screams louder than my worst nightmare, reaching an intense pitch as it builds and builds. Whatever Laurentz told his father about me has only given the Electorate proof that I am a dangerous creature. I thought telling him the truth would help me. I was wrong. He's going to alert the bishop. I'm going to be taken back to the Drudenhaus and burned at the stake in the courtyard like I should have been.

I will die, just like my mother.

I shoot a desperate look toward Laurentz. Oh, why won't he help me?

The Electorate is out of his seat and walking toward me, and no matter how I push and push to move my chair away from the table, it will not budge; my hands are slick with sweat and slip from the polished wood beneath them. His hand is outstretched for mine. I have no choice. I will go quietly, and then he tells me, "Come, my dear. It's time you met your mother."

Chapter 35
Laurentz

*N*ight falls quickly when it has the help of a forest to eat the setting of the sun. Candles deliver an eerie light throughout the room, and Rune's eyes are large and hollowed out by fright. She is no longer the girl who hides a dark secret, but is more like something of a nightmarish world—a story told by a fire, a fairy tale born from the Black Forest to explain the ghostly chill that claims those who venture in alone.

"Father." I rise to my feet. "What is going on?"

In a flash I am at her side, helping her with her chair and taking her hand. That strange fleeting moment has vanished and now I see her as she really is. She is Rune. She is the beautiful girl I saved from the hedge, the tortured soul I saved from the stake, the one who has magickally cast a spell over my heart. I see in her pale face that she believes my father is about to send her to her death.

"This way," my father urges us, "There is something you will be interested in seeing."

I have no idea what has gotten into my father's head, and I wonder if my bringing Rune to Eltz has backfired. Down the endless hall we follow him, passing through the gallery where faces from my family's past look down at us. Vivid paintings of fox hunts and ladies having tea beneath willow trees—I'm sure Rune does not see the brush strokes and beauty, but instead, wonders if any of them knew her mother, if any of them helped bring her to her death. I wonder the same and am overcome with years of guilt, a weight given to me by my own family's name.

We follow my father to the library, a place I have not visited in years, and Rune stifles a gasp. Lying on the table is her bag of fortune stones, the cloth laid out next to it. Books are strewn about, showing that my father has been very busy, and I wonder what with.

"I believe this belongs to you." He picks up the cloth, fingering it with care. "Can you tell me where and when you came to be its owner?"

Her eyes will not leave the cloth, as if looking away will make it disappear again. "It was Matilde's. As long as I can remember, the stones have always been wrapped in it," she replies. "She read the stones the day my mother gave me away. That's how she named me."

"And you were *given* to this Matilde?"

Rune gives a slight nod, "Yes."

"Do you remember your mother?" he asks.

"No," Rune tells him. "I was just a baby."

"Wrapped in this?" he holds the cloth to the light.

Rune is quiet, the look on her face is incredulous and lost at the same time. "What do you mean?"

My father steps around the table and edges closer to where we stand, his face still tight. "This is what's left of an infant's cloth. A blanket. Swaddling. It's very possible you may have been wrapped in it the day you were given to Matilde," he tells her. "Any number of things could reveal who you are, Rune. But let me ask you this—why is it that *you* are accused of witchcraft? Is it because of Matilde? Was she the witch? Did she steal you long ago?"

"No!" Rune's face is suddenly white with fear. "Matilde wasn't a witch, and she loved me. She raised me like her own."

"You were given to her by the witch who died later that day in the village square?" Moments of silence pass and my father presses further. "So you believe a woman who was burned at the stake sixteen years ago gave you away, for whatever reason, to hide you, to protect you. *She* was your mother?"

"Yes," she nods quickly. "Yes."

"What makes you believe she was your mother? Have you proof?" My father's voice grows louder, filling the room.

"Enough!" I shout. "Whatever is this for?"

"To be sure, Laurentz! We must be sure." My father sets his sights on me now, his intense expression showing me that finding out all we can is of utmost importance. He turns to Rune, who is on the verge of splitting into pieces from all the questions fired at her.

"This is important, girl. How can you be so sure the witch was your mother?"

Rune lets her body slide weakly to the cushioned chair that sits next to the desk, her face cradled in her hands as she weeps.

"Because she speaks to me," she whispers, and both my father and I lean closer, straining our ears to be sure of what she's admitted.

Even I look at her with disbelief. "She speaks to you?"

Rune nods and looks up at me with tearstained cheeks. "She whispers. Tells me things."

My father kneels closer to her. "What does she tell you?"

"Horrible things. That the village must pay for what they've done. That I must bide my time."

Rune's hands shake uncontrollably with fear. I'm certain she believes what she's told us will seal her fate. My father nods, as if he understands fully what Rune is telling us, and he gently places his hand upon her shoulder.

"Did your mother ever tell you her name?" he asks.

"Not directly," Rune tells him through gentle sobs. "I heard her name inside my head... It was Liese."

Nothing prepares me for the look upon my father's face. Each line held tautly across his forehead has smoothed; his cinched brows rise high with curiosity. He even lets out an audible breath he must have been holding in for a very long time.

"These are yours." He pushes the bag of stones closer to her. "And so is this." Rune and I watch quietly as he opens one of the books on the table, and slides it over to the light. It is a map of the southern tip of Germany outlining the noble holdings that lie at the edge of the Black Forest. An area is circled in black, and in the center of the land is a circled star.

The castle of Pyrmont.

Chapter 36
Rune

*P*yrmont.

I should know that word, but I don't. I am almost afraid to ask. There's a heavy stirring inside me. My mother is near, and something snaps into place. Her whisper, hidden and lodged inside me, becomes a breath, a deep exhale that leaps from its resting place. It doesn't lash out. It doesn't will me to do anything unspeakable. It too is silent, watching and waiting. Calm.

His hand turns the page where a colorful family crest has been painted across the creamy parchment, and he lays the rune cloth next to it. "The coat of arms was reinvented some time ago to be different from the original," the Electorate tells me. "As you can see here, the stitches are almost the same."

"Why?" I ask softly. "Why was it changed?"

"My guess is to protect you." When he looks at me, he doesn't seem so frightening any more. He points to the map. "This is your family's home."

"I have a family?"

The two men exchange solemn looks, and then the Electorate shakes his head. "Plague has dealt a swift and deadly hand. Unless there are others, you are the only surviving heir to Pyrmont."

"Is that why I would need protection? Because I'm the only one?" I wonder out loud. "But I wasn't always the only one. What makes me so special?"

"It seems great pains were taken to protect your identity," Laurentz tells me, looking into my eyes. We watch as his father opens a small box on the table, producing a metal skeleton key. He slips the key into one of the many little drawers along the top of the desk.

"I suppose *she* is the reason you were hidden away."

Before I know it he is sliding a small oval frame across the table to me, and my hand lifts to my mouth. It is a miniature painting of the girl in the looking glass from the bath—the girl trapped in the silver dome from the dining room. I want to say it is me, but I know it isn't. It's *her*, enclosed in glass.

"She was beautiful, wasn't she? They say the glass prevents her soul from rejoining the living," the Electorate says. "And if she was as powerful as they say she was, then her daughter would perhaps hold an even stronger power, one that would warrant hiding her away."

I almost laugh at the superstition, but that is the rational side Matilde instilled in me. *I was hidden away…*and I know how very alive my mother is inside me. Is this the power they speak of? That she would live through me, even after her death, to wield a terrible power against those who crossed her? How silly to think that a thin sliver of glass could be enough to prevent her wrath. But it's hard to look away from the vibrant face beneath it. There is something about her that calls, beckons, and keeps me. Though it is like looking into a mirror, I am sure I don't have the same effect on others—on Laurentz. I've seen my reflection. It makes me shudder.

"You knew her? You never told me." Laurentz shifts his gaze from the painting to me, and I know he's marking the similarities in his mind.

"She was a friend of your mother's," he nods toward Laurentz. "Her name was Liese."

As soon as he says her name a prickly feeling crawls up my back. In an instant I'm back in the bishop's courthouse, a strange voice speaking through me. Even after all the times my mother has whispered to me, that one moment when she spoke *through* me has felt like a dream. Now I know I hadn't imagined it.

His voice is reflective and gravely as he continues, "No one knew she was expecting a child."

"Do you know who my father is, then?"

The Electorate looks at me. He is composed, yet there is a strange sense of confusion that I feel from him. "Your mother was the Lady of Pyrmont."

"That would make her the rightful heir," Laurentz interrupts.

"Yes, but why place you in hiding? Why deny you your heritage, your parents? The Electorate and his wife had no other children."

"Or simply because your mother practiced that which he didn't approve of," Laurentz says reflectively, but he suddenly peers at me from the corner of his eye. I'm not offended, though. I know what I am.

Laurentz leans across the desk for another look inside the frame.

"Perhaps my father was ashamed," I say beneath my breath. "Perhaps he would have never wanted me, anyway."

All I've known about my mother has been in secret. Little stories told to me, whispers here and there. In this tiny frame, though, she appears spirited and captivating, her skin glowing with a faint blush, hair dark and cascading with waves and curls collecting about her shoulders. Her eyes shine with a light that belongs to someone other than the voice I hear in my head.

I slide the portrait back across the table. The menacing voice I so often hear couldn't possibly belong to the beautiful woman in the frame. That woman is much too kind-looking—

full of life, not vengeance. I remember the harshness to her words inside my head—her pleas, her urgency. I am not sure why she hid me long ago in the forest. I'd like to think she kept me a secret so that I might live, even if it was to do her bidding, and I briefly wonder if those remaining in the village since the day she burned are the only ones who fear her wrath. I wonder if perhaps there is someone else. And then I realize the importance of the glass. My heart begins to beat faster. To anyone who fears her, she *is* still alive.

And I do. I fear her with all my heart.

Chapter 37
Laurentz

My father steps outside into the hall and closes the doors behind him, leaving Rune and me alone in the library. I imagine he is eager to be away from what has just been said. The past often feels like a heavy lingering cloud that will suffocate us if we stand beneath it for too long, bringing back memories that a man like my father would sooner forget.

"I don't understand," Rune says. "Why would she give me away? Why would I spend sixteen years living in a forest everyone fears, when I could have had grown up knowing I had a place to belong to?"

She doesn't wait for my response, but keeps thinking out loud. "I never would have known what it feels like to be hungry. I never would have had to hide my face away from the others in the village, enduring their whispers, the way they pointed their fingers. I never," she pauses, swallowing the deep sob collecting in her throat. "I never would have had to lose Matilde."

I bend on my knee in front of her and take her hand in mine. "I have no answer for you other than the very fact that you wouldn't be who you are today without Matilde's influence. That girl who has me so charmed—the one I am willing to risk everything for in order to make sure she is safe. Would you have been the same person growing up elsewhere?"

"I would have known my family."

"No, you'd be alone. They are all gone, except for you."

Her sigh is heavy. "Matilde is gone. What's the difference?"

"I never would have met you. There's no hedge surrounding Pyrmont for me to pull you out of."

This earns a small smile from Rune, and I finally feel it's time to tell her I too have lost someone close to me. I close my eyes and take a deep breath. This room reminds me of my brother.

"My brother used to read to me when I was little, after our mother died," I say softly.

She leans her head to the side and waits for me to tell her more, and before I know it, I'm telling her about Friedrich and how I miss him, how I wish the past could be revisited and altered all at once, and how the only thing altered now is me—first because of the deaths of my brother and mother, and second, because of her.

"When did he die?" Rune's hand touches my arm. It is warm, and I let it stay there. As soon as she asks, I'm surprised how easy it is to tell her.

"Years ago, when I was eight." I breathe. "I wanted my father to think I was ready to join his Guard. I was only a boy, but you couldn't tell me that. I was strong, and willful, and capable in my own eyes. My mother was gone. It was a house full of men. Well, not Cook. But she wasn't my mother. Friedrich told me I couldn't balance the crossbow, but I wanted to prove him wrong. I wanted to prove my father wrong."

I haven't spoken of that day in so long. All I've wanted was to forget, and even when I thought everyone else had, something would happen to upset my father, and I would know he had not forgotten, and never would.

"It was an accident," she tells me.

"No. *I* was the accident. If it weren't for me, Friedrich would still be alive."

"If it weren't for me, Matilde would still be alive," she says. "She died for a careless mistake I alone was responsible for. And I watched it happen. I watched them dunk her in the stream over and over again." There's silence, and then she says, "I did that. I killed Matilde."

I know what it feels like to carry a heavy stone in my heart, like she does. I wrap my arms around her and hold her close, and she lets me. Her body is thin and frail beneath my touch, but she's warm, she's alive. She's Rune—the girl who continues to heal me, inside and out, whether she knows it or not.

Chapter 38
Rune

Somehow, between the moment he told me I was an heir of Pyrmont and the moment he left us alone in the library, Laurentz's father made the decision to trust me, not to fear me so completely, and to let me try to put a stop to the terrible illness threatening to claim his wife. The halls of Eltz are hushed as Laurentz and his father lead me to her chamber, like the castle itself knows it is about to be placed under a spell, that unfamiliar forces will be tapped into, and that perhaps a miracle will happen.

My heart beats faster than my footsteps, and two voices register as we walk—my mother's that follows me, and the other that pulls me forward. They are almost alike, overlapping, pleading, and by the time we come to a stop I am facing the ornate chamber door I had been led to earlier on my own, after my bath. With trembling hands, I push it open. A body lies still upon the bed, already so close to death there may not be enough time.

I knew you would come, she seems to say though unmoving lips, and I peer over my shoulder at Laurentz, positive that they too have heard her, only they haven't. With every pained breath her body screams her name so that I will know it's hers.

Angeline. I peel away the sheets that cling to her with dried sweat, feeling inside me how her body trembles at the cool air touching her sallow skin.

Laurentz and his father move to stand at the foot of the bed, giving me room but watching closely. They think I have a power to fix what has been done. They believe I can perform magick so her dying body will have another chance at life. Part of me wonders if they watch so intently to see if I really am capable, if I truly am a witch—which makes me notice someone else. My mother's presence is terrifyingly close. I stumble a bit, suddenly unsure where to begin, or if I should even begin at all.

I ignore the dread that seeps into me and continue to survey my task. I turn from the bed to grab the ends of the brocade draperies, yanking them until the glass pane of the window is exposed and the moonlight pours into the room. I need to see her. My hand runs lightly across her forehead, feeling the fever beneath the skin. The heat is deep, near her bones. It pulses and pushes against my palm until my hand aches and fills me. A peculiar feeling spreads inside me, and I feel sick. My body feels shaky, as if it has lost control of itself, but I stand firm and tell myself I am only nervous.

The remedy that comes to me is what I've seen only Matilde do. It isn't magick. It's common sense. It's using the precise amount and selection of herbs, and knowing that they will do what we ask because we give it time.

"I'll need much more than this," I say, holding up a half-empty pitcher of day-old water.

The Electorate steps forward and I see the gleam of desperation on his face. Every line around his eyes comes from crying over this woman. Every whisker in his chin is grayed over the idea of what the next day will bring. His eyes show how he has foreseen her death for months. He is relying on me to stop his misery, as well as hers.

I rattle off the list of herbs and concoctions that suddenly spring to my memory. I want to smile, in spite of the task that lies ahead, because Matilde would be proud of this moment. I've paid attention. I remember. Despite the dark feeling as my witch mother watches over me, I am doing this on my own. "I'll need Wormwood and a handful of Meadowsweet," I begin. "See if the kitchen has fresh Sage, Camphor, and a bit of Elecampane Root." The list grows, and it takes several trips between the two of them to bring it all back to me. I work diligently to add the ingredients to the mortar and pestle, grinding them all together to create a poultice. I ask Elsie, who has quietly shown up at the door, to fill a cooking pot with muddled Juniper berries and a touch of vinegar, warming it somewhere accessible so that she might bring it in to the room as we need it.

I lay my hands across Angeline's chest, feeling the shallow beat of her heart buried beneath the pain. I feel the poison searing into me. I don't know how, but I do, and my hands fly from her chest to the folds of my dress, where I hide them as if they've been burned.

I lift the bedclothes with a careful hand, hearing the illness call to me. What I find yanks a gasp from my throat—the tips of her toes have begun to blacken. With absolute care, I take her fingers into my hands and inspect closely. Sure enough, there is a darkness spreading beneath her nails, as if she is slowly beginning to rot inward from the furthest extremities. Laurentz comes to my side, his eyes wide.

"She was not like this yesterday." He places a hand over his mouth. "Is it Plague?"

"No, I think not. There are no buboes." I try to reassure him. While I am certainly no expert, I know that he and his father would have fallen ill by now if it were the Black Death, as would the rest of the household. Not to mention their frail patient would have been dead long ago. "It's something else. Something rather clever, for it leaves no trace of itself."

I cover particular areas of Angeline's body with the herbs—the tender skin beneath her arms, the space between her earlobes and jaw, all the while whispering softly to her, and then to Elsie for more when the bowl runs dry.

"Sacred Mother, help your daughter. Take away the poison that fills her veins. Heal the darkness that marks her skin." There is a whispering beneath my words that is not mine, but I ignore it, only paying attention to my voice.

"Matilde, help me," I whisper back. "Fire against fire, light against death…"

I feel the energy that belongs to my mother surge with me rather than against me. All at once, my hands burn and I yank them away, seeing the red marks they have left on Angeline's body. All is silent around me. Laurentz. The Electorate. The servants who have congregated in the room and spill out into the hall to watch. All stare and pray. They wait for the magick to work. My hands burn so tremendously that it takes all I can to hold in the screams. Instead, I curl up on the floor at the foot of the bed and press my face into the sheets.

Footsteps rush to me. I know it's Laurentz. He helps me to my feet as an audible gasp fills the room. We both turn to see his father standing over the bed, his hand to his mouth. He slumps to the bed, weeping, as his wife slowly opens her eyes and looks up at him, smiling.

Chapter 39
Laurentz

Rune won't stop looking at me, pleading with me with those dark eyes of hers to tell her what's wrong. This is what I wanted; this is what my father wanted. Like a dream, my stepmother has conquered death and opened her eyes, after all these weeks of waiting.

And Rune did this, just as we asked her to.

Then why can't I look at her? Why can't I thank her and bring back that moment when we stood together in the library, just the two of us?

I know the answer, and it's killing me, because I didn't expect to feel this way. I saw her heal my arm in the forest, but somehow, this is so much more, and my mind cannot grasp what I have just witnessed.

My father doesn't notice how I slink past everyone who is in awe of Rune—past Angeline, who now sits up in bed fully awake and alive, overwhelmed by the smiling faces that fawn over her. He's too immersed in getting back what he almost lost.

I, on the other hand, have lost everything in this one moment.

Rune leans against the corner of the bed, wordless, weak. She struggles to see me past the people who stand between us. I shake my head. I don't want her to follow. I know she doesn't understand.

All I know is that she is a witch. She is a full-blooded, second-generation spellcaster, and this room feels too small. This castle feels too uncomfortable. My own skin feels alien and the thoughts coursing through my head threaten to burst and corrode everything I felt earlier.

Was the library all part of her magick, too? Did she cast a spell over me and force me to tell her about Friedrich? That was my own doing, wasn't it? Now, I'm not so sure.

I don't pay attention to where my feet take me. All I know is I need to breathe. I end up in the chapel. I don't know why. I didn't plan on coming here, but it is quiet and the furthest place away from the room where I know they still gather.

I pass the rows of box pews and begin to pace, my legs aching to run from something I don't understand. Yet I saw it with my own eyes. Finally, I do the unthinkable and fall to my knees at the foot of the altar.

I ask God to help me separate miracles from magick...or are they really one and the same?

Did I witness witchcraft? Did I witness medicine? My mind whirls, coming up with only questions, no plausible reasons to explain sensibly what I just witnessed. And why must I be the one to question it all? Everyone else is still upstairs, rejoicing.

My head aches and I press my hands to my eyes.

Behind me, a woman's voice speaks softly. When I turn, there is no one there.

I have lost my mother, my brother, and my father. The girl I was with in the library was an illusion. Now, it seems, I am losing my mind. I shift my weight upon my knees, preparing to stand when my leg catches on something sharp. On the grout between the floor tiles shimmers a tiny speck of red. It is a strange stone, familiar yet confusing, and I pocket it, not wanting to waste my time on figuring it out just yet.

I rush to the barn, harness my horse, and ride to the tree line at the base of what belongs to Eltz. If I look up, I will see her face peering out the glass after me. It is all I can do to keep my head down.

The woman's voice comes again but shifts in the wind until I hear the unmistakable voice of my brother coming from deep within the woods. Without hesitation or looking back, I yank the reins, feeling the muscles of the mare beneath me, and charge after it in hopes of finding something I once lost.

Chapter 40
Rune

*C*an you forgive me? Laurentz's breath grazes my ear. Having brought someone back to life has earned me a place here, and tonight, he steals into the chamber, luring me from my warm sleep.

I reach for him and touch his face. *Of course I do.*

Only I can't remember why he needs forgiveness. Was it the look in his eyes when he saw what I had done? I'd tried to tell him that it was the herbs that brought her back—tried to convince him it was the little training I had, but he insisted otherwise. *He knew.*

And so did I.

I remember saying words—my words, not my mother's. I remember a tremendous ache inside me as I pulled what was dark and ugly from Angeline into my own body. I've been weak for the three days and nights since, but I'm not on the brink of death. I'll live through this.

You shouldn't be so trusting, he says again, confusing me. His voice is low and hushed, familiar as it trades tones, and soon, my head is filled with a single word.

Witch...

I bolt up, and I am alone.

I creep out of bed and tiptoe toward the door. Shadows play beneath it.

Someone is there.

For the last few days I have heard noises such as this from behind corners, from over my shoulder. They don't think I notice, but I do. Or maybe that is their intention—to let me see, and hear, to frighten me away. The good I did is now past its welcome here among the staff at Eltz. What held them in awe now gives way to suspicion and lies that remind me of the village back home. Angeline tells me to ignore them, but she too shows a cautious detachment whenever I visit her chamber. For the Electorate's sake, she tries to be my friend, but she only knows me as the witch girl who brought her back from death. She doesn't know the real me, and I firmly believe she'd like to keep it that way.

I dress in the quiet dark of the room, knowing that, despite my unwanted presence here, I will act as if it doesn't bother me until it is time to leave. My arms push through sleeves and smooth the pleats of my dress with my hands. I am nearly ready when I step on a loose floorboard. The sound sends the shadows outside my door scattering.

Angeline is sitting up in bed when I enter her chamber, and I immediately notice the rosy color that fills her cheeks, glad that she is no longer pale and sickly.

"Rune," she smiles, patting the thick duvet, but I cross to the foot of her bed and pretend not to notice how I make the chambermaid nervous. The girl stokes the fire crackling away in the hearth, then sets about plumping Angeline's pillows, avoiding my eyes all the while. She pretends to give us privacy, but I know why she leaves so quickly. I make everyone uncomfortable.

When it's just the two of us, I smile lightly and sit at the foot of her bed like she wanted.

"You look better," I tell her.

"I feel better, thanks to you." She reaches for the water goblet, but in her hurry to leave us, the servant girl placed it just beyond Angeline's reach. I hand it to her, then walk to the window, looking out at the trees.

"You aren't happy here," she says quietly behind me. "Is it because he hasn't come back yet?"

I know Angeline makes idle conversation with me. My palm presses against the glass. Funny how I've gotten used to the height and no longer feel as though the glass is an illusion, holding me up, waiting to topple me out. I can't help, however, letting my eyes drift toward the horizon where the other day a thin tower of black smoke rose from the Drudenhaus. It felt like Laurentz and I rode for days that afternoon—that we had surely placed a much greater distance between the horror of the courtyard and the protection of Eltz. From this height it appears we are not really all that far away, and the trees there look like giant green teeth.

"Partly," I admit finally, and peek at her from the corner of my eye. "Only…"

"Only?"

"Eltz is a dream I will eventually wake up from, and when I do, I'll have to face things again. I'll have to face what's waiting for me," I stare at the forest, "out there."

"But you're safe here." Angeline frowns. "Why would you ever want to leave?"

I don't feel safe. I feel lonelier here than I did on my own in the forest. I often think of asking the Electorate to take me to Pyrmont. I have yet to see it. I have yet to walk its halls. But what do I know of running a castle? I am only sixteen. I am a girl living in a man's world. I think I understand that my mother tried to change that. She tried to become something bigger than she was ever meant to be. And it destroyed her.

I turn away from the wild world outside and bring myself back into the room, to the woman whose delicate beauty hides the fact that days ago she was nearly dead. She sits atop layers of silk and fluff. Fresh flowers adorn her night table. There is a gleam in her eye. But ours is a friendship that is not genuine yet. It's based on the fact that I gave something back to her.

Is she afraid that, if she doesn't act appreciative, I might take it away? Will I always be the person everyone fears? I know Laurentz fears me, and I will never forget the look on his face the last time I saw him.

"When Laurentz returns he'll surely ask for you to be married." Angeline's soft voice breaks the silence, and I watch her as she lifts the water goblet to her lips.

I stiffen. "That will never happen."

"And tell me why not?" Angeline shifts her weight, leaning forward on her stack of pillows so she can see my reaction better. "My husband has had the chance to fill me in on all I've missed. You're of noble blood and are the rightful heiress of Pyrmont. It's a perfect match."

"You and I both know it will take a long time for me to claim Pyrmont, if I ever do. According to the law, I own nothing. I have no rights. Besides, we all know it's more than that. I'm a descendant of…"

"Ah, yes, the infamous Witch of Bavaria." Angeline nods her head, acting as if it's not a weighted subject.

"The Witch of Bavaria?"

There is a fresh gleam in Angeline's eyes that tells me she is getting better, returning to the vivacious woman she must have been before falling ill. "Are you surprised I know something about your mother that you don't? Oh no, your mother was quite the lady, so much more than an Electorate's wife. She was a wild thing, one I do believe her husband felt nearly impossible to contain."

After all the trivial conversations Angeline and I have shared, this one is most surprising. She leans closer so that I can see how the sparkle in her eyes makes the circles beneath them darker.

"You know there are others like your mother."

"Other Electorates' wives? Or others being accused and burned at the stake?"

She shakes her head, keeping her voice low, savoring the chance to gossip. "No, others who practice. Some who followed your mother, and others who have gone off on their own."

Angeline's hand feels heavy on top of mine. It makes me feel like I'm sinking.

"I don't want to be like my mother, Angeline. I will *never* be like her."

"You're right. You will be what the Sacred Mother has planned. You'll see."

My breath catches in my throat. She notices and her smile grows. "I see I've surprised you by my knowledge of the Great Mother."

"Did you…" I swallow hard. "Did you follow my mother?"

Angeline sits up straight, and her face switches from sneakily playful to serious. "Let's just say I knew of her many years ago."

I don't know how, but I've offended her. I feel something strange pass between us, and I worry that Angeline is darker than I understand her to be. I wonder if I should be careful around her, and without being aware of what I'm doing, my body inches away.

"Rune, you can trust me."

Can I?

"Oh poor Rune, you've been without a mother for so long."

There's pity in what she says, but she's wrong again. Matilde has always been a mother to me. I haven't gone without.

"And poor Laurentz. He's been through so much."

We are interrupted as a young girl enters, carrying a tray. She sets at her lady's bedside a plate of Schupfnudeln, rolled dumplings made of rye and potato, but my presence disrupts her duty and she topples the entire plateful onto the floor. Angeline curses the girl for her clumsiness. The girl mutters apology after apology, that she herself will ride to town for more rye, as it seems Cook's supply has run low.

It is a side to Angeline I never would have imagined witnessing. The room has become quite warm, and I stare at the flames in the fireplace—a volatile element tamed. I am beginning to wonder if I've been foolish to think Angeline has been my friend.

"Yes, he's told me of his brother." I continue our conversation after the chambermaid has left us.

"I'm not speaking of Freidrich. I'm speaking of the first Lady of Eltz, his mother," Angeline says. "I don't follow witches like she did. I don't run off looking for trouble, believing in what is child's play. Oh," she says innocently, seeing my reaction to her words. "You don't know about the Electorate's first wife? Did you know for years Laurentz's father has covered up the fact that his first wife was murdered?"

"Murdered?"

"She was among those found in the woods that terrible morning just outside your village all those years ago."

Horror spreads across my face. Images flood my mind. The girl hanging from the tree, her heart cut out of her chest. A girl lying in blood-soaked leaves. No wonder Laurentz ran off after watching what I am capable of. No wonder he and his father exchanged strange looks after I told them who my mother was, when I told them where and how she had died. I lift myself off the bed and begin pacing, ready to burst from my skin. But it's more than that. It's Angeline. It's *why* she is telling me this.

"Laurentz's mother knew your mother. His mother and yours are dead. Is that a coincidence?"

I have no doubt Angeline is feeling better, stronger, for she seems intent to wound me with her words. She doesn't appreciate what I've done for her. She only sees me as a threat, a witch, and the friendship I thought we might form is being challenged with every question that bounces back and forth between us.

"Was Laurentz's mother a…"

"Witch? Goodness no. They found Laurentz's mother on the other side of the stream, Rune." She picks up the goblet, tilting it this way and that. The water sways back and forth, creeping up the sides of the glass, then slipping back down. Angeline takes a long, exaggerated sip, then smiles and says, "You and I both know witches can't cross water."

Chapter 41
Laurentz

"Friedrich!" I've called out into the dark for hours, getting closer, yet further away.

Behind every tree I hear his voice. Around every bend is the distinct crunching of hooves. I was convinced he'd led me here, but I can't find him. I never will. And what would I say if I did? I would break down at his feet and ask for forgiveness. But what sort of forgiveness would he give for taking his life? Mine has been haunted by my guilt. Isn't that enough?

Finally, I can take no more and lean over my horse's neck, willing this outrageous goose chase to come to an end. My brother is not here. This is a trick of the forest—an illusion. I should have known better. This is how men die in the Black Forest—seduced by the voices they think they hear, like pirates falling to the whims of the sirens at sea.

I will my heart to stop beating so quickly. I will the voice of my long-dead brother to fade away, to let reality set in. In the end, when I do, there is only one voice I hear, and it is hers. I try to let that fade, too. It is apparent that for hours I've done nothing but ride in circles, becoming completely turned around, and the part of the forest I am in is not familiar to me. My horse leads me wherever it wants to go. At this point, I don't care where I end up. I know, after what I've done, I can't go back to her.

But there she is, tall and majestic, whispering to me through the treetops as if telling me she's been watching over me all along. It isn't really her, but Pyrmont's Keep, that I see. My horse, it seems, has led me to *somewhere* after all, as opposed to the *anywhere* I originally set out for.

Softly, we approach, following the thinly marked path along the ground. As soon as we reach the briar bushes lining the walk, I pull the reins hard and cover the mare's snout with my hands. Two carriages are parked beside one another, and my blood runs cold as I tread closer, immediately recognizing them—for one belongs to the Prince Bishop, and the other belongs to my father.

I jump down from the saddle and approach the door, my hand resting just above the latch. Knowing my father and the bishop are inside disturbs me greatly. This place is a tomb, a death trap, yet they are within these walls, placing themselves in great danger if Plague still lingers here.

The latch turns beneath my touch, and the door slips open, letting me step into the past. I imagine ghosts still walk these halls after having been torn from this earth too quickly— ghosts that will forever be bound here. I think of Rune living among them one day after she claims her inheritance. Only this is not where Rune should be. She belongs in the Black Forest where the trees create an eternal night, where the fern blows wild in the breeze, not penned in by stone walls.

Inside, a strange sound finds me—a wailing that is soft and desperate, that makes me think of Anna's crumbling little house in the village. The sound drifts to me from the upper floors, and I follow it. I nearly cover my mouth with my sleeve for fear the infection has not cleared, but then realize Plague must have been a game of deadly foolery. My father would never have set foot here otherwise. I soon find myself in a hall facing a half-open door. Movement stirs within.

"Shhh. There, there, my little one," a woman, who is very much alive, whispers. She cradles something in her arms no bigger than my shoe. It squirms and wriggles, and soon the bundle is set down carefully, as if it could break with the slightest movement. The room comes fully into view and I see now that there are dozens of other cradles filled with more squirming bundles.

It is a nursery.

I stay close to the wall, peering in. The woman is familiar to me. I know her—the way she bends over, her meticulous movements, the way she inspects each bundle as she walks past row after row after row. She turns to the side where I can see the angle of her face, and I am stunned to see it is the woman from the village, the woman who stood waiting for the glassblower to make the witch bottle, the one who met the bishop's carriage and took the money in exchange for the bellermine. She was the one who I saw sneaking away from the Drudenhaus.

A familiar voice comes from the open door at the opposite end of the room and in walks the bishop, robe-less and in plain clothes, paying no mind that the house could still be carrying contagion.

"A reformation, you understand, is the only way to preserve our society," he says. "We shall build a new society, a pure society, governed by the Church."

Have I wandered into a hospital for children who have lost their families to pestilence? And why is it that there are only cradles I see, and not beds? Unless there are rooms full of other patients, other children tucked safely away within the halls of the house.

The bishop cups his hand beneath the woman's chin, and I am taken aback by the closeness. She is obviously someone with whom he is intimate. He drops his hand as two more women enter, each returning a bundle to a waiting crib. Both glance at the bishop with nervous eyes as they gather up other children and scuttle from the room.

"So many souls." The bishop surveys the number of cribs in the room.

The woman bends to tuck in the edge of a blanket and quickly recoils her hand from the crib.

"See there?" A worried look spreads across her forehead as she points. "What do you suppose we do with this one? She has a funny little mark."

"Dispose of it," the bishop tells her plainly.

I am frozen to this spot watching this peculiar moment unfold in front of me, horrified that he can so unsympathetically tell the woman to kill a baby.

"Before long, these children will be cured and spared the memory of their parentage," he continues speaking, not allowing the little matter of a birthmark stop him.

"And how can you be sure the lineage will not be a problem?" A second man asks from the far threshold, and my anger boils inside me until I fear I won't be able to contain it any longer, giving myself away, as my father steps into the room.

"The line ends with the parents, be it either the mother or the father who carried the trait," the bishop replies, happy to make his point. "Each one of these children has been orphaned, and will grow up without the face of evil tempting them. They will grow up in a world void of sorcery. They will never know of witchcraft in the way their parents did. Denying them the temptation will allow them to see the world for what it truly is, and that most of what we do with our lives is unfortunately the work of the Devil himself." The bishop motions with his arm, leading my father away from the woman, so that they might speak privately. His voice drops to a near-whisper. "There is, however, one last issue to be addressed before the Viscount's visit to the friary. Has there been any success finding the girl?"

He means Rune. I am sure of it.

"No, I'm afraid not," my father replies back to the bishop. "There is no trace of her."

He does not reveal that Rune is alive and well, staying under his roof, and I am glad of it, because his willingness to lie to the bishop tells me she is safe.

"Nonetheless, you will give word as soon as she is found."

"Of course," my father nods as he places a leather pouch in the bishop's hand.

The bishop nods acceptance, a delighted grin raising his ruddy cheeks. "Your donation to the Church is always appreciated."

I don't miss how my father's eyes linger on the pouch, almost regretful that it has been handed over. I wonder why this disturbs him. I try and read him—his actions, his emotions. And while I draw a breath of relief that my father honors my wish to keep Rune a secret, today I am convinced I do not know my father at all.

Chapter 42
Rune

Laurentz will find the letter I've pushed beneath his door when he returns…if he ever returns. I will be gone by then. I'm much too wild to be kept here. There is something in me I don't understand; while I try to, I must be alone.

These walls are too thick for me to breathe, lined with too many eyes that watch me. I don't believe it is because they are curious. I feel that, without Laurentz here, I am stripped of an unseen protection I otherwise would have had. No, I need to go. I need to escape into the forest. It's the only place where I feel I can truly protect myself.

My slippers are soundless as I hide in the shadows of the pantry. Cook has already prepared lunch and will not be looking for ingredients among the shelves anytime soon, and from here I have the best view of the barn from the servants' entrance. I wait, holding my breath until a young stable boy crosses the lawn, leaving the barn door open just a crack.

I slip outside, cross the warm sweet grass, and disappear into the stable. I don't know why I haven't come here before; it's the closest thing to being in the forest. The hay is sweet and reminds me of the lichen that grows between the roots of the trees. It smells like the moss that carpets the hillsides and the pungent earth as the stream swells from the rain.

I long for home in a way I am no longer able to contain. The boy who left must have just saddled the young stallion for a ride, but I take it as a sign from the Mother that it is for me and climb up, not needing anyone's help. Once I am seated upon the beast's back I begin to doubt my escape. I peer over the animal's enormous neck and feel dizzy, feeling his body sway as his hooves take tentative steps, confused that I have not given him direction. I swallow hard and press my heel into the horse's side. I feel his muscles tighten as he starts out through the back of the stable and into the open air. My arms wrap around the steed's neck and I imagine it to be Laurentz's back, feeling safe as the trees inch closer. I smell the pine, already feeling the cool shade from the trees as, with a strong leap, the horse scales a downed tree trunk and we become part of the black that inhabits the forest.

Chapter 43
Laurentz

"Laurentz." My father's eyes widen as I step into the makeshift nursery.

"What is all this?" I walk around the cradles. There are more than I thought, now that I am actually in the room. The woman stands off to the side, stifling her gasp as she recognizes me, and I can't help wonder if one of these infants came from the witch prison where I saw her last. "Am I correct to assume Pyrmont is no longer a victim of the Black Death?"

The bishop, not my father, is the one to walk toward me. His eyes tell me he is skeptical of my visit but his arms are open. "She is clear of rats, fleas, and sorcery, my good boy. Allow me to introduce you to the next generation of Bavaria. Before long, this area will be cleansed of all evil and a new generation will guard its borders. I'm sure in time, when you are Electorate, you will be proud to live in a pure and reformed Germany."

"I may not be Electorate for a number of years." My eyes dart over his shoulder, resting on my father's face. I refuse to promise my allegiance. I refuse to tell the bishop anything.

"No matter," he says simply, as if it isn't a matter worth worrying over yet. "By that time, any number of the infants here might be worthy of serving in your Guard, Laurentz."

"Who are these children?" I walk up one of the rows, looking down. The colored blankets signify whether the infant resting inside is a boy or a girl. Otherwise, each is marked only by a number. No names. No identity. Nothing that reveals who they are, or who they belong to.

"Laurentz." My father's tone urges that I don't ask too many questions.

"It's all right," the bishop intervenes. "If the boy is to hold a position of power one day, then why not give him a taste of it now? Once he understands the importance of removing witchcraft and heresy from our villages, he'll be _with_ us, rather than against us."

The glimmer of his plan is becoming clear in my head. The bishop alluded to this that day in the chapel, and I see that his plan has been executed.

"These are pure souls, Laurentz—each one a victim in its own right. Each one a product of a parent who has been stained by evil, and destroyed so that the sins they've harbored will not pass to the younger generation."

"These children were born to people accused of being witches?"

It's such a tainted word, _witch_. The woman's face reddens before she slips through the door.

"Your son is perceptive." The bishop turns to my father. "He's a leader through and through to have picked up on such matters. Yes, Laurentz, do you remember that day in the chapel? I came to speak to your father about the prospect of contamination throughout our regions. You showed interest. If that interest is still there, perhaps you'd like to join us. We have one more to collect."

"I don't collect babies."

His laugh cuts through me. "No, she's not a child." He leans in, and I see the strong wish for power in his eyes. "She's the very reason for the rectification of the sovereigns. Hers is a soul so black, it's like peering into the eyes of the devil himself."

He doesn't know her like I do. She isn't what he says.

"What do you plan to do with her?" I ask. "Keep her in an orphanage?"

The bishop releases a tight laugh from his throat. "What a funny boy you are. Of course not. She's beyond help, and she's a fugitive, the only person to escape the Drudenhaus, as well as her own execution. No normal person could have done such things." He tilts his head and watches me. "No indeed. She should be put to death immediately, just as she would have been the day she escaped." The bishop steps closer. "You wouldn't happen to know anything about that, would you, my good boy?"

My father stands rigid and determined. He gives an almost imperceptible head shake, and briefly, I wonder how loyal he is to the bishop.

I shake my head. "No. I don't."

The seconds grow long as he looks at me. What is it that he thinks he might find by breaking me? I will never tell him about Rune. I will never give her away. I owe her that, and so does my father, yet his involvement in this does not fully reflect that debt.

"Very well," the bishop says.

He turns away from us to stare out the window. "It will not be a moment too soon the day she is captured," he says. "Sixteen years ago, the greatest witch of all Bavaria was put to death. For sixteen years this land has been spared." He turns back to face us with dark, determined eyes. "Until now. This girl is a most dire threat. She must be stopped before she has the chance to become just as strong, stopped before she can ruin my plan to rid Bavaria of all evil."

He holds his hand out to me, and the garnet ring catches the light.

"Your father has pledged his allegiance to me. Will you do the same?" the bishop asks me.

If I respect him, I will kiss the stone, pledging that I side with him. Beneath their stares I have no choice and let my lips bend to his hand. When I pull back, I see the hairline sliver in the stone nearest the filigree edge of the band. So small is the portion missing from the setting, I nearly miss it as I lean away to stand up. I remember the red stone from the church and know it still lies at the bottom of my pocket.

"I trust I have your loyalty, as I do your father's?"

I nod, knowing what I agree to is a lie.

My father holds up a hand, keeping me silent, and walks to the window. Once the bishop's carriage has rolled away, he turns back and points to the open doorway, reminding me we are not entirely alone. The woman who is nursemaid to these orphans is still here, and there must be more wetnurses. And I have no doubt the woman the bishop so openly favors will report anything questionable to him.

"You're funding this." My open arms create a wide arc above the cradles.

"For now, yes." With heavy eyes, my father lowers his voice. "It's best that we leave now so I can explain it all to you."

I pitch my voice low. "I think I've heard enough." Ignoring his stricken look, I continue. "I know where your loyalties lie."

My father steps closer, but I back away.

"This isn't about loyalty," he explains. "This is about honor."

I follow my father down the stairs, away from those who might have reason to eavesdrop.

"What about Rune? What about her honor? What she's done for you means nothing?"

"You are too quick to make that assumption, Laurentz. There is more at play here than you are capable of understanding."

"You're right. I don't understand it. You've protected Rune, didn't give away her whereabouts when he asked you, yet you've agreed she's dangerous. And this," I gesture back toward the room with the endless rows of cradles. "*What is this?*"

"There are reasons I don't tell you everything. Things that could hurt you. The money bag is hush money, Laurentz. The bishop must believe I am loyal."

"Are you?"

"I would have hoped you'd know me enough to answer that for yourself, but I've purposely kept myself at an arm's length from you all these years. Keeping you safe has been my only intention, Laurentz."

"I don't understand. Safe from what?"

My father shakes his head as if saying he cannot, *will* not, answer that question for me just yet. "I've raised you in a grim world of alliances, raised you to question each card dealt to you. I suppose now is when I ask myself if I've done well in this."

Like Rune, my father has become a mystery I now need to solve. Everything he ever was to me, is to me now, is uncertain.

"And have you?" I ask.

He looks into my face with worry, loss, and years of distance, all collected into one deep stare. "I don't know."

"The bishop has dealt a new card, hasn't he? One you are afraid of."

I am onto this. He nods slowly, telling me we tread on thin ice.

"It's a game he's been playing for a very long time." He expels a long sigh that echoes around us. "What you feel for that girl of yours is a card you must hide beneath your sleeve," he says carefully. "She left Eltz. Take your horse and ride until you find her. Find her before anyone else does."

I've never seen my father like this before. He won't allow me to take measure of our conversation for too long. He won't allow me to waste time trying to figure all this out. As soon as we reach the bottom of the steps, far away from the nursery, my father turns to me. "I have seen things I cannot explain, been privy to secrets I should know nothing about. For years I have offered my loyalty to him and kept quiet. But mark my words, my son; sometimes it is best _not_ to know. Find that witch of yours. Find her and hide her someplace safe." He leans closer, his eyes dark with dread. "Both of your lives depend on it now, for the bishop is a dangerous man."

Chapter 44
Rune

I've known the forest all my life, and yet how I see it right now has never been so magnified, nor so dangerously beautiful. I am acutely aware of what I see between the boughs, of what is ahead of me, as well as behind me. I've learned to listen to the slight sounds muffled against the forest floor, learned to distinguish what comes from the horse I ride and what I must be alert for. As I lead the horse through the trees, further away from the safety of Eltz, I hope that his black coat will hide us from what goes undetected.

Wind, please make our journey swift.

Somewhere to the right of the tree line lies the road to the city of Bamberg. Even amongst the chaos the day Laurentz helped me escape the Drudenhaus, I recognize it, and I stay away from veering too close. It's quite possible they still search for me, that a bounty is upon my head. If the city is anything like my own village, then the townspeople will be hunting for any way possible to put extra food on their tables, and a witch hunt will bring a high reward. My mother was the Witch of Bavaria. If Angeline knew that, then the others will, too, and my capture and execution will be a spectacle sure to draw an even larger crowd than the first time.

Do they believe the witch's daughter could be worse than she? More powerful? More cunning? Though uncomfortable, I talk myself into using that status to give me strength. Instilling fear in others may be the only way to ensure my survival.

I smile at the familiar gurgling stream that cuts a pattern through the earth. What began on the property of Eltz has now transitioned into the little trickle flowing next to where the horse walks. The stream closest to the cottage was never wide, but narrow in odd places as it wound around the trees and roots, sometimes flowing beneath the ground, and then poking back out. The water I follow is doing just that, and I know if I continue along it, I will find my way home.

Fear and worry distort my sense of time, but not direction, and I don't know whether to laugh or cry out loud when I see the forest floor rise into a horizontal wall of green a few yards away. The fading afternoon light reveals I've reached the beginning of the hedge. I am just feet from the line of the village, and as much as I'd like to walk closer to it, just to make sure it's really there and not an illusion, I steer the horse the other way.

It's been too long since I've felt this joyful, but I don't let the happiness shadow my need to stay invisible. No one can see me or find me. I'm as good as dead if they do. And then I see the crumbled ruins of my home. I slip from the saddle and fall to the ground, nervous I've made too much noise, but no one comes. My bones ache like I have aged a thousand years. I wonder how anyone can ride for days without breaking every bone in their body. Night envelops the forest, but the rising moon gives edges to the shadows. I give the stallion's hind quarters a slap, sending him off into the forest alone. I have no need for him anymore.

I'd like to run to my home, but I stay quiet and guarded. No matter how ruined, how sad it is, Matilde is here, in every stone and slab. I am here, too. It never occurred to me how much of my old self I had to leave behind. I wonder if I had a looking glass if I'd even recognize the girl I used to be.

Whatever was left after the fire has been taken, and I'm sure the lonely little structure has now become part of the grisly tales of this forest. It is a new tale now, perhaps living forever in the minds of children at their bedtimes. How the old cottage from the Black Forest, the one where the daughter of a terrible witch lived, burned to the ground one night. What once held visions of the future is a place now lost in the past, haunted. No one will ever come back, and because of this, it is safe for me to spend the night here.

Rocks slip and tumble off to the left of where I stand, and I begin to wonder if I am wrong to think this place is safe. I crouch low just as a black boot steps into the ruins. I see the outline of a figure, but it is concealed in shadow. I've gotten this far on my own—I can't let myself be seen. Who knows what would become of me? Witch or not, I'm a girl alone in the dark, in the forest.

I quietly fit a large, jagged stone into the palm of my hand, ready to use it if I have to, and then I look up and see the shock of hair that has become tousled from riding. The familiar strong jaw lining his face catches the moonlight falling between the trees. He doesn't speak, but I hear him, and he sighs with relief as I stand and the moon reveals us to one another.

I land in his arms, just where I've aimed. Even here, in this broken place, it is the way he holds me that tells me I am home. The ruins may hold the echoes of who I used to be, but when I look up into his eyes, I only see who I am now—the girl in his arms, the girl who forgives him for being frightened and running off.

"How did you know?"

"I knew you would find your way home." Laurentz bends closer, resting his head wearily, thankfully, upon my forehead. "Would you also believe my father told me to come after you?"

I let out a tired sigh. "No, I don't believe that one."

He takes my hand in his, pressing his thumb to my palm. "People are scared of what they don't understand. They make rash decisions; they panic. You are far too valuable to be at the mercy of one mistake, especially mine. Rune, you frighten me."

"I scare you?"

With a smirk, he admits, "Very much so."

Part of me revels in this. My mother would be proud.

"But after I left, I was frightened most about what my life might be like without you in it."

Laurentz looks around at what is left of my home. Even I find it difficult to recognize it without its walls, without the furniture or all the other belongings Matilde and I once filled it with. The memories are still here, though. Those will never go away.

"You can't stay here."

"And I can't come back with you, either." I know he only means to protect me, and I made incredible strides in earning his father's respect and trust, but I am no longer welcome in Burg Eltz. I cannot return to Angeline.

"But you're not safe." Laurentz hold my face between his palms.

I'm safe right here, I want to tell him. *Right now.*

"Come back with me," he says again. "Not to Eltz, but to Pyrmont. Fight for it."

"But you and your father told me it's an empty tower of death."

"You could fill it with light and love and happiness."

"It doesn't feel like it belongs to me."

"But it does," he argues gently, "by birthright."

He doesn't need moonlight to know I am shaking my head.

"This is where I belong." I step carefully over the stones and look out at the darkness that surrounds the tiny house. "I belong out there. You know I do."

"And what about the village?" Laurentz walks to my side. "When they discover you here, they will take you again. They won't think twice about who you are, or where you think you belong. They will kill you. Rune, the bishop wishes to destroy you, and he won't stop until you have burned, just like your mother."

"Then maybe that's what is meant to be."

Laurentz grabs my arm and makes me look at him. What I see in his face is disturbing—fear and anger, loss that threatens to repeat over and over again. I don't want to do this to him, but he doesn't seem to accept that he can't keep me. I am not like him.

"I've seen what you can do. You are powerful. You can change everything, Rune." Laurentz's eyes shine. "You don't have to follow the footprints your mother has left for you. Make your own. Make them all see that, as a witch, you can do good, not harm."

"What you ask is impossible."

"Then prove me wrong." His voice changes to a meaningful challenge. "The bishop has turned Pyrmont into an orphanage. Help me do something about this."

"An orphanage? His heart isn't that generous."

"No, it isn't. These are children taken from those who have been tried for witchcraft. Dozens of cradles filled with infants—no one older. He believes he can make them pure. A new Germany, he called it."

"Laurentz, what do you mean, 'taken?' Weren't they already orphans? Please tell me that they were."

He shakes his head from side to side. He doesn't know. But I do. I've seen it with my own eyes, heard the stories with my own ears—babies taken from their mothers moments after birth by pitiless guards. I thought the babies were taken to be destroyed. That's what Anna and I had thought. I'd forgotten my promise to her until now. Could her daughter be inside the castle? If her tiny birthmark has gone undetected, then yes, it's a possibility, and I must keep my promise.

"My father's warned me to keep you safe. The bishop has something terrible planned, not only for Bavaria, but for you and me as well. Going back to Pyrmont means I will intentionally disobey my father. And it places you in grave danger. So tell me what to do and I'll do it, after I've made certain you're out of harm's way."

"And I am to arm you with herbs that will heal you, should something happen," I whisper, "rather than stand at your side, fighting for what is right?"

"Yes."

"It's not that simple. Magick will only protect you if it's wielded from my hands."

"Then you must help me some other way," he insists. "I won't place your soul in danger. It's far too precious."

"And what of *your* soul, Laurentz?"

His face may be cloaked in shadow but it cannot hide how he scoffs at this. "Mine has much to make up for."

An owl stirs above the roofless cottage. It is out of the question that we light a fire tonight, so I nestle into him, the two of us keeping each other warm. Despite knowing he will leave tomorrow, that old feeling of being protected is back, and I hold onto it.

I drift off to sleep in his arms, waking to a paling sky and a warm embrace. I move to sit up, causing the contents of the rune bag I have tied to my wrist to clink.

Laurentz opens his eyes. "Do you know how to read them?" He points to the bag.

"Not really. I suppose I have much to learn if I'm to be a *real* witch." I spill the contents onto my lap. The stones clink together. It's such a comforting sound that, if I were to close my eyes right now, I might hear Matilde's voice deciphering the meanings of the little symbols. I wonder if my fortune has changed. I don't tell him what I'm doing, but I hold my hand over the pile, knowing it's dark enough that he won't become curious and ask. Immediately there is a pull, and I choose two stones. Only two. Strangely, the others are quiet.

When I turn them over, I see the symbols. Man and Woman. I feel the warmth of him next to me, and as the thin light of morning brightens between the trees, I smile at what the future holds.

Murgia

"I've almost forgot, I have my own stone to show you," and he pulls a tiny broken gem from his coat pocket. "I don't know if it has anything to do with the future, but I do think it's a secret to the past."

He places it in my hand and I turn it over, not quite sure what it could be. At first I think it's nothing, perhaps a piece of glass, but I don't want to hurt his feelings, and then the voice of my mother surges within me with an unforeseen vengeance, and I am most certain he has found a key to a puzzle.

Chapter 45
Laurentz

"*W*hat is it?"

It's not the stone I ask about.

She holds her hands to her head as if it's splitting open. Words tumble from her lips in a voice that is not hers, and when finally her own pushes forth, I hear a word that sends my heart racing.

"Mother."

I grab her hand and pull her with me, stumbling down the broken rocks to the muddy ground. "I'm taking you back to Eltz."

But Rune has another agenda. She pulls her hand from mine and rushes away without me.

I run through a forest of nightmares that are vividly real, of darkened trees that obliterate the dawn, of howling calls and whispers that jump out from around every bend. I am scraped and sore. I bleed. We must have moved back toward the village, because the green of the hedge rises to my right. Rune continues into the forest and I follow without question. She stands at the edge of a small stream and points. When she doesn't cross, I step into the freezing water and up to the other side, facing her.

"What now?" I hold my hands up at my sides, waiting.

Words hit me. They are inside my head, but they are not mine.

They are not Rune's, either.

They are *hers*.

If you love her, you will help her...

Find it...

Across the stream, Rune's arms are at her side, and I know she waits for what I've been told to do. I begin searching the ground and the trees closest to where I stand. If I'm to look further than this, I will lose sight of Rune, and I have a feeling she will not be standing there when I return. My hand brushes the sweat from my forehead. I don't know what it is I'm supposed to look for.

Dig...

I drop to my knees and pull at the earth with my bare hands, grabbing clumps of brush and stone, flinging them aside. The ground is soft and tender here, unlike the clay that lies beneath the rocks near the cliffs of Eltz. Here, my hand can do damage instead of the other way around. Rune screams, and I look up. For a second there is a vaporous image of a body tied to a tree, and then it is gone.

The word comes to me again. *Mother.* And this time, it is my own voice that repeats it until my throat is dry.

This is where my mother died.

Not Rune's, but *mine*.

Chapter 46
Rune

We have run out of time.

Hooves thud against the forest floor and they send my heart racing. Dark shadows move among the trees and flickering torches sway, forming a line of orange as flames bob in the breeze. The light pauses briefly, and I feel the fear that has lived deep within the villagers' hearts. The hedge has always meant more than a simple border—it is the dividing line between their safety and the tormented forest. It is the thin armor that protects them from the haunts that live among the trees, the nightmares, the witches...and yet, the fire they bring lights their way, and soon feet cross the hedge, leaves crumpling beneath, and I know they've done the unthinkable. They've crossed to the other side to see the bishop finally capture his witch.

Laurentz digs and digs as I watch helplessly from the opposite bank. Shouts close in on us—the bishop's guards, from their livery—as one spots us and alerts the others.

I cannot run without Laurentz. I will not leave him. Just as he finds his footing in the soft earth, he closes his hand around something small embedded in the ground. But it's too late for us. A burly guard pulls him to his feet.

A carriage comes to a stop and releases its footplate in a symphony of metal and wood. Straining, it moans beneath the weight of the bishop as he steps down. "I cannot believe my luck today." He pauses, taking in the fear that fills our eyes. I wish for Laurentz to come back over the stream—certain the space we have placed between us has sealed our fate.

Almost reflectively, the bishop walks toward the tree that is closest to the water, the very tree where the image of the hanged girl appeared, and he touches the bark, as if feeling the past beneath its peeling skin. "What is it about this spot that calls to a witch?" Then, without warning, he crosses the ground and grasps Laurentz's chin in his hand, squeezing hard. "You play with fire, boy."

Fire...

Laurentz struggles against the bishop's grip. When he is released, he backs away, rubbing his chin, but I see his fist remains tight around what he has unearthed from the ground.

The bishop arcs his arms wide and motions toward where I stand across the stream. His mouth twists in a cruel grimace. "Have you earned the love of this witch? Have you done her bidding?" He does not take his eyes off me, and every part of me shudders, feeling the enormity of his hatred. "It's easy to become bewitched, isn't it, my young lord? It's easy to lose your heart, your mind, and become spellbound."

"Is that what happened to you?" Laurentz's husky voice adds a fierce layer to the already thick forest air. "Were you under the spell of the Witch of Bavaria?"

He is answered by the bishop's chortle—a dark, grating noise. "Everyone was under her spell, boy." A dark look passes between them. "Careful, Laurentz. Someone of your standing must watch where he treads."

The guards converge on Laurentz, and while I try to reach him with my eyes, he won't look my way. If he pushes too hard, they will take him down, and I won't be able to do anything but watch.

The guards are ordered to step aside. Although I stand many feet away, I can hear perfectly what Laurentz and the bishop whisper, as if they are no farther than a footstep in front of me. I listen with my mother's ears. She is everywhere and everything in this forest.

Wait for it, daughter. Wait for him to say it…

Say what, Mother? What must I wait for? I ask back to the voice in my mind, but she is quiet again, watching like I do.

With a tilt of his head, the bishop inches closer to the boy across the stream. "Tell me what you know."

"I know four girls gathered here, in this spot, sixteen years ago," Laurentz's eyes are cold as he meets the bishop's gaze. "The coven held only three, but they needed a fourth."

Yes… Tell them…

I thought the words would come from the bishop. My mother told me to wait for him to say it, only I had no idea it would come from Laurentz, and I am shaken by the fact that he knows more than I—and had not told me.

"They needed my mother," Laurentz says. "You remember, don't you? After all, you were there."

Though I cannot see her, I can tell that my mother's ghostly form stands protectively behind me and I feel her tremble with a strange energy, as if urging the ensuing argument to develop further.

The bishop leans close to Laurentz's tormented face and whispers softly, "She would have ruined everything for your father. I stepped in and prevented her from making that grave mistake."

"Yes, you silenced her, and killed the others as well."

"How dare you!"

The guards are quick to surround Laurentz, but just as they draw their swords a rustling fills the air and the trees move. The villagers have found us. Their eyes jump from me to the group across the stream, and back again. They recognize me at long last, seeing the resemblance of my mother in me, knowing I am the girl who lived with Matilde. They refuse to step closer,

murmuring amongst themselves—*She is the one!... Witch!...*—
and several pull clothing over their noses and mouths in haste
for fear of breathing something that will send them to their
deaths. Some are so fearful they turn and run back toward the
hedge, as if it will protect them once they return to the safety
of the village.

With a thick sway of his robe, the bishop turns to the
crowd, his eyes wide and innocent. "I am a peaceful man of
God," he says to us all in a loud, convincing voice, "and I have
just been accused of murder." He shakes his head like this is a
ridiculous notion, then turns back. "You, Laurentz, will watch
what you say, if you want to be Electorate of Eltz one day. I
am your greatest ally. Are you willing to allow a few poorly
chosen words to ruin that?"

But the crowd that has gathered is still and watchful, and
the bishop adopts a newfound vigor to entertain his expectant
audience.

"Sorcery is at work here!" he says in a ferocious voice.

"Yes, as it was sixteen years ago." Laurentz challenges, and
we all watch in curious silence as he reaches into his pocket to
produce two small garnet chips.

"And what are those?" the bishop asks, peering into
Laurentz's open hand. "Do you intend to stone me to death
with ridiculous pebbles?"

"Stone the witch instead!" cries an elderly woman from
behind me, and soon the crowd that has gathered is in an
uproar, ready to lay blame.

"This I found in the chapel." Laurentz holds up the tiny
red chip for all to see, his voice rising above the others. "The
ground just gave up this other. It's from the setting of your
ring," he turns to the bishop. "Why don't you explain why it
was found where my mother took her last breath?" Laurentz
squares his shoulders. "Admit it broke when you killed my
mother and the other girl."

A guard steps closer, intending to inspect the ring for himself, but the bishop pushes him away. "Proof, boy." The bishops laughs. "You're going to need proof."

"Is this not enough? You're the only one who wears such stones—a gift from the church that allows you to do what you please. To let the villages starve, to condemn the innocent." Laurentz pauses to catch his breath. "Even to kill."

The bishop opens his mouth, but Laurentz presses on. "All the stories of the Black Forest—the nightmares fed to us as children, the dark tales of the horror that is here—were stories you used to your advantage so these poor people would live in fear. I will never forget the day I overheard you and my father. You told him of the unspeakable evil that supposedly lurks here; you told him how to instill fear in the villages so he would never lose his grip on them—and you told me, that day in the chapel, to fear the cunning woman in the woods. For unlike yours, her soul was not worth saving."

Like lightning, the bishop's hand flies out, colliding with Laurentz's open hand; the two gem chips are lost to the air.

"Laurentz!" I cry out.

No! You cannot… my mother hisses in my ear as I step into the water, wrestling with the fact that I cannot cross the stream to help him. Tiny bubbles erupt around my ankles, then still as if encasing me in hard stone.

"You helped invent stories of darkness and magick to keep people from venturing into the forest. Tell me, bishop, what were you afraid they would find?" Laurentz asks. "Would they find the stones from your ring and wonder why you had been here? Would the good people of this village realize they'd been fooled?"

"Milk curdling in winter! Explain that!" shouts a man who dares to hobble closer.

Laurentz breathes heavily, his forehead knotted, "An unfortunate circumstance for you, but not the work of a witch. Perhaps you left the milk too close to your hearth?"

A trembling old woman steps forward, wringing her hands. "My poor son and his wife were afflicted years ago. The witch painted his skin the color of tar, and when he tried to escape her, his fingers stiffened and fell off. His wife died soon after, her flesh burned with St. Anthony's Fire even as they laid her in the ground. Now their children tend the bishop's fields."

"The baker's son had a fit once," says another. "His neck twisted as if unseen hands were breaking it clear off his body."

"The miller and his wife! They both have red burns on their faces, like they've been slapped by demons."

Laurentz takes a step toward the crowd. "So it seems all who fell sick had been exposed to rye from the bishop's fields."

Rye grows in the bishop's fields. My brain whirls around something familiar, and then I remember the servant girl who brought the tray to Angeline. *Could the bishop have poisoned the rye himself in order to strike fear into the people? Could he have done this to place blame upon my mother?*

The bishop turns his attention to the stream. "You!" he points to me. "You put him up to this! To blame me for the horror that happened here years ago!"

"My mother was blamed for those deaths," I whisper and my heart twists in pain at what that day has brought not only myself but for others.

"I remember!" an old man cries out. His eyes are clouded with a thick white film, but he speaks as if the past plays out before him. "I was with the men who went into the forest. I remember the bloodstained ground, the icy wind that blew through the trees as we came to this very stream and found the bodies of those poor dead girls."

A frail woman hobbles up to him and places her hand upon his arm. "I can still recall the day the girl came screaming into the village. May God have mercy on their souls."

They think that day is gone, but the dead still linger, whispering secrets few ears are capable of hearing. I try not to look, for out of the corner of my eye a dead girl still hangs from the tree, her blouson bloodied where her heart used to beat. A whimper floats to me from across the stream, and at first I believe it is Laurentz, but it is not, and I am too afraid to look at the ground he stands upon, for I know I will see an image so ghastly I might scream forever.

"But something is not right here." The woman squints her eyes and stares ahead at the streambank. She takes a daring step forward and I begin to fear she sees and hears what I do. "The stone from your ring was found *across* the stream."

"The witch killed them!" the bishop screams in fury.

"No, you're wrong. My mother could not have killed them. You seem to have forgotten that witches can't cross water," I whisper.

All eyes are on me now, watching as my skirt floats across the surface of the all-too-still stream. The water, though crystal clear, does not flow as it normally does, but instead has become an invisible, ice-like vice to trap me, preventing me from moving toward the opposite side of the bank. For a moment the forest blurs, and my head fills with the whispers of my long-dead mother. I feel her icy hand upon my shoulder, feel how her presence creeps around me like the water at my feet, only her movement is fluid and crackles with an energy unlike anything I've ever felt. Her ghostly fingers cover my eyes, as if intending to shield me, but instead, she murmurs in my ear.

See, my child… See what the others cannot…

Chapter 47
Liese

Bottles line the stone table, filled with strange yellow and green fluids. He mixes them, fails, then tries again—almost... A feminine laugh tugs at his attention. Her finger reaches across, points to an open bottle and summons a swirling purple haze to billow up from the narrow neck. The room is suddenly filled with birdsong.

"Ahh, you are a clever thing," he whispers against her ear —his eyes full of wonder at the magick her slender fingers produce.

Her hand grazes his and places a cold dagger into his open palm, then she whispers something delicate, something dangerous, into his ear. He repeats her words, though they are unlike anything he's ever allowed his lips to say out loud—they are foreign upon his tongue and twist uncomfortably in his mouth, yet he tries to imitate exactly as she'd spoken. The dagger swipes through the purple mist and then, to his wonder, coins of gold clatter to the table before him.

In a breathless tangle they embrace, intertwine... He kisses her shoulder...and the sky opens with a crack of thunder. But the storm does not come from the window, it comes from the chamber door, and soon she is yanked from the happy arms of her beloved and back into the angry grip of her betrothed. She must never allow the other man to touch her again—and he is angered, convinced this game was hers all along.

In the thin morning light of the forest, he watches, hidden by branches, as four young women prepare gifts for their unseen queen, the one they call Mother. Offerings are made—wildflowers from the earth, a tin of water from the nearby stream, a kiss blown into the air from the mistress of Pyrmont… He emerges from his hiding place and strikes, his rage too much to bear. One is thrown across the water and her head splits against a large stone with the help of his fist. To a tree he binds another. When he sees that the others have fled, he cuts out her heart so that she may never love, not even in death. Had he paid more attention to his lessons, he would not have needed to use brute force, but he does not possess the magick of his love, and now she has run away, fearing for her own life. He does not see her hiding among the trees, unable to look away.

The weeks that follow find her lonely and sick, and while the man she thought owned her heart has been removed from the castle, he is a constant stain within its walls. Her husband curses her, then points his sword to her swelling stomach, for he has his suspicions.

Through the forest she runs, her feet stumbling upon the uneven ground until at last the small cottage with the sagging roof peeks through the thick trees. She knocks upon the door and is greeted by an old woman, bent and frail. Thrusting a handful of coins into the woman's bony hands, she begs for the herbs that will rid her of the child growing in her womb… for the man she loved has told her husband she has been unfaithful, and the lie is far more convincing than her pleas for forgiveness.

But the old woman tells her the herbs will not expel the infant—it has grown too large for such medicine to work. "The magick inside you is strong," the old fortuneteller Matilde tells Liese. "For it wants to live! You must not ruin what the Sacred Mother has planned. You must bring the child forth into the world."

Beneath the light of the full moon, in a clearing just past the cottage and the stream, the baby draws its first breath and the Sacred Mother vows she will possess a power greater than the witch who has birthed her. Matilde will raise it as her own, and none will be the wiser.

At sunrise the baby is handed over, nameless save for the swaddling wrapped around its tiny limbs. With the infant's cries at her back, Liese walks toward the village and steps silently into the square. The hamlet's guards seize her almost immediately. Her body is strapped to the stake *and the straw beneath her feet is lit. She screams with pain as the fire gnaws at her skin, but it is her child's cries she hears, not her own. Her eyes search the sky for the Mother, and she tries to smile, for the offering of fire has finally been given—only the Mother will not end her pain.*

Chapter 48
Rune

areful, my daughter... My mother's words shake me.

"I didn't believe it until I looked into your eyes in Bamberg. They are *her* eyes. The witch's eyes!" Hate flies from his lips. "I demand you take her immediately!" he orders his guards. "Burn her!"

"Do you still see her when you look at me?" I ask as I struggle to inch closer to the stream's edge. "She's everywhere." I tell him. "You see her, just as I hear her."

Growing hysteria laces his too-high laugh, "Voices! She hears the voice of a witch, and you won't take her away! Tell me, girl, did she tell you I am a murderous liar?" He leans toward me with a threatening grimace.

My eyes drop to the muddy edge of the stream. There is only a foot between us—a foot of water and moss and hatred.

"You loved her once."

"I *loved* what she could do for me. Do you think I wanted *this*?" he hisses, pulling at his heavy brocaded robe. "Pyrmont was to be *ours*. My brother's love for the military and territory balanced my obsession for science, physics...alchemy. He would rule the villages of Germany while I ruled the air it breathed." He stares up at the sky and inhales deeply, as if remembering a time when all was simple. "And then *she* came into our lives. My brother knew nothing of what she was capable of, but I did. He had no idea that it was I she shared her secrets with…that together, Pyrmont would be a force to be reckoned with. But she chose *him*. And he rid himself of me, ordering my vows, choosing her, *a witch*, over his own flesh and blood."

His foot balances on the unstable edge of the bank, the hem of his robe deepening to a shade of blood as the water tastes it. "*This* was my brother's way of 'curing' me after I told him his new bride was unfaithful, after I *accused* his wife of witchcraft. *This* was my brother's way of sentencing me to a cruel death while he surrounded himself with finery and a village that adored him. He took all that I had, all that I was, and destroyed me, ordering me to pledge myself to God so my soul might one day be forgiven. Only I don't blame my brother. I blame the witch who shared his bed."

His breath reeks with blame, and I am struck with the realization that *he* was the reason my mother gave me away. How evil he must have been that day, ending the lives of those girls. How evil he still is.

"Had I known my brother's witch birthed an heir I would have killed it and taken what was rightfully mine. So you see, the witch was clever to keep you hidden from me. From her own husband as well, I imagine." He takes a step closer. "Her execution was my vengeance. But it seems my work is not yet finished."

He does not know my mother is alive today—in this forest that surrounds us, in me—and a horrifying vapor manifests between us.

The bishop's back stiffens and his eyes go wide. He loses his footing and slips along the loose rocks at the edge of the stream, tumbling into the cold water beside me. Catching himself, he grabs onto my arms, nearly knocking me over as he struggles against his robe, which is drenched and heavy with water, and then he looks into my face. He looks long and hard.

You may have destroyed me, but my daughter will be the end of you...

If ever there had been horror laced among the words my mother whispers, it is now.

The hatred in the bishop's eyes turns to fear as my mother's vengeance settles in my bones.

Laurentz looks at me. He's worried. He cannot hear or feel what I do. My hands burn as my mother's spectre prepares to use me as her vessel. The forest that surrounds me feels horrifying and dark. Across the gurgling stream, Laurentz's eyes beg me to tell him what is wrong, but I cannot.

Where would I even begin? I am witch-born and possibly more powerful than my mother, but how do I tell him that my veins are filled with such vengeful blood?

Even worse, how do I face Laurentz, knowing the bishop is my father's kin—and that it is my family's blood that destroyed his mother all those years ago?

Chapter 49
Rune

*Y*ou cannot escape the past... my mother warns. I stare back at a man who has become more evil than any witch. He is far more cunning than any of us could have ever imagined.

"Trickery!" he yells. "Even in death the witch has cast a spell that I would believe you are of my blood!"

Gasps grow behind me as the others take in his words... but more audible than their rising voices is the silence that comes from Laurentz as he stares at me.

"Fools! All of you!" The bishop's fists shake as if they still hold the little magick my mother taught him so long ago.

One of the older villagers has stepped closer and stares at us both. "It was y—" His voice cuts off as the bishop's hand punches the empty space between them. He utters strange, terrifying words and swipes his hand from left to right. It is like the dagger from the vision my mother allowed me to witness, and suddenly there is a ghastly gurgling. I spin around in time to see a thick line of blood form where an invisible blade has separated the loose flesh of the man's neck. He falls to his knees. Without hesitation I climb out of the stream and drop to the man's side, pressing my skirt to his throat.

In this moment, the bishop is an evil more real than the tales of the forest witch, and the villagers scatter, some tossing their torches to the ground, running from what will surely be their end.

The dry leaves quickly ignite and the forest is awash with a blood-orange glow.

"Rune!" Laurentz cries for me, for I am stuck now on the side that burns.

"What a vile enchantress your mother was," the bishop seethes. "Pushing me aside so she could rule what should have been mine."

His words are hollow and muffled as the crackling fire inches its way closer to me and the moaning man I hold onto. A woman wails nearby, and I am certain it is his wife. She did not leave with the others. I wonder if she cries for him, or for what she fears I will do.

I stretch my fingers across the ground and am relieved to feel a patch of Sphagnum Moss curling against the rocks. Pulling at it, I yank a cluster free and press it against the dying man's throat. His eyes darken with confusion until I slowly take my hand away. His wife's tears are silenced at what I have done, yet her eyes are still filled with fear, for the fire looms.

A harsh hand clutches at my hair, yanking me to my feet. My scalp screams with a searing pain as I am dragged along the forest floor toward a patch of dry brush not yet consumed by the flames.

"I didn't have the pleasure of watching her die," he tells me. "I thought it would break me. But now I think I will like very much for you to meet your end as she did." His face twists with a dark smile.

My back scrapes the tree as the bishop pushes me against it, his weight leaning into me so that I cannot move freely. "*You* are the embodiment of all who have wronged me, and for that, your suffering will be magnified a thousand times more."

In his eyes I see how dark his soul has blackened, and his thoughts—vile images of how he'd like to see me die—slip between us.

Beyond him a dark shadow forms, stretching, undulating, a ghostly forest tale come true. He pivots at the cold presence at his back. A loud crunch echoes, and the blackness fades to reveal the man I have just healed, standing shakily, a large rock tumbling from his hands.

The bishop stumbles against me, the forest now aglow in heat and orange and fear.

"You," he spits, but he does not have the chance to finish, for a stillness washes over us and then comes a whisper...

Forgive me, my Sacred Mother, for I never thanked you for your most glorious gift...my child...my daughter...who will prove to be all that I never was, never could be...

He hears her as clearly as I do, and his face is a stricken mask as a tiny breeze spirals at the water's edge before us, growing, spinning, pulling the flames inside it as it cyclones closer... closer... It grabs onto the bishop's robe and consumes it, the water from the stream hissing out of it, leaving him to flail and scream in a wall of flame...and I know, as all falls to a deafening silence, that this is my mother's final offering to the Sacred Mother.

Chapter 50
Rune

*L*ike a gentle breath extinguishing a candle, the fire in the forest fades. The bishop is gone. It is as if nothing had ever happened. But I know that is not true, for his empty carriage still sits, his impatient horses waiting to ride from this haunted place. My birthright has never been more than a dream to me—and it will remain as such, one I've conjured in my head to hide the ugly truth.

"Rune." Laurentz stands across the bank, upon the leaves that once knew such violence, and my heart breaks for him. "Do you see what they are doing?" he asks me and I turn, looking back toward the village. It seems as if the hedge has been replaced by skin, arms…people. A human fence separates the village from the Black Forest and it moves, not away from the witch, but toward, and not with torches or flames or angry accusations, but with smiles and hands reaching forth to touch me.

Leading them into the forest is the old man, his wife dabbing at old blood now staining the skin at his healed neck. He is frail, yet moves along at a steady pace as he assures the wary group there is nothing to fear.

For I am just a girl…

Behind him a young child limps, an old woman with white-blind eyes steps softly upon the mulch ground, and a woman, heavy with the child that grows inside her, follows. They come to me as those before them sought Matilde in this wild place, and a thickness grows in my throat.

Beyond the trees, a tower beckons and in my bones I feel the silent cries of the children there. They wait for me, as does the boy across the stream. He follows my eyes and wonders if I will choose the forest over him, his face creasing with worry the longer I stand here contemplating the borderless, limitless future waiting for me.

And when the morning light finds the stones from the bishop's ring scattered among the pine needles, my eyes drift to them. They tell me that Laurentz and I are bound to each other with a power much stronger than we know.

I step into the water, feeling it swirl around my legs, moving with me as I make my way to the other side. My mother's whispers are at my back, softening, fading with each step I take, for while I am a witch, my power shall know no boundaries as long as it serves the Mother, as I was taught long ago. My foot lifts onto the bank. It slips in the mud, making an ugly scar in the earth. The water will wash it clean. It will heal. Laurentz stretches his hand out to me, waiting, and I take it, lifting myself out of the stream, and onto the soft moss that greets me.

The End

Author's Note

While this novel is a work of fiction, there are historical references I feel I must mention. All places, including villages, castles, and streams are real—only the circumstances involving them within these pages have been bent in order to tell a story.

When we think of witch hunts, it is the most often unfortunate circumstances of Salem or England that come to mind. Germany—particularly Bavaria and other southwestern territories—prove to be most significant in modern European witch-hunting. The hysteria peaked between the 16th and 17th centuries in an attempt for religious and territorial control, and thousands of women, children, and men were tried and executed in the city of Bamberg alone. When found "guilty" they were often taken to the Drudenhaus, a famous witch prison built in 1627. Known for its rooms of torture, those on trial would endure countless hours of horror and pain, often coerced into admitting their association with spells and sorcery.

The Black Forest has been shrouded in mystery for decades. Rumored to be haunted by witches and banshees, it has carved its place within old German folklore. Matilde's cottage, however, did not exist. If it did, it's coincidence.

The village of Württemberg was a duchy and did not join with the nearby village of Baden until 1952, becoming a Federal Free State of Bavaria. I recently found out my own family hails from these parts of southwestern Bavaria, fueling my imagination to dig deep and write this story. It is not surrounded by a hedge, as depicted in the story; however, old European villages often referred to the boundary between village and forest as a "hedge," and oftentimes, an herbal practitioner lived there.

All plants and herbs mentioned in the book are native to the Black Forest, as are the afflictions of the time period—famine, Bubonic Plague, and a disease called St. Anthony's Fire (now known as ergotism). Ergot of Rye played a large role in the witch hysteria. Its symptoms include hallucinations, trance-like states, rashes, and uncontrollable twitches and convulsions. It is now believed to have played a major role in the Salem Witch Trials.

The Electorate of Eltz's territory did not fall as far south as Württemberg. His region was Mainz and Trier during the Holy Roman Empire, but I felt Castle Eltz was so perfect for the story that I created an extension to his region. As far as I know, he did not have a son named Laurentz. Castle Eltz is a place of wonder and thousands of tourists visit yearly. And yes, Pyrmont Castle is its neighbor, a short three-hour hike away.

As for the Witch of Bavaria, she is quite real, although cannot be named as one particular person. Thousands of innocent women were accused of witchcraft and executed. The *idea* of a Witch of Bavaria encompasses all of the souls lost during this hopeless time in our history.

∽❦∾

A Spell of Thanks

A whole lot of magic goes into creating a book.

You need inspiration: AKA as an intuitive literary agent who looks into her scrying glass and informs you that you MUST write this book. Amanda Luedeke, you are priceless to me. Thank you for pushing me to be my very best and for finding the perfect home for my story.

The universe must align: Kate Kaynak, thank you for falling under my manuscript's spell. All is well in the world when an editor shares the same vision as the author. Nothing can compare to the warm arms Spencer Hill Press has embraced me with.

A pinch of encouragement: Cyn Balog & Molly Cochran, I am grateful for our friendship. Thank you for being the first to read *Forest of Whispers* (back when it was a little file called *The Hedge Witch*).

A veil of mystery: Lisa Amowitz, thank you for creating such a hauntingly beautiful cover. You are indeed the other half of my dark and twisted brain.

A dash of spice: Otherwise known as Publicist Extraordinaire. Brooke DelVecchio, I am in awe of you and the creativity you wield.

A bloodline: I always knew my family had secrets…including one my mother traced back to pre-Germanic times and a hint of a great, great, grandmother…who was a witch.

A flame: Tremendous thanks to my Coven of Secrets Street Team for virtually whispering about my book to the world.

A cauldron: There's nothing like family to help stir the past into present. Thank you to my parents for always encouraging me to walk my own path and for my grandmother, who will gladly sit and listen to me talk about writing over a cup of tea.

The elements: Immense gratitude to my husband, Chris—and my children, Christian and Megan. The journey would be nothing without you along for the ride.

Whisper Falls

Elizabeth Langston

BOOK TWO in the WHISPER FALLS SERIES

A Whisper in Time

Elizabeth Langston

BOOK THREE in the WHISPER FALLS SERIES

Whispers from the Past

Elizabeth Langston

Get lost in the past...

A. R. KAHLER

...or the future.

MARTYR

THE HUNTED : BOOK ONE

THE ZODIAC COLLECTOR

LAURA DIAMOND

BETWEEN

MEGAN WHITMER

About the Author

*J*ennifer Murgia writes Young Adult Fantasy and Contemporary novels. She has long loved the dark and speculative—and it's from these dark places that she weaves fantastical stories, often hoping to find truth in them. She is the co-founder and coordinator of YAFest: an annual teen book festival in Easton, PA. She currently resides in Pennsylvania with her husband, her two children, and a very spoiled cat.

CPSIA information can be obtained at www.ICGtesting.com
Printed in the USA
LVOW08s1357231214

420062LV00005B/6/P